ANDERS'S MIND WAS SPINNING, GRASPING AT new facts and then tossing them at him, as if they were supposed to somehow help everything make sense.

I transformed into an ice wolf.

Rayna transformed into a scorch dragon.

But we're twins, so that's impossible.

Whether it was some trick of the dragons' or some kind of mistake, he didn't know, and he didn't know how to start figuring it out.

He pushed to his feet, picking his way across the grass, keeping away from the edge of the roof to be sure nobody would see him.

He *had* to find his sister. That was all that mattered.

ALSO BY AMIE KAUFMAN

Elementals: Scorch Dragons

Unearthed
coauthored with Meagan Spooner

THE STARBOUND TRILOGY
coauthored with Meagan Spooner

These Broken Stars

This Shattered World

Their Fractured Light

THE ILLUMINAE FILES
coauthored with Jay Kristoff

Illuminae

Gemina

Obsidio

ELEMENTALS:

ICE WOLVES

BY

AMIE KAUFMAN

HARPER
An Imprint of HarperCollinsPublishers

Elementals: Ice Wolves

Copyright © 2018 by HarperCollins Publishers

Illustrations by Levente Szabo

All rights reserved. Printed in the United States of America.

No part of this book may be used or reproduced in any manner whatsoever without written permission except in the case of brief quotations embodied in critical articles and reviews. For information address HarperCollins Children's Books, a division of HarperCollins Publishers, 195 Broadway, New York, NY 10007.

Library of Congress Control Number: 2017944338
ISBN 978-0-06-245799-8

Typography by Joe Merkel
Map by Virginia Allyn
19 20 21 22 23   BRR   10 9 8 7 6 5 4 3
❖
First paperback edition, 2019

For Meg

My magic, who transformed me.

CHAPTER ONE

RAYNA WAS CONFIDENTLY LEADING THEM IN THE wrong direction. Anders hurried through the crowd after her, ducking as a woman nearly sideswiped him with a basket of glistening fish. The stink washed over him like a cloud, and then he swerved away, leaving it behind as they ran through a stone arch.

"Rayna, we're—"

She was already turning the corner and running out across Helstustrat, nipping in front of a pair of chestnut ponies that were hauling a wagon full of barrels over the cobblestones. Anders jogged from one foot to the other, waiting as they rumbled past, then took off after his twin sister again. "Rayna!"

She could hear him—he knew that when she flashed a quick grin over her shoulder, white teeth gleaming in her brown face. But she didn't slow down, her thick black braid bouncing as she jogged. He was stuck trying to catch up again. This *always* happened.

"Rayna," he tried, one final time, just as they rounded the corner to see the roadblock ahead, manned by guards clad in gray woolen uniforms. Without breaking stride, Rayna whirled back the way they'd come, grabbing Anders by the arm and yanking him with her around the corner. His heart thumping at the close shave, he leaned back against the cool stone wall.

"Guards," she said, tugging her coat straight.

"I know! They're on every street on the north side of the city," he told her. "Checking everyone who comes through."

Her gaze flicked back toward the corner. "Was there another dragon sighting? Or are they just doing extra patrols before the Ulfar Trials?"

"There was a dragon in the sky just last night," he replied. "I heard them talking about it in the tavern when we were climbing down from the roof first thing." He didn't point out that Rayna had missed that information because she'd been too busy telling him their plans for the day. "They said they saw it breathe fire and everything."

That silenced even Rayna for a moment. Dragons had been gone from Holbard for ten years now, but lately they had been seen in the sky overhead. Anders and Rayna had seen one themselves six months before, on the night of the last equinox celebrations.

It had breathed pure white fire as it circled above the city, then vanished into the darkness. An hour later, a set of stables in the north of the city was ablaze with the ferocious, white-and-gold dragonsfire that was almost impossible to put out, leaping from place to place faster and fiercer than normal flames.

By the time the buildings had been reduced to ashes, the dragon was gone, and with it the son of the family that lived above the stables. Dragons always took children, the stories said. The weak, the sick, and the defenseless.

"Maybe the guards think the dragon from last night could still be spying in the city, hiding in human form," Anders said. "Or planning to start a fire."

Rayna snorted. "What, and they think if they ask people, they're just going to admit they knew where a dragon was but decided not to tell anyone?"

He nodded, lowering his voice to do his best impression of an upstanding citizen. "Yes, Guard, in fact I hide scorch dragons on my roof, because I want to be roasted alive and I don't believe in public safety. I feel a little bit guilty about it, and I've been meaning to confess to somebody, but I wasn't sure who would want to know."

"At least you'd be warm." She giggled, kicking at a

slushy, melting pile of snow.

He returned to his own voice, her giggle helping chase away his own nerves, as he had hoped it would. "You never know if you don't ask." But though he smiled along with her, even the words put a twitch between his shoulder blades. *Scorch dragons.* They were the one thing every person in Holbard knew to fear, whether they were locals or traders from across the sea. There were new rumors every day that dragons were near the city again. Rumors they'd burned a farmhouse to the ground just last week, the farmer's family still inside.

"How far south do we have to go to dodge the guards?" Rayna asked, jolting him from that thought. It went without saying that they'd avoid them. Guards asked questions like "Where are your parents?" and other inconvenient things related to adult supervision.

"At least ten streets," he replied. "A couple of them were in wolf form, and I think they smell it if you're worried."

"*Ten streets?* That doubles the distance to Trellig Square! Anders, if you knew we were going the wrong way, why didn't you stop me?" She was all indignation, hands on hips.

"Well, I—" But he gave up before he started. Maybe he *should* have tried harder. It sort of *was* his fault they'd come so far the wrong way. "I'm sorry," he settled on. But she was already moving again, heading south.

"We'll go over the rooftops."

He was tall and gangly to her short and strong—though the twins shared the same black curls and warm brown skin, in almost every other way they were different. So being taller, Anders boosted Rayna up until she could grab the guttering and haul herself onto the nearest roof. Then he scrambled onto a barrel and climbed after her.

When he straightened up, he could see the rooftop meadows of Holbard spread out before them. Each square of grass was at least twenty houses long and twenty wide, rising and falling with the pitch and slope of the roofs.

The rooftops were covered in bright patches of wild-flowers, red fentills tucked down in the gullies, yellow-and-white flameflowers bobbing in the breeze on the slopes, as well as the occasional herb garden, where some-one had a window big enough to climb out and tend to their plants.

Thanks to the street children of Holbard, wherever there was only an alleyway between two stretches of grass, rather than a wide street, a plank of wood was almost always propped in place to serve as a bridge. You could travel half the city up here without ever needing to set foot on the ground.

Anders and Rayna ran across the grass together, climbing over the tops of the sloped roofs. It only took them a few minutes to find Trellig Square, which wasn't as big as the larger town squares in fancier neighborhoods, or down by the docks, but was always guaranteed to be packed with shoppers.

Below them they could see at least a hundred people doing their shopping at nearly twenty different stalls all squeezed in together, selling everything from flowers to eggs, secondhand clothes to hot sausages in bread.

On a rooftop on the opposite side of the square they saw Jerro, a dark-haired, dark-eyed boy of about their age, with pasty white skin hidden under a layer of dirt. He was a notorious pickpocket, and ran with a couple of his brothers, who looked like smaller versions of himself. Today, he studied Anders and Rayna for a long moment and then turned away, apparently confident the twins weren't a threat.

Down in the square, there was a puppet show setting up for one last performance before dusk fell, the players assembling the wooden box they'd hide behind to work the puppets, while out front a self-playing harmonica sucked in wind and spat out tunes. It was an artifact—an invention that channeled essence, or magic—and probably worth more than the rest of the puppet show put together.

The twins flopped down on their fronts, propping their chins up on their elbows as the harmonica fell silent and the show began. They couldn't hear the voices of the performers from up here, but they could still tell which story it was. The troupe was performing the last great battle, the time ten years before—when Anders and Rayna had been toddlers—when the dragons had attacked Holbard, and the Wolf Guard had defended the city.

A bunch of little wooden human puppets jumped and danced across the stage, going about their business, blissfully ignorant of what was coming next. They were beautifully made—from creamy white polished pine through to darkest mahogany, they were as varied as the citizens of Holbard who stood watching the show.

Anders heard the gasps from the audience below when red dragon puppets suddenly appeared, swooping low over the little people puppets, who scattered and ran about the stage, bobbing up and down on their sticks. One swooped to pick up the smallest puppet, kidnapping a child.

"How are they going to show—" Rayna began, but she got no further. Somehow a dragon puppet breathed *fire*—not a cascade of white-and-gold fabric, or some silly trick, but *real fire*. The flames raced along the fabric of the people puppets' clothes, curling around each seam and enveloping the tiny figures until there was nothing left.

"How do they make it white?" Rayna whispered. "And with those gold sparks? It looks like real dragonsfire."

"It's a kind of salt, I think," he whispered back. "And iron filings for the gold sparks. This is the best battle show we've seen."

The puppets who hadn't been reduced to ashes ran around the stage even more frantically. Anders and Rayna leaned over the edge of the roof in anticipation. They'd seen one tribe of shapeshifting elementals, the scorch dragons, making their attack, and now it was time for the other—the ice wolves, the heroes of the battle.

Another set of human puppets popped up on the stage, all clad in gray, and Rayna pointed. "There's the Wolf Guard, watch!"

Beneath the wooden box the puppeteers worked some trick, and in the blink of an eye the Wolf Guard puppets turned themselves inside out—and on the inside of the puppets was sewn their wolf form! Now they were no longer guards in gray uniforms, but actual wolves, howling and creating spears of ice to drive out the dragons. The high-pitched noise was audible even above the gasps of the crowd.

"Those are some fancy puppets," Anders said as a pair of Wolf Guards—real, living ones, one just like the pine puppet and the other like the mahogany—walked through the square on patrol, and nodded their approval as a dragon puppet came crashing down, defeated. Another dropped the tiny, kidnapped child puppet, and Anders winced. He wasn't sure making a dragon drop a child from a great height counted as "rescue," but he probably wasn't meant to be thinking about that.

"Sure are fancy," Rayna agreed. "But fancy puppets won't feed me dinner."

When Anders looked over, she was pulling her fishing rod from inside her coat, screwing the sections together until the handle was complete, and taking up position at the edge of the building. There was a sausage seller right below them, a wizened little man, only his gray hair and thick green coat visible from Anders's vantage point. Rayna lowered the hook, and when he wasn't looking, she carefully snagged one of his sausages.

Below them the crowd was still gasping over the end of the puppet show and handing up copper coins for the performers, arguing about how the dragon puppet had been made to breathe fire.

Rayna reeled the line back in quickly and carefully, swinging it around toward Anders, who unhooked the sausage. He rolled over onto his back and made it swim up and down like they'd just caught a fish, or like it was one of the puppets below.

"Don't play with your food," she laughed, looking down to see about getting another. It had been a genius idea of hers to use the fishing line. Nobody ever looked up for a thief.

Well, it wasn't as true these days that nobody ever looked up, not with rumors about dragons in the skies again, but it was still better than thieving on the ground. They'd have to do that tomorrow, to get their hands on some coins.

Anders sometimes worried about the stealing, but Rayna always shrugged. "There's no other way," she'd say. "We'll take care of us, and they can take care of them."

Rayna was frowning as the sausage seller handed off the last of his wares to a customer and began packing up his stall, and she dismantled her rod, wandering over to peer down into the alleyway behind their rooftop.

"Pssst," she called, waving Anders across to join her a minute later. "Look at that window."

With a sinking feeling he crossed over, then leaned out to take a look. He was pretty sure he knew where this was heading. There was a little window down there, half open. "Rayna, no way," he tried.

"Pffft, your legs are long enough," she said. "And just think what might be inside."

"A person!" he said. "A person might be inside!"

She waved a hand in dismissal. "A window that small,

no way does it lead to a main room. It'll be the bathroom, or the pantry. Nobody'll see you."

There were a dozen more arguments about why this was a bad idea, but Anders didn't bother making them. He knew how it would end, no matter what he said. So instead, sighing, he handed his coat to her, then lowered himself off the edge of the roof.

He ended up dangling by his hands, his feet feeling around for the window ledge as Rayna gave instructions, and he began to worry he'd have to let go. It was going to *hurt*, if he landed on the cobblestones.

Just as he was really starting to panic, he finally found the little ledge, getting both his feet onto it. He balanced carefully as he walked his hands down the stone wall, until eventually he was low enough that he could feed himself in through the window.

He landed lightly in what turned out to be the pantry, arms windmilling as he tried to avoid tipping over into the shelves lining the small room. He stabilized and breathed out in relief.

That relief lasted about ten seconds, before he heard the sound of the front door opening. The breeze it created pushed through the rooms, and when it reached Anders in the pantry, it slammed shut the little window above him. He whirled around, reaching up to push it open again, but his heart was sinking even as he turned.

Sure enough, the lock had clicked into place. And he didn't have the key.

He stared at his lost escape route in horror. Why did these things always happen to him?

Footsteps approached, and he spun back, searching the tiny space for a good spot to hide. After a couple of seconds of desperate consideration, he crammed himself behind a brown glazed pot almost as big as he was.

He grabbed the lid off the pot, the brine of pickled vegetables wafting up to tickle his nose, and balanced it on top of his head where he crouched. It was dark in the pantry, and if he was lucky his warm brown skin would blend in with the pots around him. Though in his experience, Anders was rarely lucky.

The footsteps stopped just outside the pantry door, which was still ajar. Through it, he could see a woman who looked like she wanted to stand out as much as he wanted to blend in. She wore a truly magnificent hat adorned with piles of expensive flowers. Her dress was large and purple, designed to take up lots of space, and she wore matching purple powder on her brown cheeks. She was clearly wealthy, and she had a haughty tilt to her chin as she leaned in to inspect herself in the hall mirror and adjust the hat.

"That Dama Barro," she said to herself, indignant.

"And Dama Chardi. I'll show them whose sweetcakes are flat. We'll just see who's laughing at the next contest, won't we?"

Anders stared at her. Was she talking to herself? How long was she going to take? And *how* was he going to get out of here? If she caught him, she'd report him to the Wolf Guard for sure.

Just as he was trying to remind himself to breathe slowly, there came a knock at the front door.

Seriously?

The woman and her hat bustled away to answer, and a moment later he heard Rayna's cheerful voice, though he couldn't make out her words. One thing you could say about Rayna was that she always jumped in headfirst, whether or not she had a plan.

Suddenly, the woman's voice grew nearer again. "I told you, I really don't want—"

Rayna didn't let her get another word in edgewise, and suddenly Anders realized she'd forced her way into the house. "As I said, we're offering a free sausage to every house, today only, as a sample of our wares. I think you'll find we sell the finest sausages in the city of Holbard, Dama! Perhaps in all of Vallen!"

He watched as Rayna strode past the pantry door, followed by the woman, who was clearly trying to get her out of the house. They looked in that moment as though they could be related—if Rayna wasn't in a shabby dress, and the woman wasn't in fancy clothes, they could be mother and daughter. This could be his and Rayna's home.

Suddenly he realized that his moment of daydreaming had distracted him from the fact that the woman wasn't between him and the front door anymore. He dumped the lid he was balancing on his head and climbed out from behind the jar.

He took a deep breath, then hurried out of the pantry, sneaking toward the front door.

"Hey!" The woman's voice sounded sharply behind him! He ran for the door.

"Enjoy your sausage," Rayna shouted as she followed close on his heels. She threw him his coat as they ran through the square, squeezing past the crowd and pushing their way into an alley on the other side. They were out of sight before the woman made it out her front door.

"Whew," said Rayna. "That was close. What did you get?"

"Get?" he echoed, pulling on his coat. "What do you mean?"

"Get," she repeated. "It was the pantry, wasn't it? What food did you take? I had to give her the sausage to get you out. It was a good sausage too."

"I . . . I didn't get anything. I was too busy trying to figure out how to hide, once the window closed," he admitted.

Rayna was quiet for a moment, but then, as she always did when he messed up, she grinned and slung an arm around his shoulders. "Doesn't matter," she said cheerfully. "We saw a puppet show today, that was pretty good."

Dusk was falling, and they both knew it was time to hole up for the night. It wasn't a good idea for twelve-year-olds to be out after nightfall. So they made their way over the rooftops of Holbard until they reached a tavern near the center of town.

The Wily Wolf, the sign outside said. They had to move all over the city to scrounge up enough to stay fed, so they couldn't always make it back to the Wolf at night. But whenever they could, they did. The Wily Wolf was special.

On the ground floor it was bustling with business, golden lights coming on one by one, noise spilling out into the street. But it had two more stories above that, fairly tall for a building in Holbard, and it was on a small hill as well.

Together they climbed up to the roof and lifted a hatch they'd found years ago, all overgrown with grass. Inside was a tiny attic, really just a space between the grassy roof-top above and the flat ceiling beneath. There was no way to get to it from below, and it wasn't large enough for an adult to even sit up inside. But it was just big enough for the twins to curl up and stay warm.

Anders always thought that curling up inside the roof of the Wily Wolf was as close as he could get to coming home. It was their special place—their secret.

Rayna wriggled down first, and Anders paused halfway in to look around and take in the view, which was quickly vanishing in the dusk. Thick city walls circled Holbard, the plains and mountains beyond lost in the dark. The rooftop meadows stretched away in every direction, and to the east of him was the glint of the sea, the masts of the ships in the harbor.

Just as he was about to pull the hatch down, he heard a soft mew from nearby. He waited another few moments, and a small black shadow with bright yellow eyes slipped out of nowhere, darting down to join Rayna. It was Kess, a cat that sometimes slept with them at night to keep warm.

Anders pulled down the hatch on top of the three of them, and Rayna spread the blanket over the two humans, Kess curling up by their feet. Anders's stomach was growling with hunger, and he was sure his sister's was too, but neither of them mentioned the lost sausage. Or the fact that even surrounded by food, he hadn't thought to shove any in his pockets. Safe together in their secret spot, the evening didn't seem so bad.

Still, he had to say something. "Thanks for coming to get me," he whispered.

"Don't be silly," Rayna whispered back. "What else was I going to do? We're a team." She wriggled one arm out from under the blanket to wrap it around him. "We'll always be together, Anders. We'll always take care of each other, I promise. Right?"

"I promise too," he said, because of course it was true.

But as they settled down to sleep, and he lay there in the dark, waiting to drift away, he knew the truth. Rayna would never need him like he needed her.

CHAPTER TWO

THE NEXT MORNING, ANDERS AND RAYNA WERE
on their way to the docks early. The monthly Ulfar
testing—the Trial of the Staff—was one of their best
pickpocketing days, so neither of them wanted to miss a
moment of it. And it turned out to be a good thing they'd
started out early—the Wolf Guard were still on street corners, far more of them than usual. The twins were forced
up onto the rooftop meadows again, which was safer but
took longer. Finding ways to cross the streets often meant
going out of their way by several blocks.

Their goal, the dockside square, was bordered by tall,
thin, colorful houses on three sides—yellow, green, and
blue, with square white window frames and polished
wooden doors. The houses were squeezed together, two
and three stories tall, often with more than one family living in them.

On the fourth side of the square was the harbor. From far away the docks looked like a forest, masts sticking up from a flotilla of ships from all over the world. Vallen wasn't a big island, but everyone always said that you didn't need to leave the capital city of Holbard to see the world—the world would come right to you instead. And that was because of the wind guards.

High above the entrance to the port were the huge, metal arches of the wind guards, the biggest artifacts in all of Vallen. They had protected the harbor for generations.

The arches were marked with runes forged all along their length—the runes were the sign of an artifact—and were big enough for even the largest ship to pass under. But though Anders could see straight through them to the ocean on the other side, the guards magically kept out the wind. Even when a storm raged beyond them, the harbor was always peaceful.

The docks were where newcomers arrived in the city of Holbard from all over the world. The safety of the harbor meant that people from every place Anders could imagine—and some he couldn't—came not only to trade, but to live as well. From what Anders knew, most cities were a mix of people from all over, but perhaps none were quite as varied as Holbard.

The dock was where traders waited for news of their

goods, where merchers and fishers plied their wares, and where Anders and Rayna picked pockets once a month, during the trial—and occasionally on other days too.

The Trial of the Staff was a spectacle, and it meant a square full of visiting merchers who were usually so busy gawking at the twelve-year-olds on the dais that they never noticed the twelve-year-olds right beside them, slipping a hand into their pocket or basket. The visitors all knew of the elementals found in their homelands, but ice wolves—and scorch dragons—were unique to Vallen, and nobody wanted to miss seeing a child transform into an ice wolf before their very eyes.

Anders was never entirely easy at the docks. He and Rayna had no idea where they'd been during the last great battle, ten years ago. But Anders thought perhaps they'd been here—there was always something about the place that made him nervous. He would look at the scorch marks on the wooden doors, and for an instant he'd think he could smell smoke. The crowd would jostle him— which never bothered him anywhere else—and it was as if he heard a scream, quickly snatched away. Sometimes he had nightmares about it.

Today the twins climbed down from the rooftops a couple of streets away and made their way on foot to the square. As they reached the edge of the crowd, a warm, salty smell came wafting in their direction, and Anders knew it immediately. Somewhere, a mercher was selling roasted veter nuts, their favorite. They'd only managed to pickpocket two coppers on the way down to the docks, but . . .

He and Rayna whispered the same words at exactly the same time: "What about—" They both paused to snicker, then finished together: "Breakfast?"

"We'll have more money before the morning's out," Rayna said. "Let's have a treat."

They squeezed their way through the tight press of bodies, following their noses. And sure enough, there was a woman in a bright green coat roasting glossy brown veter nuts in a large cast-iron pan. There was no fire underneath to warm it, but there were runes carved all around the outside of the pan, marching along its edge in a neat procession, and it was heating itself without any fire needed.

"A copper a bag," the mercher said, noticing them looking.

"Usually it's a copper for two," Rayna protested. "Are they some kind of special nuts?"

"They're artifact-cooked," the woman replied. "The heat's more even than you'll get over any fire, and you'll taste the difference. No burned bits."

Rayna grumbled, but Anders knew her mouth had to

be watering as much as his, and in the end she handed over their two coppers. The woman handed them each a fat paper bag the size of their fist, stuffed full of roasted nuts, and they drifted into the crowd, munching through them as fast as they could. It was nearly time to start.

They dodged a pack of four Ulfar Academy students—teenagers who had passed the monthly trials already, and would one day be Wolf Guards—who wandered by in their gray uniforms, trimmed with white to show they were students. They were often in fours, Anders noticed.

Suddenly everyone's attention turned to the dais on one side of the square, and though Anders couldn't see over the heads of the crowd, he knew the trial must be beginning. He licked his fingers clean and stuffed the last of his veter nuts into his pocket.

It was the start of spring, and the only remaining traces of the snow were the gray lumps around the edges of the square, but he was still wearing his winter coat. It was lined with pockets where he could stash his takings, and the cold wind that still blew meant it wasn't out of place.

He and Rayna drifted along the edges of the crowd, where the people were less tightly packed, looking for their first target and pretending not to know each other. The siblings might have the same curly black hair and the same medium brown skin, but somewhere like Holbard, where people came from every place there was, that was no reason to think they were related. And everything else was so different about them that they looked nothing like twins.

Anders spotted a woman with her head craned back, staring up at the sky nervously. The rumors about dragons were everywhere. Her expression was distracted, and her clothes looked expensive, which might mean good pickings. He bumped his shoulder against Rayna's, nodding in the woman's direction.

Rayna stopped to fiddle with the buttons on her coat, looking over his target from beneath her lashes. Then she shook her head, just a fraction. "Zips," she murmured.

Anders shuffled a step to his left, taking a surreptitious look at the woman's pockets. He sucked in a quick breath. No wonder she was so absentminded; she had no need to worry about her pockets at all. They were lined with chunky metal zips, and hanging from each zipper was a small metal charm, engraved with a pair of runes.

He'd nearly reached for a thiefcatcher. If he'd laid his hands on the zips to open her pockets, the charms would have started blaring a quick, high alarm, turning every face in the square toward him. It would have been a disaster. *Trust him to get it wrong.*

He bit his lip, and Rayna gave his hand a quick

squeeze—*never mind*, the squeeze said—and led him onward. He let her pick the next target. He wasn't as good as she was at pickpocketing anyway—or at lock picking, or at anything, really—but he was always worst of all in the square, where he was nervous.

Rayna chose a mercher just as the leader of the wolves—the Fyrstulf, Dama Sigrid Turnsen—took to the dais. The mayor of Holbard and two members of Vallen's parliament already stood waiting for her in their finest coats and gold-linked chains of office, but everybody in the square—everybody from Vallen, at least—knew where the real power was on the wooden stage. Sigrid Turnsen was a pale woman with short, white-blond hair, lean in her gray uniform, the opposite of the man Rayna had picked for their target.

Their mark was a broad-shouldered man with a bright red-and-blue jacket of thin, silky material that fluttered in the breeze. The red on his coat was their first clue that he would be an easy target—it was the color of a dragon, so locals rarely wore it.

The flimsy materials and the long, sweeping sleeves of the mercher's coat suggested he came from the Dewdrops Archipelago, and that he'd most likely arrived recently, since he clearly hadn't planned for Vallen's cold winds. As a newcomer, all his attention was probably on Sigrid

Turnsen right now. And possibly on how much he wished he had a more practical coat.

"Now, more than ever, we must remain vigilant," the Fyrstulf was saying, her voice ringing out across the square as Anders took up position. He'd heard this speech every month since he was six, but it never sounded boring. The power in the Fyrstulf's voice always kept a part of his attention on her. Rayna did a pretty good impression of the speech, but Anders could never find it in himself to laugh at Sigrid Turnsen.

"After ten years of peace," she continued, "the dragons wish to turn toward war once again." Well, *that* part of the speech was new. Things really must be serious if the Fyrstulf was acknowledging them out loud.

"Ten years ago the Wolf Guard drove them back from Holbard to their refuges in the mountains, and now we stand ready to do so again. We know that anyone here could be of scorch dragon blood. Could be a spy, willing to risk the safety and stability we have worked so hard to build in the last decade across all of Vallen."

Anders stared at her as she spoke, a shiver running through him that had nothing to do with the nerves the docks usually awoke in him. Even though she spoke about the battle each month, reminded the Vallenites of the danger and the sacrifices the wolves had made, this month she was more intense than usual, an edge to her voice.

Casually, Rayna slipped into place just in front of the mercher, apparently choosing that moment to retie the tattered ribbon at the end of her braid. She adjusted her copper hairpins and fiddled with her bow a little, tucking in a stray black curl, and then flung the braid back over her shoulder. In the same movement, she released a pinch of finely ground pepper from between her thumb and forefinger. It wafted straight up to the mercher, who was already drawing breath in indignation at having Rayna's hair shaken in his face.

Anders's job was to slip two fingers into the man's pocket—a thumb was too bulky—and let them graze along the silk of the lining until he found his coin purse. Quickly he eased it free, then dipped inside his own coat, dropping the purse into one of the waiting pockets. It felt light, though—probably just a couple of coppers.

He left the man in the middle of a sneezing fit and slid sideways, past a pair of local merchers in brown coats. Rayna would meet him away to the man's right, as always. Together, they set off in search of their next mark.

Anders extracted a small purse from a woman in a yellow dress busy gossiping with her neighbor, while Rayna politely asked them the time, keeping away from the front of the crowd.

The Wolf Guard lined the edge of the dais as the Fyrstulf spoke, all alike in their gray uniforms, hair cut short, eyes narrowed as they swept across the crowd. It was like they were beaten into the same shape when they walked through the doors of Ulfar Academy, each one turned out from the same mold.

Sigrid was speaking again. "Who now claims ice wolf blood and, having reached their twelfth birthday, steps forward to be tested? Many Vallenites proudly claim at least one wolf in their ancestry, but few have the gift that will allow them to transform." The words gave Anders a shiver. The gift she was talking about could change someone's life forever in an instant. "With this rare gift," the Fyrstulf said grandly, "comes great responsibility: an obligation to enter Ulfar Academy. To train to join the Wolf Guard, and devote one's life to protecting Vallen. It means life as a soldier. It means—"

A brutal gust of wind tore through the square, ripping away her words. The crowd staggered and some fell, screams rising all around Anders.

In an instant he was in the middle of the memory this place always tried to bring back. The screaming was terror, the wind was carrying smoke, and as Rayna grabbed for him, he saw movement out of the corner of his eye.

He whirled around to see something huge moving

amidst the sea of ships' masts, and his brain conjured up the rumors from the night before—conjured up the memory of the dragon he'd seen with his own eyes just half a year before.

His mind made the billowing ship's sail into a dragon, swooping in toward the port—and then the wind was gone, and he saw the dragon was no more than cloth, and realized the screams were dying away. His heart slammed in his chest as the people around him picked themselves up.

"The artifacts are failing," a woman wailed nearby.

"The dragons are doing it," another hissed.

Up on the dais, the Fyrstulf was looking as calm as ever, as if nothing had happened. "The wind arches sometimes require venting," she said, raising her voice over the hubbub of the crowd. "That should have been arranged for the nighttime, when nobody would have been disturbed. My apologies. Now, let us continue with the Trial of the Staff. Who seeks to join the Wolf Guard and play their part in protecting our people?"

The crowd was still murmuring as five children his own age walked up the steps to the dais, three girls and two boys. They were each dressed in their best, and the last girl in line was shaking so hard Anders was pretty sure she was going to fall off the stage before she made it up to the Staff of Hadda and the Trial itself. Anders was still trembling pretty hard himself after the fright the surge of wind had given him.

There were at least two dozen more children queuing for their chance to make it up onto the dais. Most of them wouldn't succeed. In a good month, two or three candidates would successfully transform. Anders always felt sorry for the ones who failed.

The first boy stepped up to stand front and center as a member of the guard handed Sigrid the staff. Sigrid nodded, and the boy's face drained of what little color it had, until it almost matched his fine white coat. When he spoke, he was so nervous his voice shook as he lifted it to be heard over the noise the crowd was still making.

"My name is Natan Haugen. My grandfather is Bergur Haugen, who was a member of the Wolf Guard. My great-grandmother was Serena Andersen, who was a member of the Wolf Guard. My brother Nicolas Haugen transformed three years ago and is a student at Ulfar Academy. I claim ice wolf blood and stand for the Trial."

Sigrid and many of the crowd nodded as Natan looked sidelong at the Fyrstulf. Even from his place in the crowd, Anders could tell that Natan was gazing at the amulet hanging at the woman's throat.

The amulet was a small ring of gray polished metal suspended on a leather band, engraved with a complex design in runes. There were stories about what the amulets did—that they allowed a wolf to tell when you were lying, that they gave a wolf the strength of ten people, or perhaps just that they were the only way of knowing a true member of the guard. Whatever they were for, Natan was staring at Sigrid's like it was his ticket to a new life, and in a way, he was right.

It was a life Anders would never have, though—he'd never belong to anything as important as Ulfar, and he'd never have a family lineage he could recite like that. Rayna was all he had—*and she was more than enough*, he reminded himself.

But sometimes, especially on the hungry days, he wished he too had a mother or father, aunts or uncles, or grandparents.

The boy reached for the Staff of Hadda, then hesitated. So many hands had gripped it over the years that the pale wood was worn smooth, a long strip of engraved metal wrapping around it in a spiral. The staff was one of the most important artifacts in Vallen. Only the most powerful were named for their creators, and for the wolves the Staff of Hadda transformed, it was a ticket to a new life.

Bracing himself, Natan grasped the staff, and the whole square held its breath—even Anders and Rayna paused, standing side by side.

Nothing happened.

Several heartbeats later, Sigrid reached out to rest her hand on Natan's shoulder, slowly guiding him back and away from the staff. "Vallen thanks you for your willingness to serve," she said, but as she released him, and he stumbled to the edge of the dais to walk slowly down the stairs, she was already looking hungrily at the next girl in line. Anders bit his lip, watching the other boy's shoulders slump.

The next girl didn't transform either. Rayna grabbed Anders's hand, giving him a squeeze as reminder that they had work to do. They picked their way through the crowd, scoring a copper here, another two coppers there, Rayna doing the bold work of distraction, Anders carefully taking hold of the money and trying not to alert his marks or mess it up.

The familiar ceremony wore on in the background as candidate after candidate recited their lineage as proof of their right to undertake the Trial, and trembling, grasped the staff. The mood in the square grew darker as every single one of them stubbornly stayed in human shape.

Now, more than ever, Vallen needed more wolves, more members of the guard, more defenders. But this month yielded up none at all. Anders couldn't remember there ever being *none* before.

He slid his hand into a tall man's fancy coat pocket as

a frail-looking girl made her way down the steps, head low. The twins were a little closer to the dais—and a little farther from an escape route—than Anders liked to be. Rayna was completely confident as she tossed her braid again and accidentally bumped into a pair of merchers, but Anders didn't have her courage, and his hand was shaking as he tried for one final coin.

He couldn't help watching the girl making her way down from the stage, feeling bad for her. Her shirt and trousers were neat but plain, a little old-fashioned. She'd come in from the countryside with her parents, most likely, and it would be a long trip home with nothing to show for it.

He curled his fingers around a coin that felt heavy— silver, perhaps. And maybe because his mind was on the girl, imagining the creak of the cart as they drove home in silence, he caught his wrist on the seam at the edge of the pocket, and for an instant his hand was stuck. He cursed inwardly, easing it free, lifting onto the balls of his feet so he could step back the moment it was clear—but it was too late. The mercher turned his head almost in slow-motion, eyes widening, mouth opening to shout.

"Thief!" he bellowed, one hand clamping down on Anders's wrist with an iron grip. Anders only had time to drop the coin back into his pocket before he was yanked off balance, hauled forward so the man could get a better look at him. *No, no! Why did he always mess things up?* "This boy was picking my pocket," the man announced, glaring down at Anders, his thick blond brows crowding together in disapproval.

"I wasn't!" Anders protested automatically. "I don't have anything in my hand!" *Because I just dropped it back into your pocket.* But he knew that wasn't going to be enough. When he lifted his head, he could already see a member of the guard jumping down from the dais to push through the crowd toward him, and the people around them were drawing back, like they wanted to distance themselves from the crime.

"You're a thief," the man insisted, as Anders tried in vain to stop himself shaking, forcing himself not to look at Rayna—he couldn't afford for her to be caught too. "And if you have nothing, it's only because you're a bad one. In a minute, my child, you're going to wish you'd been good."

CHAPTER THREE

ONE MOMENT ANDERS WAS STARING UP AT THE mercher holding his wrist, trying not to whimper at the pain of his wrist bones practically grinding together, breath stuck in his throat as terror crept through him. And the next moment, Rayna was at his side.

"Don't be ridiculous," she said, barging through a pair of women to reach Anders. "Get your hands off him, you bully! He was just trying to get past."

"Past?" the man repeated, blinking. His grip on Anders didn't slacken, but like most people confronted with Rayna, he already looked a little overwhelmed.

"*Past*," she repeated, rolling her eyes, as if he needed the word spoken a little slower so he'd understand. "You don't look like you're twelve to me, so unless you're here for the Trial, you need to get out of the way of those of us trying to get in the line. You're standing right here in front of it, blocking the way, so what did you expect? It's not this boy's fault he's too polite to shove through."

"And who are you?" he asked, drawing himself up to his full height, pulling Anders a stumbling step closer. Anders winced. Rayna was as nimble with her words as she was with her feet, but Anders didn't like the way this was heading.

Rayna didn't miss a beat. "I'm the girl who was trying to get behind him in the line," she replied, as though it was obvious. That was the first rule of defending each other—never admit you were twins. People believed you more easily if they didn't think you had anything to do with the other one. "Now, can we get to the dais or not?"

The dais? Anders froze.

By now a member of the Wolf Guard had arrived—a tall woman with a flawless gray uniform, her cloak hanging open to reveal the crisp shirt and trousers below, black boots shining. The crest of Ulfar—a fierce wolf guarding the city of Holbard itself—snarled down at Anders from where it was fixed on her chest. "You're here for the Trial?" she asked, gaze falling on Rayna.

"We both are," Rayna said, at the same time as the man still holding Anders tried to protest they were here for nothing of the sort. But his grip slackened, and Anders yanked his wrist free, rubbing it with his other hand.

"Then you should be on the dais," the woman said, turning to lead the way back toward it without another word. Before the man had a chance to protest, Rayna grabbed Anders's hand and hauled him toward the dais in the woman's wake.

People were turning toward them from every direction, and Anders kept his head down, face hot. Rayna had got them out of the frying pan and into the fire, as always, and he was left trying to catch up, wishing that for once *he'd* been quick enough on his feet to know the right thing to say, the right thing to do.

But instead, he was climbing the wooden stairs to the dais, only a few feet from the Fyrstulf herself, every face in the crowd turned toward him. He glanced out at them, knowing what they saw—a gangly boy in patched and battered clothes, blinking awkwardly at all the attention, with hair in need of a cut and face in need of a wash.

He knew as well that he was thinking about his appearance to avoid thinking of the hundreds of pairs of eyes on him, all waiting for him to do or say something that would reveal he had no right to be on the dais at all. He and Rayna had no idea who their parents, let alone ancestors, were, but he was sure there was nothing special about them.

What happened if you touched the Staff of Hadda

without a single drop of wolf blood in your veins? Perhaps they'd get out of this yet—just fail the Trial and manage to slip away before the angry mercher caught up with them. The crowd was still nervous after that huge gust of wind, which might make it easier to disappear.

Rayna was standing ahead of him—after all, she'd physically hauled him up the stairs—and she shot the Fyrstulf her most winning smile, stepping up front and center to present her family history. *This should be interesting.*

"My name is Estrid Larsen," she announced, which was news to Anders along with everyone else, though he wasn't surprised. If the first rule of staying safe together was never admitting you were connected, the second was never giving your real names. "And my family is strong in ice wolf blood. My grandmother was Ida Larsen, who was a member of the Wolf Guard, and—"

"What was that name?" Sigrid Turnsen, the Fyrstulf, was frowning.

"Ida Larsen," Rayna—uh, Estrid—supplied helpfully.

"I don't recall her," Sigrid said, still frowning.

"Oh, she was from out of town," Rayna assured her glibly.

"But to be a member of the Wolf Guard, she must have lived in Holbard," Sigrid pointed out. The crowd was looking far too interested in this turn of events. Including the mercher, who had made his way to the front to wait for his turn with Anders.

"She had terrible eyesight," Rayna said, confident as ever, as Anders tried to hide his wince. "She couldn't actually serve, it turned out. She lived a quiet life up in the mountains."

"In dragon territory?" Sigrid's frown was now a permanent furrow between her brows. "But all members of the Wolf Guard live at the Ulfar Barracks. You're about my daughter's age; I'm sure I'd remember your grandmother."

"Did I say in the mountains?" Even Rayna was faltering now. "Lower down than dragon territory, obviously. More like foothills, really. Still! The most important thing isn't who else successfully transformed, it's whether I can, so I'll just reach across here if you don't mind, and—"

Sigrid clearly did mind, but Rayna was already reaching past her, fingers outstretched toward the Staff of Hadda. Anders silently urged her on. The sooner she touched it and turned into nothing at all, the sooner they could make their escape. Even if he *was* going to have to recite his own imaginary lineage first.

Rayna bit her lip, and wrapped her hand around the smooth wooden staff, gripping it tightly. As she did, Anders realized he was holding his breath, even though as far as he knew she was about as likely to transform into a cabbage as a wolf. He and Rayna had started out in an orphanage, then raised themselves after that on the streets of Holbard. They weren't wolves waiting to happen.

Abruptly, Rayna screamed, her eyes popping wide open, back arching as she flung out her free arm, drawing gasps from the crowd. She staggered back a step, swinging the Staff of Hadda so the two members of the Wolf Guard behind her were forced to jump out of the way.

Stop, Anders urged her silently, wanting to sink down through the dais and into the ground, the hot flame of embarrassment taking over his body. This was Rayna, always selling the story, always so dramatic. But right now, the last thing they needed was more people looking at them.

Rayna screamed again, dropping the staff and doubling over to brace her hands against her knees. She turned her head to cast a desperate glance at Anders, and like a crashing wave of ice-cold water had hit him, the embarrassment was gone.

This was real—his sister was terrified. And this was nothing like any transformation he'd ever seen.

He stepped forward, reaching for her, but she screamed again, raw and hoarse, staggering forward to fall from the dais, crashing to the flagstones below.

The crowd jumped away as Rayna rolled onto her

back, arms outflung. Her face darkened to a deep, unnatural burgundy, then shifted to shades of bright crimson, as if all her skin were bleeding at once. Hints of gold, bronze, and copper snaked in, glinting in the sun, racing down her neck to disappear beneath her clothes.

As Anders watched in horror, frozen to the spot, her arms and legs seemed to stretch impossibly long, and the arms of her coat stretched and split, the tearing noise of the fabric lost beneath the screams of the crowd.

The fabric shredded and vanished in seconds as Rayna's body grew, doubling in size, then tripling, her neck lengthening, her mouth open in a hoarse, unending scream. Crimson, bronze, and copper wove together into glittering scales as they snaked across her skin, and a heartbeat later, Rayna was gone.

In her place lay a scorch dragon fifteen feet long, sprawled on its back, claws raking through the air as it roared over the sound of the crowd. It scrambled, rolling onto its side and clambering to its feet, wings spreading wide, tail lashing in a long arc.

This was impossible! Waves of heat washed over Anders, as if he were far too close to a fire—his skin stung, the lining of his throat burning as he dragged down air.

"Attack!" the Fyrstulf screamed beside him, jolting Anders from his horror.

The dragon's tail swept toward him, catching him in the ribs and knocking him clean off his feet. Pain rippled through his body, and he couldn't tell whether the heat—it was coming from the dragon, for certain—was burning him, or just blasting him. All he knew was that there was a dragon right above him, roaring so loudly the sound itself was like a living thing.

He scrambled desperately off the dais and fell backward just as the long snake of a tail smashed through the supports on the stage, reducing it to so much firewood.

He grabbed at a plank where it lay across his body, trying to shove it off him. Gasping for breath he sat up, pain shooting along his ribs. The Fyrstulf, Sigrid, lay beside him, dazed, a cut on her forehead bleeding.

The dragon's tail thrashed about again, and he ducked, rolling onto his hands and knees. Where had it come from? What had happened to Rayna?

It *was* Rayna.

The people in the crowd were screaming, and the dragon was roaring again, but somehow that realization cut through Anders's thoughts, stopping him in his tracks. However it had happened, that dragon was his *sister*.

All around him, the members of the Wolf Guard were transforming, their uniforms seeming to melt into their skin as they dropped to all fours, shaggy coats appearing where gray wool had been a moment before, teeth bared as they lifted their muzzles and snarled. Anders had never seen a wolf transform so close before, and their deep-throated growls were terrifying.

The ice wolf beside him reared onto its hind legs, then crashed back down to earth. As its front paws hit the cobblestones, two long spears of ice burst from the ground, sharp and jagged, flying straight at the dragon's gleaming side. They were like huge, deadly icicles with razor-sharp points—Anders had never seen them outside a puppet show or a play, but he knew immediately what was happening.

Where they struck Rayna, her scales instantly turned gray with cold. She screamed, spreading her wings, and more wolves brought down their front paws on the ground, launching ice spears at her as Anders was forced to drop to his belly. He sensed them slicing through the air more than he saw them, like clean, cold arrows through the confusion of the heat.

The dragon brought her wings down in a great sweep, and with her tail thrashing and her claws grabbing at the air as though to lift herself, she somehow took off. The down-draught flattened Anders, and he scrambled for the shelter of the wreckage behind him as the ice spears flew, and the crowd screamed, and the wolves howled.

Then, beside him, he saw it—the Staff of Hadda. It was half buried in the wreckage of the dais, along with Anders. That smooth, worn pole had somehow triggered this dreadful transformation. He had to find a way to use it to transform Rayna back, but as he tried to make himself reach for it, he found himself yanking back his hand instead.

What would happen to *him* if he touched it?

Above him, the dragon—Rayna—screamed again, and he made himself grab for the staff.

Pain rushed through him, setting his arms and legs on fire, and the screams of the crowd grew unbearably loud, his ears filling with the high-pitched wall of noise, his nose suddenly filled with the scent of sweat, of wet woolen clothing, and the musk of wolf fur. He felt his shirt tearing, and as his senses overwhelmed him, he could only think of one thing—*run!*

He dug his fingertips—his claws (his *what*?!)—into the flagstones, scrambling free of the wreckage and pushing through the crowds, shoving a pair of knees aside and hurtling through a forest of legs. He suddenly broke free, tearing up a street, past the stationary wheels of a wagon and the legs of two rearing horses, past the houses and the wooden doorways that still showed their singe marks.

Finally he turned a corner to find an alleyway, a stack of crates at one end offering a place to hide. He scampered in behind them, his breath coming in quick, short pants, his tongue lolling out as he tried to slow his thoughts, force himself to calm.

All around him was the scent of the moss and mildew that grew in the shady alleyways the sun never reached, the muddy mush of melting snow, the wet wood of the crates.

The lines of the alleyway were perfectly crisp, but the colors of the world had faded, subdued, as if night were falling—as if he'd run so fast he'd left all the bright shades of Holbard behind. But he was free of the crowd.

Shaking, he looked down, and saw two gray paws stretched out in front of him. He tried to shout, but all that came out was a yelp.

Suddenly seized by panic, he spun in a circle, stretching out his tail to catch his balance, and he—*his tail!*

Understanding caught up to him in a rush, and he heard himself softly whimper. Rayna was a scorch dragon, and *he was an ice wolf.*

He forced himself to stay silent, to stop panting, and again tried desperately to collect his thoughts. He had to find her.

He had to explain to somebody that she was no dragon, she wasn't the enemy—she was his twin, and it was impossible for the same family to transform into both wolf and dragon. The wolves defended Vallen *against* the dragons. It was forbidden to even befriend one, let alone share a family.

Somehow this had been done *to* her—he was positive she was his twin, so there must be trickery involved—and he had to make the Wolf Guard understand that she wasn't on the side of the dragons before they hurt her.

But first, he had to find a way to become human again, so he could speak. Though he was unquestionably still himself inside this new body, the influx of extra information his suddenly sharp senses insisted on providing was tugging his thoughts in a different direction every moment. His nose and ears kept reporting on new sounds and scents, trying to steer his thoughts in new and different directions, to pay attention to everything happening around him.

He closed his eyes and looked inside himself, trying to remember what it felt like to be human, noticing the differences and separating them out.

He pushed his mind deeper into those human feelings and memories, and suddenly he felt the change surging toward him like a sneeze. With a rush, he was human once more.

He could feel the cold cobblestones against the soles of his feet, and the tips of his fingers, and he could—but wait. If his feet were bare, where were his boots?

Forget his boots, where were his *clothes?*

Anders made a sound very like the whimper he'd made as a wolf, dropping his head. Of course he was naked. Of *course* he was. The Wolf Guard might have absorbed their uniforms into their fur somehow, but he'd felt his shirt rip. And to think he'd been stupid enough to assume just for one moment that his day couldn't get any worse.

Clearly he'd been wrong about that.

He heard a roar from the sky overhead, and tipped his head back just in time to see the dragon—Rayna—the dragon that *was* Rayna—soar past, winging her way toward the farmland outside the city. Suddenly he became aware of the screams out in the streets of Holbard once more.

"Rayna!" he shouted as she vanished. "Rayna, come back, I'm here! You can change back, you can . . ."

But Rayna was gone, and Anders had never been more alone.

CHAPTER FOUR

ANDERS LEANED AGAINST THE STACKED CRATES, despondent, then stopped leaning against them when he got a splinter in his side. His ribs were already aching where Rayna's tail had smacked into them. But that wasn't his biggest problem.

There was nothing here he could use for clothing—and even if he somehow dressed himself, he had no idea how to find Rayna. He could still hear the distant roar of the crowd, though he was several minutes' run from the port. He didn't understand any of what had just happened, didn't know what to do next, had no idea—

But just as he began to spiral into panic, he heard a growl at the mouth of the alleyway, and then a soft whine. His heart picked up speed as he crouched, peeking through a crack between two crates. Perhaps he could hide. Perhaps he could . . . *Oh no.* There were three wolves at the mouth of the alleyway, noses to the ground. Tracking him.

The largest of the three growled again, and they each blurred, then seemed to stretch, fur fading into gray uniforms as they rose up on their hind legs and suddenly became human once more. And naturally, they were still wearing their clothes. There must be some trick to it he didn't know.

There were two adults—a man and a woman—each in the neat gray uniform of the Wolf Guard, their heavy cloaks open over their shirts and trousers and neatly polished boots, their hair clipped short. The third was a girl his own age, her gray cloak edged in white, marking her as an Ulfar Academy student. She must have been there to watch the Trial.

"Are you all right?" It was the leader of the trio speaking, a big, broad-shouldered man with a neatly trimmed beard and square, black, thick-rimmed glasses. He had been silver-gray as a wolf, but as a human his hair was black, his skin a medium brown.

"Um." Anders was dying inside, but there was only one answer he could give, because he knew they'd want him to come out from behind the crates next. "I ripped my way out of my clothes. I don't have . . ."

There was laughter from the other side of the crates, and even though it wasn't unkind, Anders squeezed his eyes tight shut in embarrassment.

"Hold on," the man said, and there was a rustling sound. Then footsteps approached, and when Anders forced himself to look, a hand was reaching around the crates, holding an assortment of clothes. The girl's white-edged cloak was there, along with a far-too-big gray shirt, a pair of someone's long johns, and a belt. He was in no position to argue, grabbing the clothes and getting to work covering up.

"Did the dragon hurt you?" the woman asked.

"No, I—"

She didn't let him finish. "It's all right, she's gone."

Anders opened his mouth and then closed it again. He already knew it was all right—Rayna would never hurt him.

Except she very nearly *had*.

Instead of answering, he cinched the belt tight to keep the long johns up, and pulled on the cloak over the shirt, puzzling for a few moments over how to fasten it. Now the shock was starting to wear off, he was getting properly cold, and he could feel his toes starting to turn numb.

The three wolves were still tense as he walked out from behind the crates, but their concern wasn't directed at him—the leader was staring up at the sky, while the woman watched the mouth of the alleyway. They were keeping watch for Rayna, or some other new threat, he realized.

Only the girl was looking at him, and she offered him a polite nod, reserved but friendly. She was about Rayna's height, but as wiry as Anders was. She had short-cropped, curling black hair, a serious expression, and white skin nearly hidden under more freckles than anyone Anders had ever seen. She looked none the colder for having given him her cloak, though she now stood there in her shirtsleeves.

Then the moment was over, as the leader of the group tilted his head to study Anders, a hint of wolf in the gesture. "Congratulations on your transformation," he said wryly. "The circumstances might be less than ideal, but we welcome every new member of our pack."

Anders sucked in a quick breath. *Wait, what?* He didn't want to join a pack! He wasn't going to Ulfar, he had to find Rayna.

Behind him, the woman lifted her hand to grasp the amulet at her throat. "And we'll get you one of these," she said. "It helps your shirt stay where it belongs when you change. Helps you control when you change at all. At first it's like sneezing, you can't help it; it happens about every time you get excited, or scared, or feel anything overwhelming. But if you're wearing an amulet, it only happens when you want it to."

His cheeks were burning. But behind the embarrassment and the fear and the confusion, the gravity of what had happened was kicking in.

Anders had *transformed*.

He had become an ice wolf—one of the few, one of the chosen.

His brain wrestled with the idea, trying to shake it off on the basis that Anders hadn't been special a single day of his life, but it was impossible to deny.

"I'm Hayn Mekkinsen," the leader said, pushing his square glasses up his nose. "Did you have parents back in the square that we need to find?"

Years of practice came together instinctively, and Anders opened his mouth to lie. The rules were simple. Never admit you were connected. Never give your real names. Never admit you didn't have any parents. But how was he going to produce parents if he said yes? "I, uh . . ."

Then he realized that Hayn had made the words a *question*. Whether it was the ragged clothes he'd been wearing before his transformation—he realized with a pang he'd lost the whole morning's loot when his jacket was ripped away from his body—or his too-skinny frame, or his slightly too-long hair that had turned messy and needed cutting, they suspected. There were enough children in

Holbard on their own that Hayn was obviously familiar with the existence of street orphans.

"If not, you have family now," Hayn continued. "We take care of our pack. You'll be fed and clothed, housed and trained at Ulfar Academy."

Anders breathed out slowly, though suddenly his lungs felt shallow. He could barely imagine *one* of those things—knowing where all his meals would come from, knowing he had a safe place to sleep, going to school—let alone all of them. "No parents, Herro Mekkinsen," he admitted, feeling the thick wool of the cloak between his fingertips, absorbing its warmth, its luxury. The girl who owned it offered him a shy smile.

He couldn't have smiled back if he wanted to. He drew a shaky breath, trying to think what he could say to get away from them.

"Don't worry," said Hayn, apparently recognizing his fear but misunderstanding the source. "If another dragon spy makes it into the city, we won't miss our chance again. We were sent to find you, but others are still tracking her."

Ice slid down Anders's spine, like one of the spears the wolves had thrown at Rayna as she fled the square. These people might sound friendly, but they weren't safe, not for him.

These people were hunting his sister, which meant

they were hunting him too. They just didn't know it yet. They'd thrown their ice spears at her, tried to kill her, and they might as well have thrown them at him.

"You were near her," said the woman, frowning. "Did you know her?"

Anders shook his head stiffly. *Rule number one.* "No, Dama. We were both trying to get up to the dais, but the crowd was thick," he said, his mouth dry, the words coming slowly. "I've seen her on the streets before, but I don't know her."

"We'll find out who she is," Hayn said. "And we'll find out where she is."

Anders couldn't stay with them a second longer than he had to. If he did, he'd surely give away their connection by saying something stupid. He had to find a way to get away from them, and soon.

Rayna had a long head start on the wolves—she had been flying, after all. If she managed to sneak back into the city, he had to be waiting for her, not locked behind the towering gates of Ulfar.

The Academy itself was a huge building, housing all the children who successfully made their transformation at twelve. It was half school, half military barracks, because if you could transform, there was only one job in your future.

You'd be a part of the Wolf Guard, patrolling the

streets to enforce the law, protecting Vallen against drag-ons, or helping raise the next generation. The barracks for the adult wolves was next door to the Academy, joined to it and surrounded by the same high walls. The students were small guards-in-waiting.

The Academy students only ever seemed to come out into the city in groups of four, or with adult members of the guard. He'd be trapped in their midst when he needed to move independently to either meet Rayna or figure out how to find her.

If their positions were reversed, he knew Rayna would walk straight through anything in her path to get to him. Now it was up to him to do the same.

The wolves left him to his thoughts as the four of them made their way out onto the streets once more. Hayn and the woman reached down toward the ground, figures growing leaner in a way that was hard for Anders's eyes to follow. It was as if his brain was telling him that what he was seeing was impossible, and therefore refusing to let him see it properly.

By the time he'd finished that thought, they were wolves once more, lifting their noses to scent any approach-ing threats. The change had felt to him like his body was on fire, but they'd made it look so easy. The pair trotted ahead of the two remaining humans, and the townspeople were quick to move out of their way.

The aftermath of Rayna's flight was visible all around them. The streets were crowded with people, everyone abuzz with their own version of the story, but they stayed close to their doorways, ready to duck back inside if the dragon returned to attack once more. The middle of the cobblestone street was clear, and the wolves and humans made their way down it with every pair of eyes tracking their movement. With the girl's cloak on over his makeshift clothes, Anders knew he looked like one of the guard.

Except he knew he walked differently from the rest of them, just as he *was* different from them. There was a grace to their movements, something wolfish, even when they were human. A confidence. They walked as if they knew people were watching.

He glanced sidelong at the girl and found her looking at him. "I'm Lisabet," she said quietly. Then, her lips quirking: "Don't worry about this. There's a reason they tell new students to stay in wolf form all the way back to the Academy. There's always one that gets caught out every few years, and they don't have a dragon for an excuse. Just think, at least you didn't change back up on the dais."

Anders felt himself go cold just *thinking* about that. She was right, he could have ended up naked in the middle of the docks. He'd literally had nightmares about that sort of thing. He knew she was trying to be nice, so he made himself try to smile back.

Lisabet was the only Ulfar student Anders had ever seen without a group of four, and he wondered if there was something special about her. He felt like he should introduce himself, but he couldn't remember a single made-up name to give her. "Thanks for the cloak," he whispered back instead. She smiled again.

He'd never seen a wolf smile before, or at least not in human form. Sometimes when they trotted through the streets of Holbard in pairs on patrol, tongues lolling out, they seemed almost to be smiling at the fun of weaving through the crowd. But there was something gentle about this girl that didn't fit with the idea he had in his head of the Academy students.

Anders had never wondered before what happened to the children who made their transformation, but didn't want to fight, or train, or learn to salute and patrol as the guard members. But now he did.

He wasn't sure if these new questions were about Lisabet or himself.

They turned a corner, and he caught a glimpse of the dockside square where the Trial of the Staff had been held. He forgot about his speculation, his worries flooding back. The streets were more peopled now, merchers and townspeople making their way out to gossip and gawk at the wreckage of the dais, though everybody kept one careful eye on the sky.

In a minute they'd be in the square, where there would be even more wolves, and then past it to the Academy. How would he ever get away then?

Anders cast his gaze around desperately for a diversion. He needed something to give him a moment's head start, if he was going to run. If this had been any other day, if he'd been in any other scrape, Rayna would have been out there keeping pace with him, ready to cause chaos at just the right moment.

Now, with the seconds ticking away, Anders was stuck on his own, and this kind of thing never went right for him.

He scanned the crowd, hunting for an ally.

Plenty of the children who ran wild on Vallen's streets like Anders and Rayna spent their time around the docks, for exactly the same reason he and his twin did—the crowds were thick, the pickings were good, and there were always a labyrinth of alleyways and rooftops over which you could escape if things went wrong. Now, Anders needed just one of them to show up.

He didn't exactly have what he'd call friends—when you were competing for scraps, temporary alliances were usually the best you could expect, and anyway, he'd always had Rayna. Right now he just needed someone—anyone.

They were only a dozen steps away from the square when he spotted Jerro, the pickpocket he'd seen with Rayna on the rooftops of Trellig Square. They'd never known each other well, but they'd met plenty of times. Jerro's gaze nearly skipped straight past him—he was in a gray wolf's cloak, and nobody was stupid enough to pickpocket a wolf.

Jerro's eyes popped wide when he realized it was *Anders* in the white-trimmed, gray wolf uniform, and he stumbled a step, ricocheting off a woman who was busy muscling a huge barrel of silver fish into place, bringing her wares back out now that the danger was past.

Anders didn't waste a moment. He lifted his right hand to make a fist and extended his thumb to touch it to his right ear. *Help me*, that signal said. *It's urgent.*

According to the rules of the street, this was the most important signal there was. You *had* to help someone who gave it, and everybody did, because you never knew when it might be you giving the signal.

Still, Jerro hesitated for an excruciating moment, his gaze flicking over the guards, weighing the risks. Then he nodded, and barged forward into the woman with the barrel, bending at the waist to drive his shoulder in against her for maximum impact.

She fell against the barrel, and with a clatter it tipped over sideways, a cascade of gleaming fish pouring out onto the street. A wave of salt-and-fish smell assaulted Anders's nose, and hundreds of slimy silver fish slid under everyone's feet. The nearby townsfolk and his wolfish escort went skating across the cobblestones with cries of alarm.

Anders was the only one ready for the onslaught, and he jumped back and away from the scaly mess, pushing his way between a couple of onlookers. He peeled off the gray cloak as Jerro silently appeared next to him, hand extended. Anders shoved the cloak at him, and Jerro took off up the street, pulling it on over his ragged shirt.

Anders ducked behind a pair of men as a silver-gray wolf he knew must be Hayn took off after Jerro, the others close behind him. Hoping the smell of the fish would block his scent, Anders clambered up onto a stack of wooden crates outside the next shop along. He glanced back to make sure the wolves hadn't spotted him, then reached for the window frame on the second floor.

His bare feet were almost numb, and for a dizzying moment Anders swung from one arm, trying to make his leg lift and his toes grip. Then his foot connected, and he was reaching for the gutters, pulling himself up to the safety of the rooftop meadow. He rolled onto his back, arms spread wide, ignoring the snowy sludge that was slowly soaking through his borrowed clothes.

If Jerro could get away from the wolves—and he probably could, since he was fast, and he could climb where they couldn't—then the cloak would be a reward for his help. It was warmer than anything Anders had ever known. A quick dunk in a vat of dye and it would be unrecognizable. In the meantime, Anders would stay up on the rooftops until he was well clear of the square.

His mind was spinning, grasping at new facts and then tossing them at him, as if they were supposed to somehow help everything make sense.

I transformed into an ice wolf.

Rayna transformed into a scorch dragon.

But we're twins, so that's impossible.

Whether it was some trick of the dragons' or some kind of mistake, he didn't know, and he didn't know how to start figuring it out.

He pushed to his feet, picking his way across the grass, keeping away from the edge of the roof to be sure nobody would see him.

He *had* to find his sister. That was all that mattered.

CHAPTER FIVE

T HE NEXT MORNING, ANDERS WAS STILL
searching. He'd stolen a pair of boots from the
mud rack in the courtyard of a house the night before,
and pulled his spare trousers, even more threadbare than
the ones he'd lost, from where he kept them stashed in a
butcher's roof. As it had grown darker he'd missed the coat
he'd left behind at the docks, and the loot in the pockets
that would have bought him supper. He'd felt bad about
stealing the boots, since the home clearly wasn't a rich
one, but there wasn't much choice.

He and Rayna had a dozen prearranged places to meet
if things went bad, or to leave each other messages and
instructions. It was their way of finding each other when
they had to run for it and couldn't stay together. Slowly,
hoping against hope that Rayna had somehow managed
to turn human again and made her way back into the city,

Anders had worked his way through most of them the night before.

He'd climbed over the rooftop meadows and dodged patrolling members of the Wolf Guard in the streets, and his heart sank a little further every time a meeting place turned up nothing. He'd waited for somebody who had recognized her at the docks to start a rumor that the dragon had been Rayna, but so far in that, at least, they'd been lucky. Eventually he'd curled up in the long grass in the lee of a chimneystack for warmth, and tried to snatch what sleep he could as he waited for dawn.

This morning, he'd woken up to find Kess staring at him from a safe distance. The black cat was seated by a patch of bright yellow-and-white flameflowers, named for the colors of a dragon's flame, their buds still closed in the early morning light. Somewhere nearby herbs must be growing, because Anders could smell the sharp tang of chella and penries.

It felt like a little weight off his chest, seeing a familiar face, even if it was just a cat's. He reached out one stiff arm to click his fingers and call her. "Hey, Kessie girl. Come over here. We can keep each other warm a little longer, while we make a plan."

It felt like having an ally, just for a moment. Like he wasn't Anders, who had transformed into a wolf, been chased through the city, and lost his sister. Like he was just himself. He'd cuddle with Kess while he figured out what to do next.

But Kess just stared at him with huge, yellow eyes, the tip of her tail slowly twitching, not moving an inch closer.

"Come on," he whispered, clicking his fingers again. But she wasn't moving, so he forced himself up onto his hands and knees, crawling a little nearer to her.

Her little pink nose twitched as he came closer, nostrils flaring as she took in his scent. And then she came alive, arching her back, tail lashing as she bared her incisors and fluffed up her fur to make herself bigger. One paw lifted, claws extended, to take a swipe at him, and he threw himself back into place once more, his back slamming hard into the chimney.

"Kess, what the . . . ?"

But the cat was gone, whipping around and running for it in a quick black streak of movement. Like she'd caught wind of his scent, and it wasn't that of a boy, but a wolf.

It was like she didn't know him at all.

When he looked down to the street below, the city was transformed as surely as he had been himself the day before. The guards they'd encountered the last couple of days had been nothing compared to this. Members of the Wolf Guard patrolled in groups of four, eyes sharp, looking up as well as searching the faces of the crowd. Everyone was watching the sky, and everyone was on alert.

Anders was jumpy as well, and he kept catching himself looking up, but he didn't know what he was hoping to see. If a dragon appeared, would it be Rayna, or would it be here to attack?

Anders made his way stiffly down from the roof, jumping onto a wagon full of hay and surprising the sleepy pony hitched to it. He scrambled free, picking hay from his clothes and hair, and strolled off before its owner could return.

If Rayna was still a dragon, no doubt she'd be hiding somewhere safe, far from the city. But he'd figured out how to change back from a wolf, and he had to hope she'd figured out how to get back to human form as well.

If so, she'd have come from the farmland to the west, which meant he might still find her on the other side of town. With so many wolves on patrol, it made sense that she wouldn't risk making her way across the city to him.

They'd stopped spending any time on the west side of the city more than a year ago—the homes there were too rich, and that meant the shabby twins were too easy to spot for what they were—but there were still hidey-holes she might use.

An hour's walk later, he finally found her signal.

It was just a collection of lines drawn in chalk, high up on the wall next to a bakery. It had to be from her, though—no one else could have climbed up on top of the barrels set against the wall and fished around under the eaves until they found the bit of chalk hidden there, then drawn a picture in the exact spot they'd chosen.

But what was it? It was a half circle, flat along the top, like a bowl. There were wavy lines rising from it, but what did that *mean*? He tried to press his tired brain to work.

Eventually, he remembered. Last year he'd been down with a fever, sweating hot and cold, shaking so hard it had scared both of them. With the snow coming down relentlessly outside, Rayna had tucked him away inside a stable and made the trek across the city.

She'd climbed over roofs and pushed through snowbanks for hours, and come back blue, but carrying a stoppered thermos of the best soup in the city, wrapped in layer upon layer of cloth and paper to keep it warm. Everybody said Dama Sancheo's shop was the best of the best, and when Anders was sick, Rayna was convinced that the best of the best was what would bring him back.

And she'd been right—she'd helped him drink it, shaking with cold herself, teeth chattering, and then she'd tucked him up in the hay once more. And in the morning, the fever had broken.

He couldn't imagine how anyone was going to fix *this* problem—him a wolf, her a dragon, all of Holbard hunting for her—but he knew that somehow she would. If he could just find her, she'd find a way, as she always did.

So now he knew where Rayna must be, and soon he was standing outside Dama Sancheo's shop. He could see the Dama and her staff inside, working over steaming vats of soup, and the customers were queuing out the door and down the street.

He was just considering whether Rayna might be hiding in the laneway down the side of the building when he thought to look up. And there by the gable window on the roof was his sister, clad in a blue dress and watching him with her trademark grin.

Something in his chest released, and he almost let his knees give out so he could sink down to the street in sheer relief. But Rayna pointed toward the lane, then disappeared out of sight. He made his way around the corner, and it was quick work to climb the stone-and-wood frame of the house, until her hands were reaching down to help him scramble onto the roof, and they could collapse together onto the grass and wrap their arms around each other.

She'd already pilfered some soup, of course, or pilfered the money to buy it, and produced the thermoses from where she'd concealed them by the gable window. The early spring flowers bobbed in the gentle breeze around them, the rooftop meadow stretching for the length of the whole block. The pair of them sat with their backs to the window, out of the wind, and let the soup warm them up as they spoke.

"I couldn't believe it, I ripped my way right out of my clothes," she was saying. "By the time I figured out how to change back, I was naked in the middle of nowhere. Naked, Anders!" She laughed, shaking her head. "I didn't have a thing left, except my hairpins! How do you suppose the wolves keep that from happening?"

"They—"

But he couldn't get a word out about the amulets before she was speaking again. "Do you like my new dress?" She held up a handful of the blue fabric for him to admire, her words tumbling out. "It's better than my old one, I think. So really, I came out ahead! I stole it from a clothesline. I found a farm quite quickly."

"I hope it wasn't someone's best," he said, touching the fine fabric. He'd felt bad enough about the boots, but this dress was beautiful.

Rayna shrugged. "We'll take care of us, and let them

take care of them. I couldn't get boots there, but I got them a little closer to town."

She tugged out her copper pins, wisps of curls escaping her braid and blooming around her face, and dropped a pin into his hand. "We always said they must have a little bit of essence in them," she said as he turned it over in his fingers. It was finely crafted, beautifully forged, the beaten copper always shiny. Along one side were a series of tiny, intricate designs that they had always thought might be runes.

Anders knew that the runes were what channeled the essence—the power that came from nature, from the earth itself—into artifacts.

But if the pins were artifacts, they'd never shown the slightest hint of essence, except for having survived Rayna's transformation to a dragon. She'd had them as long as they could remember, maybe forever, and no matter how hungry the twins had been, they'd never traded them. They both felt instinctively that they were too valuable— they were the only thing they had that might have come from their past.

Anders handed back the pin, but as Rayna kept on at full speed, he couldn't help feeling the words were almost *too* gleeful, *too* cheery—this wasn't Rayna's usual confidence. Despite her cocky smile, Rayna had hugged him just as tight as he hugged her. Anders wondered if for once she'd been afraid too.

Somewhere behind that confidence, she was rattled. But Rayna didn't know any way forward except full speed ahead.

"Flying was incredible," she said. "Incredible! Every muscle in my back is aching today, but oh, I can't describe it. Soaring, once you get the hang of it . . . I have to find a way to do it again."

Anders had been so caught up in his hunt for her—in his exhaustion, in reeling at his own transformation, in his cold, stiff tiredness and his worry—that he hadn't had time to stop and think about anything but finding her since his mad flight from the dockside square. But now, as Rayna spoke, Anders did think.

"Did you see them all running away from me?" she asked. "They were panicking, it was almost funny. I saw one man run straight into a building. Little wolves and people scattering all over the place."

Anders sipped his soup, not sure how to reply to that. Rayna had always been sharper around the edges than he was, but she'd never been hard-hearted. Now, though, she seemed to think that transforming into a dragon had been some sort of game. Was it bravado, or was she really more excited about flying, about her new dress, than what this could mean?

"I thought for a moment the guards were going to really hurt me," she was saying when he started listening again. "The ice spears the wolves throw, did you see them? I've got bruises all up and down my leg from where they hit me, and there's a horrible cut on my side. Still," she continued with a laugh, "I don't think much of their aim."

"They're still hunting you," he said, so quietly she almost missed it.

"They're what?"

"I was looking for you all over the city, I heard the rumors everywhere. The wolves are hunting you. There are patrols on every street," he said. "Everyone's eyes are on the sky. They're saying you're a scorch dragon spy, that next time, they'll be ready."

"But I haven't done anything wrong!" she protested, indignant. "I might have transformed, but I'm not like— I'm not like *dragons* are. I don't want to hurt anybody! I didn't even *mean* to transform!"

"So what if it happens by accident again?" he asked.

She shook her head. "What's really been worrying me is whether you're going to turn into a dragon too, because I—"

"Rayna," he tried, but she kept speaking.

"I thought about it and—"

"*Rayna*," he repeated, louder this time, and she stopped in surprise.

"I didn't become a scorch dragon," he said quietly, forcing himself to meet her eyes. For once she didn't interrupt, seeming to sense he had more to say. And he made himself say it. "I became an ice wolf."

Rayna stared at him, speechless—though not for long. "A *wolf*?" Her voice was a squeak. "You can't, a family can only be one—dragon or wolf!"

"I know that," he replied quietly, staring down at his soup, feeling as if somehow *he* was to blame for this impossible problem. Like since she'd transformed first, he should have matched her. Like suddenly their connection was damaged because he hadn't.

"But we're twins," she insisted, dumping her own thermos to one side and leaning sideways to catch his eye. "Don't look at me like that, you know we are. It's right there in our faces."

And it was . . . but it wasn't. They really didn't look that similar, but if you knew where to look, there were small things. They both had exactly the same dimple in their right cheek, the same strong brows, the same long eyelashes. They both folded their arms across their chests when they were uncomfortable, and they both tilted their heads exactly the same way when they were thinking.

But how many other people in Vallen have dimples? asked a tiny voice in the back of his mind. *Did you learn to fold your arms that way from watching her?*

Rayna was in every memory Anders had, from sharing a crib together at the orphanage to the time they ran away when they were six, because the woman in charge wanted to separate them, to . . . today. Anders grabbed hold of that tiny, nasty voice with both hands and shoved it in a mental box, nailing the lid down tight.

Rayna was his sister. She always had been. And she always would be.

CHAPTER SIX

RAYNA WAS STARING AT HIM, AND ANDERS MADE himself reply. "Of course we are. We're twins." And then, hating the words even as he said them: "Rayna, do you think we should leave Holbard? They're looking for you here. And maybe for me too. Wolves are supposed to go to the Academy, and join the guard."

"Leave?" She looked sick at the thought. Holbard was Vallen's capital city, and really, its only large city. Anywhere else they'd be fending for themselves in a town, or worse, a village. Somewhere people would learn to recognize them quickly enough, and learn to watch out for their sticky fingers. "Let's do some reconnaissance first. Let's see how bad it is."

They both knew that Rayna should hide while Anders went out to gather up rumors and bring them back to her. Though perhaps she really was as shaken as he was, deep down—neither of them wanted to be apart, and so when Rayna suggested she trail him up on the rooftops where nobody would see her, he didn't argue.

But when he climbed down from the roof, the news was *all* bad.

There were rumors on every street, and members of the Wolf Guard on every corner. If Anders thought there had been extra patrols before, it was nothing compared to the waves of gray-clad uniforms everywhere he turned.

He checked in with the shopkeepers who sometimes slipped them scraps, other children who ran on the streets, with all the usual gossip sources, and the same words were everywhere. The whispers and worries of the day before had unfurled into fully grown facts, passed around undisputed.

They were simply lucky nobody who knew them had been at the docks—or, at least, nobody who knew them had been inclined to speak to the authorities, and thus draw attention to themselves. As the city's fear grew, though, so too did the risk that if they had been recognized, somebody might break their silence.

"There are dragon spies all over the city," said Dama Sturra, a baker who was usually good for a bite to eat if they were desperate. Her worried face was daubed with a fine layer of flour as she mixed a new batch of dough. "A whole network of them, I'm hearing. Ready to rise up and start a new war for control of Holbard."

"Another battle like the last," said one of her customers, smoothing down her fine blue dress, as if wishing she could smooth out the city's problems just as easily. "I'll never forget it. I was down by the docks when the battle came there. We jumped into the harbor in our coats and boots, we were in that much of a hurry. There were dragons diving down to burn us alive, and only the wolves and their ice to stand between us and being turned into charcoal."

"The ice wolves saved us," agreed the baker's husband, Herro Mensen, handing Anders a small cinnamon roll with a kind wink. "And don't you worry, they'll save us again."

"I heard the dragon at the dockside square was a spy," a second customer said, busy packing her purchases in her basket.

"Makes sense," Dama Sturra agreed, nodding thoughtfully. "Did she get what she came for, that's the question."

"And shame on them for using children," Herro Mensen added, frowning.

"She didn't," the customer replied with relish. "She was sent to destroy the Staff of Hadda, as I heard it. To make sure no more wolves could make their transformation, to weaken the Wolf Guard. But they have it safe, I heard it from a guard himself."

"Dragons only ever want one thing, and that's to hurt the innocent, kill if they can," said the first customer. "And yesterday's was no different."

And on it went, everywhere he tried.

When he met Rayna in a laneway and relayed the conversations to her, her lips thinned as she pressed them together. "Hurt the innocent," she whispered, cheeks darkening with anger. "*Kill* if they can. *I'm* the innocent, Anders! I'm the one who got turned into—"

He pulled her farther down the laneway and behind a stable before her voice grew too loud, and she shook him off her arm, pacing the three steps she could manage in the confined space, then spinning on her heel to stalk back again. "I'm a Vallenite, same as them," she fumed. "I should be protected. The *last* thing I want is anything to do with scorch dragons, I know what they are. I'm not wicked! Just because it turns out I can fly doesn't mean I—"

She broke off, her face even darker red than before—and as her eyes went wide, Anders realized she was *too* red. This wasn't a natural color, this was a rich crimson snaking across her skin. Suddenly there was a glimmer of bronze to her complexion.

Heat was rolling off her, hitting him in a wave,

scrambling his thoughts and sending a bolt of panic through him. "Rayna, no!" He threw himself forward, grabbing the front of her dress, as if he could somehow prevent the transformation by sheer willpower alone.

"I'm trying!" she rasped, squeezing her eyes tight shut in concentration.

"Breathe," he instructed her, keeping her close, forcing himself to resist the urge to push her away, the urge to run, find a bank of snow, throw himself into it to cool down. "The wolves told me you change when you have strong feelings, try and think of something else! Just listen to my voice. You can do it, Rayna."

She reached out to grab at his shoulders, anchoring herself. "*Help me*," she shouted, head thrown back, hands squeezing painfully.

"Stay calm, focus!"

And then suddenly she let him go, staggering a step back, the unnatural redness fading from her skin, the terrifying heat fading away, and she was simply Rayna once more. Her chest was heaving as if she'd just run a race, and his heart was thumping like it wanted to shove its way right out through his ribs.

There was a clatter from the laneway, and a young man burst into view, hefting a broom in both hands. "Get away from her!" he shouted, aiming it at Anders, who ducked.

"What are you doing?" Rayna screeched, jumping between them.

"I heard you!" the young man told her, still holding the broom at the ready. "You shouted for help."

"No I didn't," Rayna protested immediately, and slowly, puzzled, he lowered the broom. "Must have been coming from some other direction," she insisted, reaching for Anders's hand. "We don't need any help. We were just leaving."

They left him standing bewildered behind them as Rayna towed Anders straight past him and out into the bustling street once more, disappearing into the crowd as fast as she could. He kept hold of Rayna's hand as they made their way down the street. With eyes on every corner, and another transformation just a moment's bad temper away, it felt as if the walls of the city were closing in on them. He felt scared for her—protective of her—in a way he never had before.

He found his gaze lingering on the wolves. Most of them were in human form, and they held themselves the way the girl Lisabet had. As if they knew they were being watched, and they were allowing it. As if they knew things nobody else did. Anders couldn't help wondering what that kind of certainty would feel like. That kind of knowledge and power.

They were walking down a broad street a few minutes later when two little boys ran past them, one wearing a red blanket as a cape. The other caught up with him, wrapping his arm around him and tackling him to the ground, where they both landed with a thud at Anders's and Rayna's feet. For a moment they might have *been* Anders and Rayna years before, a tangle of playful brown limbs, and then one of them spoke.

"Hold still!" he roared. "I'm going to kill you with my ice spear, dragon!"

One of them was playing Rayna—the blanket wasn't a cape, it was a dragon's wings—and the other was playing a Wolf Guard.

Rayna stared down at them. "Is everyone . . ." Her voice broke, then began to rise. "Does everyone in the whole city think someone should kill me?"

Anders knew what was coming before it happened. "No!" he said urgently, reaching for her. "No, listen to me!"

But this time there was no stopping her. Faster than he could track she grew into a blaze of red, wings unfurling as she towered over him. She took up most of the street, which was one of the widest in Holbard. Tipping her head back, she roared, and the ground trembled beneath his feet. When she thrashed her tail, a shop front flew to pieces like a house of cards.

Anders staggered back as four—no, six wolves came running down the street, teeth bared in snarls. They made a semicircle around Rayna as she spread her wings again, bellowing a protest.

Everyone else in the street was turning to run now, pushing past Anders like a rushing tide of water that wanted to sweep him away from his sister.

The first of the wolves struck the ground with its front paws, just by where Rayna's blue dress lay in ruins, and two ice spears flew from the stone to hit Rayna where her wing joined her body, drawing a screech of pain and protest from her.

The next wolf struck, and she ducked her head just in time to stop it piercing her eye.

Panicked, Anders could feel his own change coming for him, the sights and scents of the world becoming sharper and brighter as his head cleared and his body readied itself to transform, the colors fading to the duller wash he'd seen last time. He tried to stay calm, tried to push it away and stay human, but pain roared through his hurt ribs and down his arms and legs as his bones reshaped themselves, and he once again ripped free of his clothes.

As he bounded forward—though he had no idea what he was going to do—the largest of the wolves howled, and

Anders found he understood the sound. It was an alert, a warning, and like the rest of the pack he tipped his head back to scan the sky.

A *second* dragon was soaring in over the roofs of Holbard, at least twice the size of Rayna, crimson, gold, and bronze just as she was, gleaming in the late afternoon sun. It roared, and in response Rayna sprang skyward, the hot downdraft from her wings knocking Anders and the other wolves off their feet.

The waves of heat coming off her, the dazzling mosaic of scents clouding his nostrils—the musty smell of the horses, the damp of the cobblestones, the sweet hint of someone baking nearby—all of it combined to send Anders's head spinning.

As he scrambled upright, there was nothing he could do except watch her wing her way up, edging his way back under the eaves of the buildings so the other wolves wouldn't see him. How could she *do* this? How could she fly straight toward the enemy?

Rayna pumped her wings, climbing steadily, then snapped them open to soar away—and he realized she wasn't flying *to* the other dragon, she was running *from* it.

As the wolves loped together along the street, staying as close to Rayna as they could manage, a man barged past Anders. Everyone else was taking shelter inside homes and shops, but this man ran out to stand in the middle of the street, looking up as the larger dragon pursued Rayna. He was dressed in a plain blue coat and wore a flat cap that hid most of his face, and but for the fact that he was running out into the middle of the street while everyone else ran away, Anders never would have noticed him.

A woman ran out to join him, dressed as he was in a plain coat and trousers, sturdy boots showing beneath them. They both looked utterly ordinary, though their behavior was anything but.

They exchanged a couple of words, and then she ran on past him, until she was a good fifty feet away. As one they dropped to a three-point crouch, one hand resting on the ground, and the crowd around Anders started to scream anew as the pair began their transformation.

Their skin turned to red, clothes melting into invisibility, and his eyes couldn't follow the way they began to swell and grow, impossibly large in seconds, copper and bronze and gold streaking through crimson so the sunlight glinted off their scales.

If Rayna was fifteen feet long, they were at least thirty each, taking up the whole street. They were impossibly, terrifyingly big, heat radiating from them like they might set the street alight any second. With a rush of wind they launched themselves, circling up with quick, efficient strokes to join the pursuit.

Rayna didn't stand a chance. Where their wing strokes were quick and economical, hers were disorganized and unpracticed—she practically clawed her way through the air, rather than flew through it.

She banked to the right, wings pumping furiously as she tried to put distance between her and her pursuers. But they were all so much bigger than she was, and they soared, closing the gap in seconds.

She roared her defiance, and she kept whipping her head around toward them—was she trying to breathe fire? If she was, nothing was happening. His heart in his throat, Anders ran along the street after the wolves who were tracking the dragons from the ground.

The dragons surrounded her, then peeled away toward the mountains, herding her with them like a helpless sheep between three sheepdogs. She tried to barge her way past one of them and it pushed her back into place, breathing a gout of flame horrifyingly close to her head.

Anders ignored the pain in his ribs—apparently that damage transformed with him—dragging down great breaths as he hurtled along the streets toward the edge of the city.

He reached the city gates in time to see the other wolves, dozens of them now, pouring out through them and onto the plains beyond. He stopped himself before he ran out onto the plains as well, sinking down on his haunches and biting back a howl of despair.

Rayna and the other three dragons were already a vanishing dot on the horizon.

She was gone, and no matter how fast he ran, he wouldn't catch her.

In a moment, the wolves would be returning to the city to report, and if he was standing here in the gateway, they'd find him. He had to run.

He had to find a place to hide, to survive, to live another day and try and make a plan, though he couldn't begin to imagine what that plan would be. This time, Rayna wasn't on her own—she was a prisoner. This time, Rayna wouldn't be waiting tomorrow with hot soup to tell him about her adventures.

Two questions beat like drums in his mind, over and over again, their urgency making it hard to think straight.

How could he find the dragons' stronghold?

Even if he did, how could he get Rayna back?

He would need to learn more about the dragons— about where they hid, about their weaknesses, about how to track his sister down and find a way to bring her home.

He'd spent most of his life scared of one thing or another, letting Rayna make their decisions. But perhaps that just meant he was good at doing things while he was scared—and he could do this too.

There were rumors about dragons on every corner in Holbard, but there was only one place they *studied* dragons, one place they learned how to defeat them, one place that could teach him what he needed to know.

All day he had been watching the wolves, seeing how sure of themselves they were. He needed that kind of power, and knowledge, and there was only one place he could find it.

He had to enlist at Ulfar Academy.

He would learn how to control his transformation, learn what they knew about dragons, and find his chance to escape and go after Rayna. He couldn't wait for her to come back. He had to find a way to help her himself. It was his only hope of seeing her again.

The huge pack of wolves that had chased the dragons out across the plains was trotting back toward the city wall in formation, coming into view.

So instead of slinking between the buildings to hide once more, Anders gave himself a shake, and feeling the grass beneath his paws, he walked slowly out through the city gate to meet them.

CHAPTER SEVEN

DOZENS OF WOLVES WERE TROTTING TOWARD him, and he found in his new form he could read and understand them as naturally as if they'd spoken. Their ears pricked up as they spotted him, and when a big wolf made his way to the front of the pack, Anders found he knew it was Hayn, the wolf he'd met in the alleyway, by his silver-gray coat and the black marks around his eyes where his glasses would be if he were a human.

With a soft growl Hayn reassured the others, and Anders the wolf could tell by the way he carried his tail high, waving confidently back and forth, that he was more senior than Anders had realized the day before.

Hayn came to a halt in front of Anders, lowering the front half of his body in almost a bow, stretching his forelegs out in front of him. For a moment Anders was confused, and then Hayn's legs thickened as his torso lengthened, and he rose to become the broad-shouldered man Anders had met from behind his stack of crates.

"Good to see you again, young man," he said gravely, pushing his thick-rimmed glasses up his nose. "Can you transform so we can talk? New wolves often find it easier to use speech at first."

Except Anders couldn't change, especially in front of dozens upon dozens of wolves. Because he still didn't have an amulet, and the ruins of his clothes were somewhere back inside the city. *Again.* He whined, unsure how to convey that information, then realized that the wolves around him all understood from the tilt of his head and the soft sound exactly what he meant. Even Hayn seemed to follow, and with a nod, he transformed down into a wolf once more, taking his place at the head of the pack.

When he lifted his head and rumbled softly, deep in his chest, Anders realized he didn't just understand Hayn's gestures, but he could make out their precise meaning: *Of course, I should have thought of that. Let's head back to the Academy.*

It wasn't that he heard the words, exactly. It was just that in the same way all his senses were reporting new information every second, he found every tiny sound or movement from the other wolves had meaning. It was utterly strange in some ways, but in others, clearer than speaking. He could already see it would be harder to lie.

A chill raced down his spine as a new thought struck him—was he unwittingly sharing his own thoughts and fears with every movement?

As Hayn moved past him, Anders turned to fall into step, loping toward the city gates in the midst of the pack of wolves. Somehow, unimaginably, he was one of them. He was fighting the urge to peel away from the pack and run for his life, stretching out his legs and finding out how fast this new body could go, but he forced himself to stay in line.

The citizens of Holbard parted for them as they made their way through the city—probably they'd never seen so many wolves in one place before, or not since the last great battle. Anders certainly never had.

They made their way up Ulfarstrat, the cobbled road that led to the Academy itself, which wasn't far from the city gates. In just a few minutes the huge iron gates of the Academy and barracks loomed before them. They were open just now, and the pack made its way through into a large stone courtyard surrounded by high stone walls.

Where the shops and homes of Holbard were colorful greens, yellows, and blues, the inside of Ulfar's courtyard was a grim blue-gray stone. It looked like even weeds wouldn't dare grow up from between the cracks. The courtyard was hundreds of feet across, and every part of it was in perfect order.

Most of the wolves turned for the Ulfar barracks, where the adult Wolf Guard trained and lived. Hayn led Anders into the Academy and along stone hallways with thick wooden rafters, well lit with oil lamps every few feet.

It felt more like a fortress than a school, and Anders felt himself slinking lower with every step, his belly closer to the ground, tail tucked close to his body, less and less certain of his impulsive decision to risk coming here.

Hayn paused at an open doorway, and as Anders halted beside him, he saw it was a storeroom and laundry. Inside, the shelves reached all the way up to the ceiling, piled high with folded gray clothes. There was a woman busy using a large, metal machine, covered all over in runes. It was an artifact, Anders realized. But even with the magical device, it still looked like hard work the woman's fair skin was ruddy from the effort.

As he and Hayn made their way inside she fed a shirt into the machine. It clanked softly, a series of metal arms whirring into quick movement. A couple of seconds later, it extended two of those arms to set a neatly folded shirt on the shelf above her.

She turned away from the folding machine for the next shirt, and saw the two of them, breaking into a smile.

"Hayn," she said, evidently recognizing his wolf form. "And I see you have a young friend."

Hayn stretched, transformed, and offered her a courteous nod. "I have a new student, Dama Lindahl," he said. "He will need some clothes before I take him to the Fyrstulf."

"Of course," she said, not even twitching a smile, for which Anders was grateful. "Just step behind that screen there, my dear, and we'll get you outfitted as soon as you're two-legged again."

Anders's claws clicked on the stone floor as he walked around behind the screen, trying to calm himself enough to transform. His sense of danger was screaming at him to run for it, and in his mind's eye, all he could see was Rayna, herded helplessly off toward the horizon. His heart kicked up another notch every time he imagined it.

Then he heard Hayn's quiet voice on the other side of the screen. "Breathe in deeply," he said gently. "Hold it for a beat, then out again. Close your eyes. If you let your mind settle, you'll find the kernel of the human inside you. When I learned, I used to think of it like taking a pair of socks that are in a ball, then unfolding them, turning them right way out. Take your human self and unfold it so it's on the outside."

Anders tried to obey, and for a moment it felt

hopeless—but even imagining something as mundane as a pair of socks helped calm him, and a few seconds later, with a bolt of pain up and down his arms and legs as they reshaped, he was human once more. And perhaps it had hurt a little less than the time before.

Dama Lindahl made him reach his hand around the screen at head height to show her how tall he was, and a moment later she passed him a bundle of clothes. He heard her talking quietly to Hayn as he dressed, her voice less jovial now. "I heard there were four."

"There were," Hayn said, sounding tired. "Three on the ground, one in the air. They left once they had their spy. It will be a different matter completely if they start setting fires."

"We've seen them off before," she reminded him, soft. "We can do it again."

"We have," he agreed. "But the price was very high."

Anders silently pulled on the clothes Dama Lindahl had given him—underwear and thick woolen socks, a shirt and trousers, all of it better than anything he'd ever owned—better than anything he'd ever touched, except when he was pickpocketing. They were all in wolf gray, but with white touches and trim, as the students' uniforms always had when he saw them out in the city. White buttons on the shirt, white stitching on the trousers.

When he finally padded out, Dama Lindahl checked his feet and dug out a pair of shiny black boots. Hayn waited as he crouched to lace them up, then turned to lead him from the supply room.

"I'll see you soon enough, I'm sure," Dama Lindahl told him with a smile. "There was talk it was a bad sign that we had no new students this month. But here you are, after all. I'll start gathering up the rest of your things."

Anders murmured a thank-you as he headed out the door on Hayn's heels. She might be friendly enough now, but she didn't know his secret. The wolves would have questions, and he wasn't sure he had answers—but Rayna was depending on him. His brain was scrambling as he tried to pull together a tale that would explain why he'd bolted on their first meeting. "I'm sorry I—when I transformed, I—"

Hayn held up a hand to stop him. "The Fyrstulf will want to hear from you herself," he said, sending a chill straight down Anders's spine. How much trouble was he in? Did they even want him here as a student? Dama Lindahl had seemed to think so, but she only managed the supply room. But then Hayn glanced back and softened a touch. "It was an unusual day," he said. "She'll listen."

"The dragons . . ." Anders ventured, not even sure what he was asking. Wondering what Hayn would say, perhaps.

"We'll see them off, if we have to," Hayn replied. "We knew there were dragon spies in the city, and now we've been proven right. The humans are starting to forget how dangerous they are. The humans forget the price we've paid to protect them."

It made Anders's skin prickle, to hear Hayn use that word: *human*. As if the wolves—as if Anders—were something else. He watched the man's broad back as he followed him down the hallway, wondering if all wolves felt so separate from everyone else, or if something had taught Hayn to feel that way.

"Don't be afraid," Hayn was saying. "We've met them before, and we'll meet them again."

Anders felt cold as they made their way toward the Fyrstulf's office, and it had nothing to do with the stone walls around him.

Hayn led him from the school corridors into the adult barracks, though Anders wouldn't have known the difference, except that the occasional student in a white-tipped uniform gave way to older, grimmer adults all in gray. The gray stone corridors with their lamps and thick wooden beams overhead stayed the same.

Eventually, they reached another doorway like all the others, except that a tapestry was hung on the wall opposite it. Stretching twelve feet long, it was of the last great battle with the dragons, bright with flames. An army of wolves was arrayed along the bottom of the scene, driving the dragons from Holbard with their ice spears.

Hayn knocked on the door opposite the tapestry, then opened it, glancing in. He exchanged a few quiet words with whoever was inside and withdrew.

"Good luck," he said quietly to Anders, clapping him on the shoulder with a grip that nearly made Anders's knees give out. Then he tilted his head to indicate Anders should head inside—a wolflike movement—and strode off down the corridor.

Anders wondered for a wild moment whether he could simply slip behind the giant tapestry and hide there. Would anyone notice his legs sticking out the bottom? Probably not.

Instead, he made his feet move, forcing himself to walk through the Fyrstulf's door and close it behind him.

The office itself was large—Sigrid sat behind a wooden desk opposite the door, with bookshelves running down either side of the room. Her pale skin and short blond hair almost seemed the same color by the light of the lamps, and she sat with that strict, upright posture he'd seen so many times at monthly Trials.

The shelves were lined with books, but more than that—in front of the books, and sometimes between them, sat small metal devices and all manner of trinkets. There was a long, coiled piece of metal, a water skin with an elaborately designed metal spout, a set of scales. *Every one of them was engraved with runes.* Anders spotted the Staff of Hadda in a bracket on the wall. If these other artifacts could channel essence as powerfully as the staff, this would be the most important room in Holbard.

Sigrid spoke, jolting him from his thoughts. "Good afternoon." If anything, she sounded faintly amused, and that snapped Anders back to his fear—why was she amused? What did she have planned for him? "Please take a seat . . ." She trailed off deliberately, and Anders realized she was waiting for his name, and she was amused because he'd been gawking at her office.

"Anders," he said quietly. "Anders Bardasen." He hadn't given his real name to an adult since he was six, those were the rules, even if his was a common enough surname. But if he was going to last here as a student, maybe for weeks, he needed something he'd actually respond to when people called him. And that meant the truth. He felt naked just saying it out loud. *And lately, he really knew exactly how naked felt.*

"Bardasen," she echoed. "I'm sorry."

It took Anders a moment to think why his name would make her sorry—he knew plenty of kids on the street with the same last name—and then it clicked into place. *Bardasen* was an orphan's name. *Barda* was an ancient word meaning "battle" that someone had dug up after the last great battle. It was the surname given to children who lost their parents in that terrible fight against the dragons. Children whose real surname was unknown.

And of course, Sigrid had been one of those fighting. He'd heard her talk about it on the dais at the trial. He'd heard her say she felt personally responsible for every death. Now her expression softened a little. For the first time in his life, his name was an asset.

"Please," she said, rising to her feet. "Sit, we should talk." The Fyrstulf nodded at the space behind him, where two couches sat facing each other. She moved out from behind her desk to settle into one. Anders noticed the cut on her forehead—the injury from when the dais crashed and he fell beside her.

Anders took the other couch, sinking down into the soft cushions, as aware of that luxury as he was of his fine clothes, and uncomfortable with both. "I'm sorry I ran," he started, stumbling over his words. Usually Rayna did the fast talking, and for some reason he found it hard to lie to this woman, as though the wolf in her could read the wolf in him, even in human form. He *had* to make this story convincing. "I thought the dragon would come back, and I—I'm not proud of myself. I should have been braver. I didn't come back at first because I was embarrassed."

The Fyrstulf met this news with silence, and as the words echoed between them, Anders could hear how weak they sounded. "And now?" she said eventually.

"Now I'd like to take up my place as a student, Dama," he said, trying to inject as much respect as possible into the words, trying to remember all of Rayna's tips. *Eye contact, but not too much, or it looks like you're trying. Don't fidget.*

"Just Sigrid," she said. "We are wolves, which means of course we have a hierarchy. Such a thing is vital, if we are to keep Holbard safe, and it is natural to us. But we use first names here. It's our way of remembering that as well as pack, as well as soldiers, we are also a family."

"Yes, D— yes, Sigrid," he murmured, the name feeling unnatural in his mouth. She was still looking him over far too keenly, and he knew some part of what he was telling her wasn't adding up. She didn't entirely believe his story. But slowly, she nodded.

"Fleeing once is understandable," she said. "I would not be so sympathetic a second time. Nevertheless, welcome to Ulfar." He had to stop himself letting out a breath of relief. Apparently she wasn't quite suspicious enough to refuse him entry. *Or,* he thought with a shiver, *maybe she doesn't trust me, and she wants to keep me where she can see me.*

Sigrid rose and walked over to her desk, picking up a mirror there. It was small, about the size of the palm of her hand, but when she held it up, Anders could see the runes on the back of it. She spoke again. "When you see Lisabet, please send her to my office immediately," she said.

Anders flicked a glance around the room, trying to figure out who she was talking to. Not him, surely? He didn't . . . though actually, he *did* know who Lisabet was. That was the name of the girl he'd met, the day of his transformation. The Ulfar student—the one who had smiled at him. Was he supposed to find her?

"Yes, Sigrid," said another voice. *Where did that come from?*

Sigrid set down the mirror and looked over at him, registering his confusion. "The mirror allows two-way communication," she said. "I have asked the wolf on duty to send us a student, who will be your guide until you learn your way around."

Anders's jaw dropped. A mirror that allowed you to speak to somebody in a completely different place? He'd seen smaller artifacts plenty of times—devices to help with cooking or trading—but never something as powerful as this.

"Lisabet will explain the Academy rules," Sigrid continued. "Show you your assigned room, help you find your classes. We will expect to see you in classes tomorrow morning, and I myself will see you in the afternoon. My duties as Fyrstulf entail leading our warriors and managing Vallen's safety for the most part, but I make it a point to teach one class for our younger students. I want all of you to know me, and to know you can come to me at any time. This includes you, Anders."

"Thank you," he murmured, weakly imagining himself bringing his one and only problem to Sigrid. *My sister transformed into a dragon. Any idea how to solve that one, Fyrstulf?*

"The dragons have us on high alert at the moment, as I'm sure you know," said Sigrid. "If they come to Holbard in numbers there will be a battle, but we will ensure you're ready to join the fight. We are always ready, Anders. Always on guard. We will always stand against the dragons."

It felt like a threat, as if she could see straight inside his head, see his connection to Rayna—as if, when her gaze bored into him, she was looking straight at his link to the dragons. Except he'd told her he'd run because he was scared. Perhaps she was, in her own terrifying way, trying to reassure him.

He was saved from the need to answer—just as he was hopelessly groping for words—by a knock at the door.

"Come," Sigrid called, and it opened to reveal Lisabet, the girl Anders had met the day of his transformation.

She shared Sigrid's upright posture, the same lift of her chin—all wolves were alike in the end—though her black, curling hair and the thousands of freckles on her face were as messy as the Fyrstulf was perfectly, flawlessly neat.

"You sent for me?" Lisabet asked politely.

Sigrid nodded. "Lisabet, this is Anders, our newest student. I believe you met shortly after his first transformation. Please help him collect his uniform and take him to dinner."

Lisabet kept up her serious expression, but as soon as Sigrid rose to walk back to her desk, and her back was turned, the girl offered him a quick wink.

"Thank you, Sigrid," Anders said, pushing to his feet. Of all the students at the Academy, they had to pick the one who'd seen him lose his clothes and make a run for it. *Of course they did.* Still, her company was less terrifying than the Fyrstulf's. He beat a hasty retreat, Lisabet close on his heels.

Lisabet spoke again once they were some distance down the hallway. "Looks like you survived that all right," she said, quirking a smile. When she smiled, it completely wiped away the serious expression her face fell into the rest of the time. "She likes to eyeball everybody on their way in. Did she give you the bit about being family, and how she teaches classes so you know you can trust her?"

"She did," Anders admitted.

"She wouldn't know what family meant if she read about it in the dictionary," Lisabet confided. "She teaches us so we'll all know her and remember to be appropriately terrified. The Trials for Fyrstulf are every five years. Last time, nobody even challenged her."

"I don't blame them," Anders muttered, and Lisabet snorted.

"Me neither."

They reached the crossroads of several different hallways, and Lisabet pointed up to a large bell hanging in the middle of the junction. "That's the class bell," she said, jumping up to tap one fingernail against it. It sang with an almost inaudible note, so light was her touch.

Anders didn't know what a class bell was, but he was also pretty sure that question was approximately number seven hundred and forty-two on his list, so he kept it to himself. He'd figure out why she thought he needed to know about it later.

Lisabet took him back to Dama Lindahl, who was waiting with the rest of his uniform.

She had a warm gray jacket for him and a thick cloak to go over it. He'd never owned a cloak before—a decent coat like the one he'd lost the day of the Trial was better. A coat had pockets you could drop the things you pickpocketed straight into, but a cloak had nowhere to hide anything.

The Ulfar crest was emblazoned on his clothes. He'd seen it before but never had the chance to examine it like this. It was a metallic blue, showing a wolf standing up on its hind legs, fierce and ready to protect the city of Holbard in the background.

While he was studying the crest, she opened the safe on the wall, producing an amulet of his very own. *Just like that*—as if all these luxuries were nothing.

And to the wolves, they were. They had no idea what it was to go wanting.

His fingers itched for a second amulet—he'd need it when he found Rayna—and he eased sideways to try and glimpse the combination on the safe, but Dama Lindahl's fingers were quick as she pushed it shut and gave the tumbler a spin, the amulets locked inside. The leather strap on his amulet was new, but now he could see that though the design was finely sculpted, it was worn. A line of wolves chased one another around the amulet's edge, runes carved inside the circle they made.

"We pass them on," Lisabet said, watching him turn the amulet over in his hands. "We can't get new ones, so we have to make the amulets we have last as long as possible."

Wondering about the wolves who had worn this amulet

before him—wondering what they'd make of him, there only to steal this amulet and stay until he knew how to find his way to the dragons—Anders fastened it around his neck. He felt a faint tingle against his skin, the metal warming, and then there was nothing.

Dama Lindahl also plunked him down on a stool and cut his hair regulation short, showing him his reflection in a mirror when she was done. Before, his black curls had been longer than his finger when he pulled a lock of hair straight. But the boy looking back at him had short hair, barely long enough to curl at all. He wore an amulet at his throat, and the gray wolf's shirt seemed to drain the warmth from his brown skin.

The boy staring back at him looked like a wolf.

He looked nothing like Anders.

With his arms full of his spare clothes, Anders was silent as Lisabet led him to his room, opening the door for him so he could carry them inside. The room held four beds (two made, two not), with a couple of sets of drawers and wardrobes for the occupants to share.

"That's mine," Lisabet said, pointing to one of the two made beds. "And that's yours." She indicated the other, and Anders walked forward to dump his new clothes on it, leaning down to press one hand against the mattress. He'd never slept in a proper bed before, as far as he knew.

He'd barely ever slept without Rayna there to curl up beside him, so they could keep each other warm.

He forced his gaze up to take in the room. The other two beds were messily unmade, and Lisabet came up beside him to eye them thoughtfully. "We weren't expecting company," she said. "That's Viktoria," she continued, pointing to the bed beside his. "She, um . . . she doesn't always remember there's nobody to make the bed for her."

Hearing her careful tone, Anders wondered what Viktoria was like. Someone used to having the bed made for her? Was she from a rich family? What would she think of a street boy like him?

"And that's Sakarias," Lisabet said, pointing at the bed next to her own, diagonally across from Anders's. Along the stone wall beside it, the unknown boy had tacked up a series of sketches of people and wolves, mostly done in ink or pencil, a few with color.

"Those drawings are really good," he said, walking over to get a closer look. The snarl of the wolf in the picture was all too real, and he stepped back.

"He's really talented," Lisabet agreed. "That's rare for a wolf. The dragons were always the artists."

Anders shot her a sharp look. Dragons as *artists*? What did that even mean? Dragons as kidnappers, more like.

A moment later, at the thought of Rayna, he was

berating himself. *Anything* could be happening to Rayna right now, and Anders was letting this girl lead him around to get a haircut and go to dinner. He had to find some way to ask questions, to search for information.

But there was nothing else he could do for now, except try to blend in. He couldn't make them suspicious. He had to trust that Rayna knew how to fool the dragons, that she'd be in there making speeches right now about how excited she was to set things on fire, how she killed people for fun in her spare time. That somehow she'd be keeping herself safe.

It was better than believing the dragons knew Rayna wanted nothing to do with them and their cruelty.

Better than believing she wasn't being shown a bedroom, but a cell.

CHAPTER EIGHT

LISABET HELPED HIM PUT AWAY HIS CLOTHES, AND he was just hanging up his new cloak in the wardrobe beside the others when a deafening bell suddenly started up overhead.

Rrrrrrrrrring-rrrrrrrrring-rrrrrrrrrring!

Anders clapped his hands over his ears, dropping the cloak and shoving himself in against the wall, though he barely knew what he was hiding from. Ten seconds later the bell abruptly felt silent, and he lowered his hands slowly, his heart thumping, breath coming quickly.

Lisabet hurried over to him. "It's all right, it's the bell I showed you, it's for the change of sessions," she said, picking up his cloak and reaching for a hanger. "It goes every hour. I'm sorry, I should have explained more. It's an artifact system—the duty professor or a senior student rings the one bell we saw, and all the others ring to match it, wherever they are in the Academy."

Anders stepped away from the wall, cheeks hot, feeling foolish. At least Lisabet wasn't laughing at him. "Do we have a class now?" he asked, exhausted at the very idea.

"No, dinner," Lisabet said. "Come on, I'll show you the way."

They closed the wardrobe door, and she led him down the hallways of the Academy, where they joined groups of other students filing toward what his nose told him must be the dining hall.

"Thank you for showing me the way," he made himself say, and Lisabet smiled, pleased. *Good.* If he could make friends with her, perhaps she wouldn't be suspicious when he crept away to try and steal an amulet for Rayna. He was already wondering how, between guides and classes and mealtimes, he was going to manage it.

They joined the queue and shuffled into the dining hall through a large archway. It was a huge room with a low ceiling and long tables seating about two hundred people, most of whom seemed to be making as much noise as possible. They were as varied as any Holbard crowd, and the youngest seemed to be Anders's age, the oldest about eighteen or so, along with a healthy smattering of adults.

At the end of a nearby table, a boy and a girl their own age waved for their attention, and Lisabet waved back.

"They've saved us seats," she said. "Let's get something to eat."

She led Anders over to the side of the room, where large serving dishes waited, and handed him a plate. His stomach knotted with sudden hunger as the smells rose to meet him, his mouth watering as he followed her along the bowls and dishes.

He piled his plate high with smoked lamb and roasted potatoes, adding dark-brown rye bread along the edges, and filling all the gaps with fried mushrooms and piles of green peas. It was more than he'd usually eat in several days, and he knew his stomach was going to protest when it was all on the inside, but there was no way he was missing a meal like this.

I wonder what Rayna's eating, said a small voice in his head. *If she's eating at all.*

He followed Lisabet over to the table where her friends were waving, slipping onto the end of the bench opposite her. "This is Anders," she said as they took their places. "Anders, these are our roomies, Sakarias and Viktoria."

Sakarias was a boy with an easy grin that showed off his dimples, and reddish-blond hair cut close to his head in the usual wolf style. "Welcome to the Academy," he said cheerfully. "Hope you don't snore." As he spoke, he was leaning over to pour Anders and Lisabet glasses of milk from the big jug in the middle of the table.

"And this is Viktoria," Lisabet said with a laugh, indicating the girl beside her.

Viktoria didn't look nearly as welcoming, her dark-brown eyes flicking up and down Anders as though measuring his worth, and finding him wanting. She had sleek, silky black hair longer than the rest of the wolves, a delicate nose and mouth, and light-brown skin. "Welcome to Ulfar," she said, and Anders knew immediately he had been right. Her voice was so polished you could just about see your face in it. This was a girl who had grown up with servants, and she probably thought her transformation was one big inconvenience, now she had to make her own bed and serve her own meals.

The four of them dug into their food, and around mouthfuls, Lisabet and Sakarias told him more about the Academy. Viktoria wielded her cutlery meticulously, and Anders watched her out of the corner of his eye, painfully aware he was holding both his knife and his fork wrong.

"There are about twenty-five of us in each year level," Sakarias was saying. "After you've done twelve months, you'll go up to the next year level. So we all move at different times, depending on what month we passed the Trial of the Staff and made our first transformation. There's about a hundred and fifty students in total most of the time. After you're done with your final year, you go train full time as a soldier, or whatever else you're going to do."

"Mostly soldiers," Lisabet said. "Viktoria wants to be a medic, though."

Viktoria looked up with an irritated wrinkle of her nose, as though this was some great secret that had been spilled. Beside her, Sakarias rolled his eyes, then stopped quickly, just before she looked his way. "Pack and paws, I'd stop being sick if you told me," he promised. "Scared not to. You'd be a great medic."

That seemed to please her, and she nodded, returning to her meal, and deigning to join the conversation. "Some of the adults here aren't wolves at all, they're our medical staff, or our cooks, things like that. But we still need wolves with those skills. Can't take a *human* doctor out on patrol with you, after all."

There was that word again—*human*. Anders nodded and tried to absorb each new name and face, each new job and piece of information. Anything could be a piece of the puzzle he needed to solve. Anyone could be the one to help him.

Sakarias's voice jerked him back to the present a few moments later. "So where are you from, anyway?"

"From?" Anders took a few moments to echo him,

and he realized with a pang that he'd been waiting for Rayna to reply, as he always did. But he had to do it himself this time.

"From," Viktoria clarified, with a toss of her sleek, black hair. "I'm from the west side of Holbard. What about you?"

Well, that piece of information certainly clarified Anders's suspicions—the west side was where Dama Sancheo's fancy soup shop was, where Anders and Rayna had stopped pickpocketing because they'd stuck out too much in their patched clothes.

"Her mother's a doctor," Sakarias supplied cheerfully, around a mouthful of lamb and gravy. "Fancy, right? But when Viktoria's a medic, she'll treat wolves *and* humans, so she'll be double fancy." He reached past her for another slice of bread. "Assuming she survives sharing a room with us, of course. That's gonna be a close thing."

"Shut up, Sakarias," Viktoria said, lifting one hand to rest the inside of her wrist on top of her head, and flick her fingers toward the back of her head.

For a moment Anders was puzzled by the gesture, but then understanding clicked into place. She was casually imitating the way an irritated wolf would lay back its ears, using wolf body language even as a human. *How had he understood that? He'd only just transformed.*

"I'm from a village near the west coast called Little Dalven," Sakarias said, not shutting up even a little bit, but at least turning his attention away from Viktoria. "Farmers, my family. Poor as can be. At night, we used to roast a single potato, and gather around it for heat, then divide it up between the nine of us."

Viktoria snorted, and Sakarias sighed. "All right," he admitted. "There were two potatoes."

Anders's mouth quirked, and he found himself on the verge of laughing. Sakarias reminded him of Rayna in some ways—always ready to talk, always ready with a quick answer, though he was a little sillier.

It would have been a nice thing to make a friend, but he had to keep himself separate. No matter what he thought of the wolves, they were Rayna's enemies.

"I grew up here at Ulfar," Lisabet said. "My mother's a wolf, and if the child of a wolf doesn't have any other family, they're allowed to stay here until it's clear whether they're going to transform or not."

"What happens if you don't?" Anders asked, realizing a moment too late he had his mouth full. Viktoria definitely noticed, but Sakarias just winked at him.

"The Academy arranges an apprenticeship in the city," Lisabet replied.

"And you have to leave your family?"

"I think my mother would have coped," she said, wry.

Sakarias opened his mouth to comment on that, but Lisabet continued, speaking over him. "You grew up in Holbard too, Anders, is that right?"

"Yes," he said, looking down at his plate, searching for the right words. "I was in an orphanage."

Everyone was silent, and it seemed like even their neighbors had been listening, because Anders saw heads turning farther up the table. One wolf leaned in to whisper to another. He could feel their confusion like an extra guest at the table. The idea that he couldn't say how he connected to the pack was *strange*—their faces told him that.

Eventually Viktoria spoke. "But what about your family? How did they know to test you?"

Anders exchanged a glance with Lisabet, who had been there. He couldn't say it had been an accident. She'd seen Rayna saying they were there *for* the Trial. That meant he couldn't outright admit that he didn't know who his wolf ancestors were, but since he couldn't say, he was stuck pretending he didn't *want* to say. It was such a tangle.

Sakarias came to his rescue, perhaps accidentally. "He said he was an orphan, not that he never had any parents. Kind of rude to ask about them when they're . . ."

He trailed off awkwardly, rather than say *dead* out loud, but it did the job.

Viktoria clearly did *not* like anyone suggesting she had bad manners. "Do you have any brothers or sisters?" she asked in a very polite tone of voice, ignoring Sakarias.

"Just me." It felt like a betrayal, pretending Rayna didn't exist, but he had to hide her. "No other family."

"Well, you have a family now," Lisabet replied.

Those were the same words Hayn had spoken, and Sigrid. *Family. Pack.* The wolves were so sure he was one of them, but if they knew about Rayna, if they knew what he wanted to do . . .

He didn't reply, and after a moment, the conversation moved on without him.

The four of them made their way to their room together after dinner was over. They chatted cheerfully as they got ready for bed, Sakarias keeping up a steady stream, barely requiring anyone else to join in. His wiry frame seemed full of endless energy, always on the move.

Anders made all the right noises, or hoped he did, and eventually they all settled in to bed. It felt strange to put on his crisp new pajamas and climb into his own bed alongside the other three. His ribs still ached. He felt crowded in by the others, and at the same time, completely isolated.

It took Anders a very long time to fall asleep, and not just because the big bed in his corner of the room was too lonely, and too soft.

* * *

The next morning Sakarias took him to breakfast, a thick porridge with berries, though Anders was still full from his meal the night before. His roommate kept up a barrage of introductions, though the names and faces soon started to blur, and Anders was pretty sure some of the wolves he met were the ones who'd been whispering the night before. He was grateful when Lisabet and Viktoria joined their breakfast table.

"Today we have Combat in the morning," Lisabet told him. "Usually it's three classes before lunch and three after, but some run long. Combat's a triple, and Military History this afternoon is a double, because Sigrid can't come back twice in the week to teach us. Once is easier for her."

Anders's heart sank. Combat he could use—if he had to brave the mountains to find the dragons, combat could be useful. But Military History? Unless they were going to tell him exactly where the dragons had fled after the last great battle, what use was that?

"Do we study—" He paused, searching for a way to ask what he wanted. "I mean, the dragons were right here in the city, and everyone says they might come back any day. Do we study them? I know we're only students, but if something happens, it seems like they'll need everyone."

"Oh, we study dragons," Lisabet replied, as Sakarias laughed.

"We *only* study dragons," Sakarias told him. "Every class is about dragons, dragons, dragons. Especially right now."

"It's not *if* something happens," Viktoria said, grimmer than the others. "It's *when*. They must have a reason to be back in the city after all this time."

That was enough to silence their laughter and chase away even Sakarias's dimples, and they were quiet as they made their way to the combat hall to wait for their class. Along with the others, Anders changed from his uniform into leggings and a tunic, comfortable clothes he could move in, his feet bare.

The group formed a long row along the edge of the big hall, every small sound echoing off the wooden floors and the rafters. Anders stood between Lisabet and Mateo, a quiet boy who seemed unfairly tall and strong.

"Professor Ennar teaches this class," Lisabet murmured as she leaned down to press both her palms to the ground in one easy movement, arching her back to a stretch. Looking up and down the row, Anders realized everyone was warming up, and he leaned down to imitate her, though the best he could manage was pressing his knuckles to the ground.

"What's the professor like?" he whispered back.

"She's . . ." Lisabet considered the question. "She's tough. She's a real soldier, she was a commander in the last battle. She and her wife single-handedly held a whole section of the city wall for an hour, until reinforcements could get through. She has a lot more than ice spears in her arsenal."

Anders wanted to ask what that meant, what a wolf could do that was more than an ice spear, but the hall fell suddenly silent as a woman with clipped, steel-gray hair strode into the hall. She was short and muscular, and despite her gray hair, she didn't look that old—her skin was as smooth and pale as the pine wolf puppet that he'd seen . . . had it only been the day before yesterday? Instead, it was as if her hair had decided to change color prematurely so it could match her uniform and be all the more wolfish.

"Good morning," she said, and everybody—including Anders—stood up a little straighter. "New boy, come talk to me," she said. "Everyone else, laps of the hall."

There was some very quiet muttering as the class turned to start running laps, their bare feet quieter on the floor than Anders had expected—even in human form, the wolves were still moving with careful stealth. He swallowed and walked over to present himself to Professor Ennar.

"Good morning, Professor," he ventured, folding his arms across his chest as he and Rayna both did when they were uncomfortable, then unfolding them in case it looked like he was hiding something.

"Anders Bardasen," she said, as if reading his name off some invisible list. Like Sigrid, she leaned a little heavier on his surname. It meant something to these wolves, who had fought in the battle he was named for, that it didn't mean to everyone else. Though he'd only been a baby, he'd lost people in the battle, just as they had.

"Yes, Dama," he said as politely as he could.

"Just Ennar," she said absently. "Or Professor, if you must. In this class, over the next six years, you'll learn all kinds of combat, armed and unarmed. You'll learn to fight as a human and as a wolf—you never know which you'll need. You'll learn to use a staff and a sword as a human, and ice spears as a wolf. Perhaps more, if this turns out to be an area in which you're particularly gifted."

Anders had to swallow down a snort—the idea that of all areas he'd be gifted at combat was depressingly funny. If Rayna were here, she'd be at the top of the class, learning secret weapons in no time. Still, it didn't matter—he would only be here as long as he needed to be.

Ennar didn't seem to notice, keeping half an eye on the students running laps of the hall. "Now more than ever, combat classes are of vital importance. The equinox is coming in just five weeks. Do you know what that means, Anders?"

He blinked. "I know it's when the amount of daylight is the same as the amount of night, but . . ." He trailed off. He didn't think that was what she was asking. How could that affect the danger from the dragons? He and Rayna had seen a dragon the night of the last equinox celebrations six months before, he remembered that much.

"True," she said. "It is also an important time of year for the dragons. A powerful time. When day and night are equal, it represents fire and ice being equal too. Both kinds of elementals, ice wolves and scorch dragons, are said to have equal power. We wolves mark tipping points like the equinoxes, but we do so with quiet learning and contemplation. Humans, as you know, celebrate the turning of the seasons.

"No wolf has ever been privy to the dragons' rituals, but it is said the dragons throw wild celebrations instead. To welcome the longer days, or show they are not afraid of the longer nights. They have a history of kidnapping children in the days and weeks before the equinoxes."

Anders blinked, his gaze snapping to her. That was *exactly* what had happened to Rayna. Well, not exactly— the people they'd taken had been in human shape—but still . . . "Do we know why they kidnap them?" he asked, afraid of the answer.

"They take our weak and our sick," Ennar said. "Always children. Those who cannot defend themselves. They sacrifice them on the day of the equinox. We must be ready, in case they attack again soon."

Anders felt like he'd swallowed an icicle, his insides going cold, pain stabbing at his gut. *Sacrifice?*

She wasn't one of them. She wasn't a proper dragon. She couldn't be, she was the sister of a wolf.

Sacrifice. The word beat through his heart like a drum.

Five weeks, his mind whispered, trying to overrule his heart. *You have five weeks, she's safe until then.*

He had five weeks to find out where Rayna was, get there, and rescue her.

This is good news, his mind whispered again, trying to silence his panicking heart. *If they want to sacrifice her, they'll have to keep her alive. This gives you time.*

But Anders still felt sick as he looked up at Professor Ennar. "I'll work as hard as I can, I promise," he said.

"I'm sure you will," she agreed. "And don't make the mistake of thinking these skills are just for battle.

Wolves keep the peace right across Vallen. When you're older you'll go out on long patrols of the island, visiting smaller towns and villages, and walk the streets of the city here. And if the dragons make good on their threat, you'll be ready to stand with us and fight."

"Yes, Professor." Anders could hear the faint hesitation in his voice.

"You'll catch up with the class quickly," Ennar promised him, mistaking the tone for something else. "Every wolf is born with a gift for this, and you'll refine yours much more quickly than you think."

She turned away, and with a sharp whistle recalled the class, who completed their lap and lined up once more, breathing heavily. At her instructions, they dragged over soft mats from the edge of the hall and began with drills in pairs.

Anders found himself standing opposite Mateo, the mountain, his heart sinking. He could see the other boy's muscles beneath his light brown skin. *Who had muscles when they were twelve?*

He was going to be mashed into pulp before he ever left to save his sister. Forget that—he was going to be pulp before he got a chance to leave the combat hall. But all this could be important, so he had to try.

The first two times they came together Anders hit the mat in under ten seconds, landing hard on his back, the air driven from his aching lungs. Each time Mateo smiled an easy smile and leaned down to offer him his hand, helping him up. As if trying to drive his spine out through his chest was nothing personal.

But it turned out that all his practice on the streets— climbing up and down the sides of buildings, running from the Wolf Guard themselves some days, squeezing into places he didn't belong and jumping from places he shouldn't have been—was worth something.

Mateo might know the moves, but Anders had the speed and flexibility. The third time, when Mateo stepped forward to reach for him, Anders ducked, then stepped in closer rather than back, lifting one foot to hook it around the back of the bigger boy's knee, and pull. Mateo's eyes flew wide open as his knee gave way and he crashed backward.

He lay staring up at the rafters as if he'd never seen them before, and given his size, maybe he hadn't. Just as Anders began to wonder if he'd made a mistake, Mateo's face split in a grin, and he moved, levering himself to his feet. "Show me that move," he said, still grinning.

"Sure, if you show me how you sent me flying last time," Anders shot back, and Mateo rumbled with laughter.

Perhaps combat class wasn't going to be *completely* terrible.

But it turned out he thought that far too soon. Ennar prowled along the rows as they sparred in pairs, correcting stances and moves, offering advice, and, very rarely, praise. And then they transformed, and things got worse.

It took Anders nearly five minutes to manage his transformation, while half the class watched, and the other half pretended not to. He'd never transformed on purpose before, and Ennar quietly coached him, offering suggestions and advice. His head was whirling with everything he'd learned, and the more he knew their eyes were on him, the harder it became to slip into the wolf form waiting inside of him.

His gaze swept across the hall and the pack of wolves waiting there, and he picked out Lisabet's nearly black pelt, almost as dark as her hair. Sakarias's fur had a hint of red to match his reddish-blond hair, but Viktoria's was a light gray, nothing like her long black hair.

Lisabet offered him a wolfish grin, one that reminded him of her usual, human smile. He relaxed just a fraction, and next thing, he felt the pain of the transformation shooting along his arms and legs.

The world looked different from down low. The smells rushed to him, telling him exactly where each of his classmates stood. It felt strange, almost uncomfortable, to be so aware of his body. To feel the quick, testing swish of his tail, and know his muscles were waiting to launch him into a run the moment he asked them to.

But at least he'd managed it—if it had taken much longer, his brain might have melted completely, what with the embarrassment of everyone staring at him.

Unfortunately, the worst was yet to come. The class lined up along the wall to practice their ice spears, taking their places by a strip of the floor made of stone. Ennar paced along the line once more. The wolves reared up onto their back legs, then smacked their front paws down against the stone floor. Ice spears burst forth from the ground, smashing against the wall.

Some were as thick as his human arm, others were thin and sharp, and a few, those of the newer students, were more like shards of ice. The air around them cooled, and Anders felt more comfortable in his own skin, taking his place in line to try and cast his own spears.

Ennar padded along the line of students to stop beside him to help, offering instruction with her soft growls and whines, with the flick of her ears and the tilt of her head. As before, he found he understood her as clearly as if she'd spoken out loud, even though the words themselves were complex. *Channel the essence all around you. The ability runs through your veins. Draw the moisture from the air, from the ground, and will the ice into being—you command it, so you need to act commandingly.*

Anders understood her words, but he wasn't sure he understood her meaning, so he copied the others carefully. He concentrated on the moisture that must be floating around in the air, trying to push all other thoughts out of his mind. Then he reared up, smacking his paws down on the ground, bringing every bit of his willpower to bear on creating a spear.

Nothing happened.

Don't worry. The tilt of Ennar's head was calm, her breathing slow. *It will come. Try again.*

But it didn't.

If he'd been a human, Anders would be burning hot with embarrassment right now. As a wolf, he knew his ears were flattening against his head, and he couldn't stop himself from sinking low to the ground, as if he could vanish right through the floor. Just as he understood every word Ennar spoke to him as a wolf, he knew that now, anyone who looked at him could see that he just wanted to be invisible.

Ennar shifted back to human form effortlessly, walking over to pick up a bowl of water from a shelf by the door and carrying it back to him. Crouching, she poured it onto the floor until there was a puddle right in front of Anders, and then transformed back into her wolf form.

Try now, she said with a tilt of her head.

Anders reared up again, smacking his paws down in desperation. He *had* to be able to do this. This was the weapon he'd need, one of the parts of his plan to rescue Rayna.

He just didn't understand what she meant—he could imagine there must be moisture in the air, and he could *see* the puddle in the ground, but how did he get it to do what he wanted? How did he summon it?

He had about as much chance of opening a door without touching it, or predicting the future. It just didn't make sense.

Don't worry, Sakarias growled, coming up beside him. *Everybody gets this. I'll bet my tail you have it in no time.*

But there was an uncertainty in the tilt of his head that told Anders everything he needed to know. Anybody else would have it by now. Sakarias didn't understand what he was finding so difficult.

He kept trying for the rest of the lesson, but though Ennar stopped by again and again, he couldn't manage so much as a snowflake. Some of his classmates tried to offer helpful advice, and others didn't bother to hide their amusement, tongues lolling and tails wagging as they laughed at him. The boy with no family, who'd avoided telling anybody what his tie was to the pack, wasn't a proper wolf. *Surprise, surprise.* Anders grew more and more painfully aware of their scrutiny, and of his failure.

He didn't understand how to sense water, or how to talk to it.

It was as if he was missing the gift that every other wolf had been given.

CHAPTER NINE

LUNCH WAS AGONIZING. HALF THE CLASS TRIED to make excuses for his inability to generate a spear, and offered well-intentioned stories about their own failings, none of which were remotely the same. Anders couldn't shake the sense of failure, or the sight of the students up at the other end of the table who were still smirking.

Sakarias tried telling him about the time he'd nearly pinned Viktoria to the wall with one of his first spears (Viktoria didn't think that story was quite as funny), and Mateo admitted that once he'd generated a spear flying *toward* himself instead of away, and knocked himself unconscious.

Lisabet mostly watched him, and Anders couldn't shake the feeling that she understood more than he wanted to tell her—that she could read his body language even as a human, and see the worry there, the impatience.

Anders chewed miserably through his fish stew as the others talked, his mind turning inexorably toward Rayna. His mood didn't improve when Lisabet, Viktoria, and Sakarias led him to Military History class with Sigrid, the Fyrstulf.

"Jai's in charge of textbooks," she said, pointing through the crowd of students to one with their back to them, hair cut short like everyone else's, clad in a gray Ulfar uniform. "They'll get one out of the supply cupboard for you."

Anders pushed his way through the crowd to see Jai about a book. Jai turned out to be a redhead with a ready grin and the sort of very pale, paper-white skin that looked like it would crisp if they ever went outside on one of Holbard's rare sunny days. They gave him a textbook and a cheerful smile and a welcome to Ulfar, and Anders tried to smile back, though his heart was sinking at the size of the book he held in his hands.

There was *no* way his reading was good enough for him to follow along with the class. He could read a little, but he and Rayna had really only ever needed it for street signs and labels on the food they were stealing. They'd left school at six when they'd left the orphanage, and his lessons had been . . . occasional since then.

There was a boy named Det sitting near him, who had

an easy smile, and hair and skin a rich, dark brown, quite tall for his age. By checking how far into the book Det seemed to be and comparing the diagrams he could see, he tried to find the right page in his own book. After a moment, Det noticed what he was doing and held up his book so Anders could see it.

He thought for a moment about confiding in someone that he couldn't read the textbook, and looked around at his options. Lisabet had her nose buried in her book. In front of him, the back of Viktoria's head didn't look inviting. Jai and Mateo were arguing about something from combat class behind him, and he didn't know Det, however friendly his smile was.

Sakarias sat to his left and looked busy already. Anders hadn't picked him for a hard worker, but perhaps—having been poor once himself—he knew what an opportunity he had here at the Academy.

The decision was made for him when Sigrid strode into the room. Everyone sat up straight as she began her lecture. Anders didn't know the names of any of the wolves or dragons involved in what sounded like an ancient battle she was describing, and his mind began to wander. He leafed through his textbook, looking at the pictures of attack formations and old battlegrounds, and artifacts the wolves had used in battle.

Next, his gaze drifted across to Sakarias again. Now he was sitting up straight, he could see what the other boy was writing. And he wasn't writing at all—he was drawing. His quick, clever pencil was skating over his notebook, bringing to life a picture of a huge stack of textbooks, with a pair of boots sticking out of the bottom of them, as though the wearer had been crushed by the mass of reading. Sigrid was visible at the edge of the picture, adding another book to the stack.

Anders's mouth quirked as he tried to hide a smile. Apparently he wasn't the only one who found the Fyrstulf intimidating.

Sigrid's tone changed suddenly, and he jumped, snapping his gaze up. Had she seen Sakarias's sketch? Had she seen Anders smiling at it?

But no. She was glaring at Lisabet, who was apparently repeating a question. Lisabet's pale skin was a little pink under her freckles, but otherwise she was unapologetic in the face of the pack leader's displeasure.

"I was asking about the treaty times, Sigrid," she said.

"What do the treaty times have to do with it?" Sigrid asked, close to a growl. "This is a *military* history class."

"Well, you need the black to see the white," Lisabet replied. "You need the warm to feel the cold. And you need to see peace to understand battle. There have been times we got along with the dragons. Decades. Some historians even say centuries."

"There have been times," Sigrid said, "when we tolerated the dragons in order to reach a goal. We have never trusted them. We never *got along* with them."

"But that doesn't seem right," Lisabet pressed. "I mean, the courtyard here at Ulfar is literally sized for dragons to land in, it's huge. We must have wanted them here to do that." Now everybody in the class was staring at her, including Anders, though he was doing it for a different reason. Listening to her tugged him in two different directions.

On one hand, hearing her defend dragons was putting his teeth more on edge. He and Rayna were orphans because of the dragons. He and Rayna had grown up on the streets, never knowing a moment's safety because of dragons.

He was alone, trying to figure out how to rescue his sister from whatever trickery had turned her into a dragon. He had no family to help him, because of *dragons*.

But on the other hand, Lisabet was the first one he'd heard even raise the idea that dragons might be reasoned with. A tiny part of him wondered if Lisabet would help him, if she knew what had happened. If she might believe that even though Rayna was a dragon, she was also a hostage. A hostage in danger of the equinox sacrifice.

"That's enough, Lisabet," Sigrid snapped. "Pack and paws, why would we dream up a danger that wasn't there? Our artifacts are breaking, one by one. If we had a way to repair them, we would. If we could trust the dragons enough for that, we would. What could be worth more than that?"

Anders blinked. What did dragons have to do with repairing artifacts? He felt like she'd made a leap he didn't understand, but it clearly wasn't the right moment to raise his hand.

Lisabet stared at the Fyrstulf for a long moment, and when she spoke, her voice was very quiet, but her gaze was direct. "Power," she said.

"Power?" Sigrid repeated, her voice going dangerously hard.

"The mayor doesn't run Holbard," Lisabet said, soft and even. She knew she was getting into trouble, Anders could tell, but she kept talking anyway. "The parliament barely runs Vallen. We do. And all because they're afraid of dragons, and they need us to protect them."

"*And we will*," Sigrid snapped, raising a hand to point at the door, baring her teeth like an angry wolf. "Because we know best. Get out of my classroom. We will discuss this later."

133

The whole classroom was deadly silent, and nobody else moved as Lisabet rose slowly to her feet, her jaw stubbornly squared. She was a solitary figure, almost . . . Anders had to search for the right word. *Almost lonely*, he realized. He'd noticed before how her face turned serious as soon as she stopped smiling, but now, it seemed something more than that.

Her footsteps were the only noise in the room as she walked through the doorway, then pulled the door closed behind her.

After a long beat of silence, Sigrid resumed her lesson.

"Well," she said, disapproving. "You can be sure that the dragons who have been spying in Holbard and who knows where else around Vallen aren't doing it because they'd like to come celebrate the year's end feast with us and exchange gifts. When you all were babies we fought them for Holbard. We lost lives preventing them from burning down the whole of this city, and as some of you in this room know"—and here her gaze lingered uncomfortably on Anders—"our personal losses were great."

There was a soft, general murmuring of agreement around the classroom. Nobody else wanted to be sent out.

"Betrayal of the pack is punishable by death for an adult, and by exile for a student," Sigrid continued. "And though I do not question Lisabet's loyalty, her softness toward dragons is misplaced and inappropriate. Now, let's move on and discuss the ways in which we estimate how long it will take a squad of the Wolf Guard to travel a particular distance."

She had the class get up from their seats and come to the front of the classroom to gather around her desk. Everyone was still tense, and tentative about speaking, but they began to relax as they studied the artifact that sat there.

It was a large metal sheet, with a knotwork design engraved all around the edges and a compass marked with runes at the top. The rest of it showed a map etched into the metal—it was the island of Vallen down to the very last detail, from the Westlands Mountains up in the remote northwest of the country to the Seacliff Mountains in the east, with the Icespire Mountains running down the country's spine. He could see the city of Holbard with its high walls, and the farmlands to the west. Rivers snaked across the landscape, and the coast crinkled in and out in a design as intricate as the edge of any snowflake.

"This map works with these two markers," Sigrid said, holding out her hand to show them two small, metal discs. "We place one in our location, and the other where we want to go. The numbers that appear in this corner here," and she tapped the map, "will tell us how many hours the travel will take for a human on foot, a wolf on foot, and a horse-drawn wagon.

"It's less accurate for the wagon," she continued with a wry smile, at odds with her usual, stern expression, and Anders didn't find it very comforting. *She's trying to calm things down after losing her temper at Lisabet.* "It probably depends on the horse. Nevertheless, you can see how useful it would be."

Anders was quiet for the rest of the lesson, as the conversation slowly came back to life around him. Sigrid's words kept echoing around his head.

Death, or exile, for betrayal of the pack.

Those were the stakes of the game he was playing.

And he didn't think he was good enough to win.

* * *

At dinner, as the others talked around him, Anders was quiet. So were Sakarias and Viktoria—like him, he thought they were probably wondering where Lisabet was. She hadn't shown up to eat.

His plate was full of food, as it was at every meal. This time it was meat and vegetables, fried up and seasoned with sharp, spicy chella that made his tongue prickle.

"This isn't strong, this is nothing," said Det, grinning. "This kind of seasoning would be for babies where I grew up."

Det had come from far across the sea, Mositala, Anders learned. Det told him that Mositala had wide plains and high mountains like Vallen, but the sun burned far hotter there. In some places, the grass was yellow, the earth dry. In others, the jungle was lush and green—compared to the island of Vallen, it sounded like it went on forever.

"Our elementals are different there," Det said. "Different animals, different elements. But when I turned twelve, I started to get sick. We didn't think we had any thunder lion blood in our family, but I undertook the changing ceremony anyway, because I was getting sick the way children do when they need to transform, but nobody has helped them make their first change.

"It didn't work, of course. But eventually, one of my aunts remembered that my great-grandmother was from Vallen. So, in desperation, my parents put me on a ship and brought me here. And sure enough, when I touched the Staff of Hadda, I made my transformation."

"Your great-grandmother," Mateo repeated. "That's so little wolf blood, and you still made the transformation?"

"Sure as I'm here," Det replied. "It doesn't matter how many wolves you have in your bloodline, as long as there's one. That's enough for the spark to live inside you. After that, it's up to chance—you're one of the ones who transforms, or you aren't."

Anders kept his head down, pretending to concentrate on his meal. Someone in his family's past must have been a wolf, he thought. But it could have been generations back—knowing it brought him no closer to knowing who he was.

Det forked up another mouthful of vegetables with a sigh. "I miss the warmth, but I can't imagine being away from the pack now."

"Det has great stories from Mositala," Jai said brightly.

Det broke into his easy, infectious laughter. "They're little children's stories," he said. "You're just easily entertained."

"Well, they're good," said Mateo loyally—he and Jai were roommates with Det.

"Anything from another place is interesting," said Det. "That's why Holbard is such a good place to live. People from all over the world end up here. Every big city has people from all over—it's the same in Mositala—but Holbard is a trading post like no other. Just look at all of us. Viktoria has stories about Ohiro, where most of her family's from. Mateo's grandmother bakes these amazing cookies from Allemhäut."

Every head in the group swiveled toward Mateo.

"What cookies?" Sakarias demanded. "How come Det knows how good they taste? Did you get cookies and hold out on us?"

"Stories from Vallen are interesting too," Det said, trying to rescue Mateo. "Anders, were there kids from all over at your orphanage?"

Anders froze. He knew what Det was trying to do—what all the others were trying to do, with their interested expressions. They wanted to include him. To let him know that at least some of them didn't care that he didn't have a family, that they weren't sure how he connected to the larger pack.

But he'd left the orphanage when he was six, and the last thing he wanted was attention drawn to where he'd come from. He didn't want to tell any of his stories about scavenging for food—Rayna's trick with the fishing pole was clever, but hardly the kind of thing you wanted to draw attention to. Looking around at their encouraging, expectant faces, he groped for something to share.

"We were from all over," he agreed.

They'd all felt like outsiders, much of the time, set apart from everyone else in Holbard who had a family. "We stuck together," he said, instead of trying to explain that unique kind of loneliness. "We had our own secret language."

Of course, that didn't throw them off the trail at *all*. He ended up teaching them the signal he'd used to enlist Jerro's help on the day of his transformation. Soon everyone at his end of the table was making a fist with their right hands and touching their ears with their thumbs.

Eventually the conversation moved on, but he couldn't doubt anymore that whatever some of his classmates felt, his friends wanted him to be a part of the pack.

The wolves and their pack weren't at all what he'd expected. From the outside, they were all crisp gray uniforms, all the same from their haircuts to their attitudes. But on the inside, he'd discovered something very different. They valued pack, and they valued order, but no two were alike.

Though Anders and Rayna had often wondered about their parents, Anders barely ever felt like he was missing out. He and Rayna were a team, and they were enough for each other. *More* than enough.

But now, he was finding that all this time he *had* wanted something more. He just hadn't known it. The feeling of family at Ulfar was hard to deny. The fact that they all managed to be a pack despite their differences only added to the feeling that if he'd had the chance, perhaps he might have belonged here.

But next moment, a pang of guilt struck him. What was he wasting time dwelling on that for? Belonging here didn't help Rayna.

And anyway, what was he thinking? He was lying

about who he was and why he was here, and he was a failure as a wolf—he couldn't even cast an ice spear. The more they knew about him, the less any of them would want him.

He gritted his teeth, and silently he renewed his promise to his sister. *I'll find you. I'll get you out of there. I won't let the dragons hurt you.*

CHAPTER TEN

AFTER DINNER, ANDERS HAD HIS MILITARY HIS-tory homework to tackle. He was too wary of Sigrid not to get it done, and he chose the library as his place to work. He figured that anybody who saw him doing his homework wouldn't have a reason to question what he was doing there . . . and maybe the library held information that could help him figure out where to locate Rayna. He wasn't sure he'd be able to read his own textbook, let alone the books in the library, but he had to try.

Viktoria gave him directions and he made his way there, carefully pushing open the stout wooden doors.

Long tables ran up and down the length of the library, thick carpets muffled footsteps, and long tapestries hid the stone walls. Shelf after wooden shelf was lined with leatherbound books, their spines etched with gold titles, their smell filling the room with a unique scent that he thought must belong only to places full of pages. Certainly there was something about the air in here he'd never felt before.

Spiral staircases led up to second-floor balconies, which were lined with yet more bookshelves. Dust motes danced in the last of the evening light that shone in through the tall windows, and Anders had the place very nearly to himself.

"Can I help you, young man?" One of the librarians looked up from her desk, managing to speak so her voice carried and yet somehow keeping it quiet at the same time. It was a kind of magic that belonged only to librarians, as far as he could tell. She had dark brown skin and dozens of small braids in her hair—the length of which suggested she probably wasn't a wolf—and a pair of glasses pushed a little down her nose so she could regard Anders thoughtfully.

As always, there was that momentary pause as he waited for Rayna to answer, then realized she wasn't there. "I was, uh . . ." He wasn't any good at doing his own talking. "I just wanted to do my homework," he said. "If that's all right."

"Quite all right," she said, smiling. "Take a table, and let me know if you need any help finding books."

He took his time making his way through the room, soaking up every detail. There were a series of locked glass cases along the wall next to the entrance, and he walked along them slowly, looking inside each one.

The contents were all artifacts—he knew that much from the runes engraved on them—though he didn't know what any of them did, or why they were on display instead of being used. He saw a set of metal buttons that looked as if they should be sewn on a shirt, as well as a series of boxes, a metal picture frame with a blank canvas, and other strange shapes.

He wondered immediately if one of these could be useful to him somehow—if he could use one of them to find a dragon, or fight one. But he didn't want the librarian to start wondering what he was doing, loitering over the artifacts. Those locks looked like they could be picked in just a few seconds—he'd just need to come back later on, when nobody was around.

For now he turned away, scanning the library for a place to sit. He'd tackle some of his homework, and then try searching the books for something that might help him—a map, or a diagram—once the librarian was used to him and wouldn't watch everything he was doing.

But there was already someone else in the library as well. *Lisabet.*

She had a book nearly as big as she was laid out on the table so she could lean over it, her freckled face serious as she studied it. She didn't seem to notice him, and he hesitated, then settled on a place a few tables over. After that afternoon's fight in the classroom he wasn't sure if she'd want company, and it suited him not to have any.

He opened his textbook and took out the worksheet he was supposed to fill out—a simple quiz on the facts in that week's chapter—his heart sinking as he counted the questions. It was going to take him *forever* to read the whole thing. What was Sigrid going to say when he showed up with nothing done? Or the students who laughed at him behind their hands? He hadn't even learned their names yet—hadn't been brave enough to talk to them. This was impossible.

He abandoned his plan to try and finish his homework, pushing away from the table and walking farther back into the library. His heart was hammering, and his head hurt.

He couldn't even fill out a quiz, let alone search the library for clues on how to locate his sister.

He turned a corner into an aisle lined with shelves that were each double-height, holding books as big as his torso, bound in dark-red leather. Each one was an oversized reminder of his failures—of the homework he couldn't finish, and of the fact that he might be surrounded by the very information he needed right now, and he could barely read it.

The shelves stretched away, dozens upon dozens,

blocking out the light from the windows and giving him a safe place to crouch down, out of sight, and bury his face in his hands.

His eyes were hot, and aching, and though he hadn't cried in years—not when he and Rayna had lost a week's worth of food and earnings to bigger children, not when he'd fallen off a roof and nearly broken his arm, not even when Rayna had flown away with the other dragons—now he thought he might.

He'd come here so full of determination to find a way to search for her, but he didn't have the first idea where to start, and if the wolves found out she was his sister, anything could happen to him, and he'd lose the chance to help her.

"Anders?" A tentative voice spoke at the other end of the aisle.

He scrubbed at his face, leaving his fingers wet, and looked up, blinking in the dim light. Lisabet stood there, watching him uncertainly.

"I was just coming to get another book," she said, pointing up at the big leather volumes, and he realized they were the same as the one she'd been reading on the table.

"Don't let me stop you," he muttered, part embarrassed at being caught, part sort of impressed that his day could deteriorate any further.

"Well, I . . ." She paused, pushing her hands into her pockets. "Okay, that's not true. I came to check if you were all right. You were sort of . . ." She shifted the way she stood, rounding her shoulders, bending her knees a little, making herself smaller, and he realized that yet again he was watching a human produce a wolf's body language. She'd understood his mood without him speaking a word.

"I'm okay," he said, pushing to his feet, trying to make himself stand up straight. "Headache." He wondered again how much he was telling the wolves around him without meaning to.

She shot him a disbelieving look. "Look," she said. "I've been starting to think that . . . I mean, I could be wrong, but . . ."

He made himself keep his breathing slow and even. What was she wondering? Had she guessed something about Rayna? Had she read that in him, too? Whatever she said, he had to be ready to deny it.

Lisabet pushed on. "Look, I was just wondering if you need any help with reading."

Anders blinked. *That* wasn't the question he was expecting. But a moment later he was wary again—would Ulfar Academy keep him if he couldn't read? Then again, he was a wolf. Did they have any choice? Would they force him into endless extra lessons, taking away his time to find Rayna? He stared at Lisabet, unsure of what to say.

"If you do need help," she said, "I don't mind helping. I want to be a professor one day, it'll be good practice." She lowered her voice, walking a little closer. "There's no need to be embarrassed. But I won't tell, if you want."

Finally, he made himself speak. He *did* need help reading, if only so he could learn more about dragons, and about where they might have taken Rayna. "Thank you," he said. "I'd like that."

They spent the next hour on the Military History homework. Lisabet said there wasn't time to have a reading lesson and do the homework as well, so she read the chapter out loud, and together they found the answers to the quiz questions. It was quiet and companionable, and by the end of it, Anders found himself almost giggling with her over the names of the long-ago dragons and wolves.

"Lisabet," he said as they marked down the final answer. "Can I ask you something?"

She put down her pencil and turned to face him. "Because I don't think they're telling us everything," she said.

He blinked. "What?"

"I know what your question was going to be," she said. "Why did I fight with Sigrid in class, when she's the Fyrstulf, and I'm supposed to be quiet and listen?"

"Um . . . yes," he admitted. "It was, actually. What do you mean, they're not telling us everything?"

"Let me start with this," Lisabet said. "I don't think we're being told the truth about dragons. I mean, I believe the battle happened, and I think maybe we disagreed with them more and more in the years leading up to the last great battle. But everything Sigrid's saying, Anders, it doesn't add up—I don't believe the dragons just attacked the city out of the blue one day. Why would they?"

Anders made himself nod, wondering where this could possibly lead.

"And look at all the artifacts we have," she continued. "Sigrid and the others want us to believe we traded for them despite the fact that dragons are cruel and untrustworthy, despite the fact that they'd rather kill ten of us than help one of us. But why would they have made the artifacts they did? Why would Hadda have forged the staff, if she didn't want wolves to transform?"

Anders held up a hand to slow her down, trying to make sense of her words. "Wait a minute," he said slowly. "You mean Hadda, as in the Staff of Hadda? As in the Trial of the Staff? What do dragons have to do with that?"

"They made the staff," Lisabet replied. "They made all the artifacts. Wolves designed them, and dragons forged them."

"Hadda was a *dragon*?"

"She was," Lisabet said. "And the artifacts are beginning to break, and without dragons we have no way to repair or replace them."

Anders was reeling. He'd lived his whole life in fear of dragons, and now Lisabet was saying the wolves had been trading partners with them? It must have been out of fear, or desperation. "Do the rest of the pack know we traded with the dragons for them?"

"Not the youngest ones," she said. "But most do. Only nobody ever questions Sigrid."

"Well, she's Sigrid," he pointed out.

"Right," Lisabet said, grim. "But someone has to ask. The artifacts are starting to break, and without the dragons, we have no way to fix them. What if the Staff of Hadda stopped working? Or the amulets?"

"Well, not having the amulets would be awkward," he said, earning himself a brief smile. "The staff would be a lot worse."

"Exactly," she said. "I'm trying to learn about them, but the professors only ever show us some of the artifacts. I need the Skraboks for the rest."

"The what?" he asked.

She gestured for him to follow her, leading him over to where the big book she'd been consulting still lay open on the table. "These," she said. "And all the ones in the aisle over there. They list all the dragons' creations."

Anders was torn between joy and despair all at once. On one hand, perhaps the Skraboks would tell him about some kind of artifact that might help him find Rayna. On the other, there were hundreds of them. A lifetime of reading, even if he could read as fast as Lisabet.

There was one artifact to each page, sketched from several different angles, with lines of careful handwriting—or sometimes not so careful handwriting—laying out its uses. Lisabet ran her finger along under the lines to help him follow as she quietly read the contents to him.

The first page was dated just over ten years ago, and it showed sketches of a pair of telescopes. The description Lisabet read was in neat handwriting:

Position the first telescope aimed at the view you want to see. You can take the second telescope anywhere you like, and it will show you the view from the first. Particularly useful for keeping watch for incoming ships or watching a road for anyone coming along it. Designed by Hayn and Felix. Forged by Drifa.

NOTE: Does not work in the dark. Does work on opposite coasts of Vallen, not tested at greater distances. Make sure you don't swap the telescopes or you won't see anything.

And then, in another person's handwriting, the letters written by someone pressing down very firmly indeed:

Seriously, be careful. The telescopes look annoyingly similar.

"Drifa was a dragonsmith," Lisabet said. "One of the most famous. And you know Hayn already. I don't know who Felix was."

Anders's eyes widened. *Hayn* had worked with the dragons?

The next page showed a metal plate with ornate etchings of storm clouds all around the edges, about a foot across according to the measurements written beside it. The text was in someone else's handwriting, a little messier:

Place the plate in the area where you would like rainfall to occur, and leave overnight. Does not guarantee rain, but makes it more likely rain will occur. Useful for new crops that require early rainfall. Designed by Hayn. Forged by Tilda.

NOTE: The rain you're attracting is coming from somewhere that probably also needs it. Do not overuse. Be cautious when using alongside artifacts designed to raise or lower temperature.

The Snowstone, for example, will bring down the temperature, but combined with this plate, it will probably just cause hail. Which is terrible news for your crops.

Facing it was a sketch of a pair of handcuffs, along with a metal belt with an ornate buckle at its front.

The wearer of the handcuffs is not able to move more than ten feet from the wearer of the belt. Originally intended for law enforcement, these were to be replicated for widespread use by all patrolling pack members, however this was put on hold due to wolf-dragon conflict. Designed by Kaleb. Forged by Eliot.

NOTE: Handcuffs are only equipped with ONE key. Given no dragons are available to release the essence forged into these devices, it is vital the key not be lost when the cuffs are being used. VITAL.

They kept on reading together, soaking up artifacts far more complex than any Anders had ever seen outside the Academy—and more complicated than most he'd seen inside as well. They flipped backward to check their theory that the artifacts were listed in order of their invention, and decades earlier, they found another Anders recognized. It was a sketch of the wind arches at the port, the blueprint drawn carefully, lines of runes listed under-neath. *Designed by Sylas*, it said, giving the name of some long-ago wolf. But then: *Updated by Hayn*. Interesting.

They returned to more recent artifacts, and eventually they realized only the lamps were now lighting the library, and it was dark outside. Anders had been right—this was a lifetime of reading, and no promise of an answer.

Looking up, Lisabet seemed to notice the darkness as well. "One more," she said, turning to the next page. It held a picture of a water bottle with an ornate metal lid, and a spout through which to drink.

Water bottle can be filled with water of any quality, and if drunk through the spout, it will be potable. Designed by Felix. Forged by Drifa.

NOTE: It is important to clean out the filter in the neckpiece regularly. This bottle will purify the water, but it will not cause chunks of debris to disappear. These must be cleared by hand.

Anders stared down at this final picture. A tickle in the back of his mind told him it was familiar, and he squinted sore eyes at it, waiting for his brain to present an answer.

Then the puzzle clicked into place. He'd seen this exact water skin on a shelf in the Fyrstulf's office. He remembered it distinctly, tucked between two books.

Lisabet said she had to put the book away and declined his offer of help—which made him wonder if she, too, was keeping secrets, so he gathered up his homework and set off for their room.

He could barely wrap his mind around what he'd learned. Wolves and dragons working together? Lisabet's questions felt *dangerous*.

And they didn't change the fact that the dragons had kidnapped Rayna. Or that he still had no idea how to rescue her.

Viktoria wasn't back in their room yet either, so Sakarias gave Anders another lesson in ice spears while nobody was looking. But Anders still couldn't understand what Sakarias tried so hard to explain. He couldn't sense water around him in the air, or under the earth, let alone imagine how to summon it or freeze it.

"Do I just . . . think at it?" he asked, frustration washing over him. "How does that work? I have about as much chance of talking to you with my mind as talking to water."

"You don't *talk* to it," Sakarias said, uncertain. "You just sort of . . . open up your mind. Sense what's there, then imagine it doing what you want it to do."

If just wanting something was enough to make it happen, Anders had a lifetime of practice at that—as long as he could remember, he'd wanted something more to eat, somewhere safe to sleep. He'd wanted to be as quick or as smart as Rayna when he was in a jam, or just to be good at something.

But wanting had never helped him before, and it didn't help him now.

They had to stop when one of Sakarias's spears actually chipped the stone wall. "We'll just cover it up with one of my sketches," Sakarias said, hastily repositioning a pencil drawing of Lisabet surrounded by stacks of books taller than she was. "We'll figure it out tomorrow, don't worry."

When Anders finally lay in bed, he could barely believe it was only the end of his first day at Ulfar Academy. Last night's meal with Lisabet, Viktoria, and Sakarias seemed like weeks ago.

He wished he had more to show for his first day, but he hoped he was moving in the right direction. The events of the day swirled together—from thumping to the ground in Combat class to Sigrid and Lisabet's fight in Military History.

Then he thought of the artifact map Sigrid had shown them in class, and the giant Skraboks full of lists of artifacts.

More and more he was sure that somewhere out there, there had to be an artifact that would help him search for Rayna.

It was up to him to find it.

CHAPTER ELEVEN

THE NEXT DAY IN GEOGRAPHY, ANDERS PORED over the map of Vallen in his textbook, trying to memorize every possible location of dragons. He might not be that good at reading, but he knew how to learn from a diagram, and every piece of information helped.

The dragons were to be found in all three mountain ranges in Vallen—the Westlands, the Icespire which ran down the center, and the Seacliff Mountains on the east coast. But where exactly they were in those mountains, nobody knew.

The city of Holbard was on the coast in the southeast, depressingly far from those mountains—though he acknowledged with a dark smile that he was probably the only non-dragon to wish the dragons were closer.

There were dozens of dragon communities, called aeries, that much the wolves knew. Scorch dragons didn't live in one big pack but preferred to spread out through the mountains.

"Though we don't know where to find them," said Professor Rosa, his Geography teacher, "we have ideas on where to search, if we need to take the battle to them. Wherever there is volcanic activity, you'll find the dragons. A scorch dragon's flame is most powerful in the mountains where the lava flows beneath."

Anders's heart was starting to sink. If there were dozens of aeries, none of which were even marked on the map, how could he possibly know where to start searching for Rayna? Even if he found one, it might not be the right one.

The more Professor Rosa talked, the more downhearted Anders became.

He made himself raise his hand. Professor Rosa turned her attention to him—she had bright blue eyes that stood out against her golden brown skin, and wore glasses that magnified them larger than anyone's he'd ever seen, so her stare was really quite something.

"If we don't know where the aeries are," Anders asked, "does that mean we don't have any way to detect them? We have so many artifacts, and none of them are for finding dragons?"

A shiver went through him at asking such an obvious question—would anyone suspect why? But he remembered how Lisabet had read his body language the day before, and forced himself to take a slow breath and sit up straight.

"Unfortunately, not anymore," the professor replied.

Not anymore? What did that mean?

Turning to the map, she tapped a spot in the Icespire Mountains, the craggy range that ran down Vallen's spine. "For instance, we know this used to be Drekhelm, their lead aerie. The only large gathering place for dragons. After the last great battle, the dragons moved. They relocated Drekhelm to somewhere else new, but our scouts have never found it."

Anders nodded, repeating the name silently to himself. *Drekhelm.* He might not know where Rayna was, but he would start by searching for their capital, unless he found some better clue soon. Perhaps they would keep a prisoner there. Until the equinox, at any rate.

Their next class was Law. Wolves had to know all of Vallen's laws when they were on patrol. The professor spoke at length about different types of theft and showed them an artifact that could be set to recognize members of a family but to ring a loud and angry bell when somebody other than the family entered a home, which made an excellent antitheft device, unless you wanted visitors.

Thinking of antitheft artifacts reminded Anders of the zippers Rayna had saved him from touching, the day of their transformation. What would have happened if they'd been caught that day and not gone up to the dais? Would they have avoided all this trouble?

Or would he have gotten sick like Det? Anders could have gotten worse and worse—nobody would ever have thought to check if a boy from the streets needed the Staff of Hadda. Some of the others had made clear enough with their whispers and glances that they didn't think a student who hadn't named a single wolf ancestor belonged at Ulfar.

As the professor kept on talking, Anders sketched the map he'd just seen in Geography to help fix it in his mind. *Drekhelm. Drekhelm. Where on this map was the new location of Drekhelm?*

But try as he might, though, he didn't learn anything more over the next several days. He ate huge meals, practiced his transformation and took his classes, and quietly had tutoring sessions with Lisabet in the evenings.

She didn't mention the artifacts again, though secretly Anders wished she would. Maybe she thought she'd gone too far during their first homework session. Anders found it difficult to sneak to the library without her to look in the Skraboks, and even when he did, his reading was far too slow.

No matter what he tried, his task felt more impossible each day.

* * *

It was most of the way through Anders's second week when he and his classmates ran into Hayn, the wolf who had brought him to the Academy. They were making their way back to lunch when Anders saw a familiar silhouette and the square, black, thick-rimmed glasses through the crowd, and the idea came to him in a flash.

Hayn's name had been in the Skraboks as the designer of so many of the recent artifacts. If Anders could steer the conversation in the right direction, perhaps the big wolf would tell him something about an artifact he could use to find his sister.

"Hayn!" he said, before the man had a chance to walk by.

Hayn pushed his glasses up his nose and took a look at Anders, then broke into a smile as he recognized him. He was juggling a huge pile of Skraboks—even for an adult, they were difficult to carry.

Out of the corner of his eye, Anders saw some of his companions tilt their heads a little, and the wolf in him recognized that they were showing their throats to a senior member of the pack, instinctively making clear they weren't a threat.

Hayn waved away the shows of respect, hefting the pile of books. "Our newest recruit," he said. "How are your classes going?"

"G-good," he said, wincing as he stumbled over the word.

"He transforms straightaway almost every time these days," Sakarias said cheerfully, and Anders winced all over again. He'd have preferred his roommate leave out that "almost."

Still, he couldn't afford to let Hayn continue on his way, so for once he was bold in speaking, jumping straight in before anyone else could sidetrack the conversation. "I saw the Skraboks in the library," he blurted out. "Your name was in lots of them."

"So it would be," Hayn agreed with a quiet smile. "I'm a designer. You'll learn more about that in third year, I think that's when the artifacts class is. Study hard in the meantime, plenty to learn."

Third year? Anders's heart sank. He couldn't afford to wait that long. So instead, he waited as everyone politely said good-bye to Hayn and hung back as his classmates made their way down the hallway toward the dining hall. Then he turned to hurry after the big wolf.

The designer blinked to find Anders still at his elbow, keeping pace with him as he made his way along the hall. "Is there something else?" he asked.

"I . . ." Anders's words stuck in his throat. How did he ask what he wanted to ask—about an artifact for tracking dragons—without rousing suspicion?

And then Lisabet's voice sounded from behind him. "Can we help you carry those Skraboks back to your workshop?"

Hayn smiled again. "That's kind of you, thank you."

Anders and Lisabet took one giant book each and followed him down the hallway. Anders wasn't sure if Lisabet was just being polite or if she'd sensed he wanted to keep talking to Hayn, but he didn't question his luck. He just set his mind to thinking about how to stay once they were in the workshop.

Hayn opened a wooden door a minute later, leaning against it to hold it open for the two students. Anders followed Lisabet in and stopped short when he saw the room waiting for them.

Packed shelves lined the dimly lit room from floor to ceiling, stuffed full of books, old pieces of machinery— artifacts, Anders supposed—and all kinds of mess. There were twisted pieces of wood, a bowl of apples shoved between two theater masks, sketches and diagrams pinned to almost every available surface, half-assembled artifacts suspended from the ceiling.

Hayn did something to a dial by the door, and the strings of lamps around the room all brightened at the same time, as though they were linked. Some kind of artifact, Anders guessed. There was no window, so the room had been almost dark without them.

"Just over here is perfect," Hayn said, leading the way and balancing his books on the edge of his cluttered desk while he moved two empty mugs, a chisel, and a pile of maps out of the way.

First Anders, then Lisabet put the books down. Anders groped for another question, a reason to stay now their task was done. "Are the maps part of an artifact?" he asked, nodding at the pile on the table. Perhaps he could steer the conversation around to locating things.

"They were once," Hayn replied. "Not anymore."

"How do you make something like that?" Anders asked.

Hayn glanced around the room at the half-assembled artifacts hanging from the ceilings and stuffed into the shelves. "We don't talk about it anymore," he said quietly. "And with good reason. Our partnership with the dragons is over."

"But look at all these artifacts," Lisabet pressed, waving her arms to indicate the whole room. "You just said it yourself, they're breaking, one by one."

She was here to satisfy her endless curiosity, Anders realized. If Sigrid wouldn't answer her questions, perhaps Hayn would. Well, that was fine—as long as she didn't get them thrown out.

Anders could tell that arguing wasn't going to move Hayn—though he was a big, broad-shouldered man, there was a gentleness about him. So he matched Hayn's quiet voice instead. "We won't tell anyone you told us," he promised. "But we really are interested."

Hayn hesitated, looking first at Anders and then at Lisabet. And then, as if coming to some internal decision, he nodded. "There are two parts to making an artifact," he said. "The design and the forging. Do you understand how essence is channeled?"

Lisabet nodded at the same time as Anders shook his head.

"Essence is the magic that's found all around us," Hayn said. "In nature, in the earth itself. When we transform from human to wolf, we channel it instinctively so we can make the change. Wherever they're from in the world, elementals always have gifts linked to nature, because nature is where we find the essence that gives us our power. But essence can also be forged into artifacts. Wolves and dragons worked together to achieve this, according to their strengths."

"What is a dragon's strength?" Anders made himself ask. It felt wrong even to think about dragons in that light—he could tell why Hayn didn't talk about it anymore.

"Well," said Hayn. "We wolves are a family. We are

organized, we operate as a pack. We are well-suited to keeping clear records on the uses of various runes and their combinations and researching new combinations. There's no set formula for the runes on any artifact—it's like inventing new words. Say, for example, you were the person that invented the very first door handle. It wouldn't have a name, would it? So you'd have to take the word 'door' and the word 'handle' and put them together, and there are other combinations you could have used. You could have called it an 'entrance maker' or a 'door opener.'"

"And if you used the wrong combination of runes on an artifact, what happened?" Anders asked.

"At best, nothing," Hayn said. "It just didn't work. At worst . . . well, once I caused an explosion that left me deaf for a week. But we wolves are careful with our records, and we don't mind the hard work of researching. Dragons, on the other hand, are quite different. Where we are a family, they are individuals. Many dragons even live alone. They are artistic, fanciful, often inconsiderate."

"But, Hayn," Lisabet protested. "You can't just say one thing about all of them. We wolves aren't all the same. I mean, even our *class* isn't all the same. Sakarias isn't careful with his records, he loses his notes every second week. Viktoria's organized, Jai's funny, Mateo's strong, Det knows how to help people get along."

Hayn sighed. "I used to think the dragons were all different too," he said softly. "But in the end, they proved themselves all the same where it mattered."

Anders could see Lisabet still didn't agree, but he caught her eye, and she fell silent. She didn't want Hayn to end the conversation either—she wanted to learn more. And Anders had to keep the conversation going until he could ask about whether there was an artifact for locating dragons.

"The dragons have the ability to channel essence into their fire," Hayn continued after a moment. "Just as we do into our ice. But as we have a gift for research, they have an ability to see what little bit of creativity an artifact might need to bring it to life."

Anders wondered how to bring the conversation back to specific artifacts. "We saw in the Skraboks that you updated the wind guards at the docks," he said, picturing the huge, metal arches, so familiar to everyone in Holbard. Surely those must be Hayn's proudest achievement. The wind guards were one of Vallen's most valuable artifacts— without them to keep the harbor safe, there would be almost no visitors or merchers sailing into the dock.

"That's right," Hayn said. "A wolf called Sylas designed them generations ago, but with the port becoming busier and busier, we needed to make improvements, which is a delicate business. I designed them, and they were forged into the existing arches by a dragon called Drifa. She was perhaps the most talented dragonsmith who ever lived." He shook his head. "They used to say that Drifa had mixed elemental blood, one parent a scorch dragon and the other a Mositalan thunder lion, so she could channel essence into both her fire and the wind of her forge."

"Pack and paws," Lisabet whispered. "Can you do that?"

"Did she?" the words spilled out of Anders, and he leaned forward, his heart thumping. Was it even possible to have two types of elemental blood? Could that explain him and Rayna? He'd always been told, as long as he could remember, that two elementals could never have a child.

Hayn shook his head. "Of course not," he said, and Anders's hopes sank. "Legend has it that the child of two different elementals would have extraordinary gifts, unpredictable gifts, but it's utterly against—well, I can barely even say 'the rules.' It's so unthinkable, there barely needs to be a rule against it. Nevertheless, there most certainly is."

Lisabet crossed her arms. "That makes no sense," she insisted. "There are lots of children who come to the Trial of the Staff who have wolf blood, but never manifest. There are probably people with dragon blood who are the same, who don't even know anymore, because the last dragon in the family was their great-great-grandmother or something. How do we know none of those people have children with each other?"

"We don't," Hayn admitted, and Anders's heart stopped. So it *was* possible that he and Rayna were twins. "But no two elementals who had transformed—who knew what they were—would dream of doing such a thing. In all my reading, I've never come across more than one elemental type in the same family, let alone the same person."

"Not now," Lisabet agreed. "But sometimes myths exist for a reason. Are we sure it's never happened?"

"Drifa was an exceptional dragonsmith," said Hayn quietly. "People look for a reason, sometimes, that people are extraordinary. But we have no reason to think her parents were both different elementals. Every piece of research we've ever found in the depths of the library says it's forbidden, and impossible."

There was something in his tone when he spoke of Drifa that didn't invite further comment, and Lisabet took the hint, eager to get a version of the story that didn't come from their teachers. "You used to work with the dragons, Hayn. How did we end up fighting?"

"There's no easy answer to that," Hayn said, sobering. "There were always disagreements. The dragons never seemed to understand, or care, that all of Vallen depended on the work we did together. Our citizens needed us to produce more artifacts for them. I'm not talking about artifacts that would simply save them a little work. I'm speaking of artifacts to keep them safe and healthy. The dragons refused to help."

"They refused?" Lisabet whispered. She sounded like she didn't want to believe it.

Anders, on the other hand, could hardly believe that the dragons and the wolves had *ever* worked together. The thought of going so near a dragon other than Rayna— of exposing himself to their flames, their talons—sent a shiver down his spine.

"They refused," Hayn said. "That's the difference between us wolves, who understand duty and family, and the dragons, who believe only in their own needs, the demands of their art."

Lisabet bit her lip against her disagreement, and Anders sucked in a breath. He could hear Rayna's voice in his ears, the words she'd spoken so many times. *We'll take care of us, let them take care of them,* she'd said. Just like a dragon, judging by what Hayn was saying. Just like she'd always been, answering his every hesitation about pickpocketing with a shrug and a quick excuse.

Could the dragon in her bring out those qualities? Was it happening already? If she transformed into a dragon again and again, were those parts of her that were so different from him transforming as well? Was determination becoming heartlessness? Were her sharp edges becoming cruelty?

He forced those thoughts away.

She was still Rayna, who had a hundred ideas that kept them fed, kept them safe, kept them together. She was his twin, and he loved her.

But Hayn was speaking again, pushing his glasses up his nose. "Lisabet, I understand you have questions about them, I've heard that from your teachers. But you have to understand, the dragons are nothing like your imagination. They care only for themselves, and what pleases them, and what they can take. . . ." His voice trailed away, his gaze turning distant. "I was there when it began."

He was quiet a moment more, gazing down at his desk, and Anders held his breath, waiting for the man to continue.

"My brother, Felix, and I collaborated with Drifa many times," Hayn said eventually. His mouth was a set line amid his neatly clipped black beard. "We were supposed to meet her that day, but I was held up."

He was speaking so softly now, Anders and Lisabet had to lean in to hear him, and Anders was sure the designer wasn't even seeing the workshop around them anymore. He was far away, and long ago.

"Felix got on better with Drifa than most wolves and dragons. I thought we were safe with her, or as safe as you can be with a dragon. But . . ." He stopped again, drawing in a deep breath before he continued. "But Felix was found dead, and Drifa was seen flying away. And after that, she was never seen again. There's only one reason she would go into hiding."

"She killed him," Lisabet said softly.

"We demanded the dragons send Drifa to Holbard for trial," Hayn said. "We wanted justice. But they refused. They said they couldn't find her. As if the greatest dragonsmith of our age would simply go missing." He snorted. "There was precious little trust between dragons and wolves to begin with. After that, there was nothing left. We worked with the mayor and with other humans to set up a guard, and keep the dragons to the parts of the city where their projects were, but that wasn't enough for them." He closed his eyes. "Eventually they attacked Holbard."

The three of them stood in silence, Hayn's eyes closed as he remembered that long ago day. Anders was remembering it too, in a way—the smell of smoke, the sparks, the sound of screaming, though he was never sure in the memory whether it was his own or someone else's.

Then Hayn cleared his throat, lifting his head. "The dragons are simply not like us. They cannot consider the good of others. If we let them get a foothold now, after all this time, I'll bet my tail they'll show their true colors again. They are greedy, and, as we learned the day Felix died, violent. So we keep watch and protect Holbard. We protect all of Vallen."

Anders and Lisabet were both quiet, gazing at him. Hayn looked at their faces, seemed to dig deep for a moment, and then produced a smile. It still looked a little sad to Anders. "All that's a very long way of saying that you should listen to Professor Ennar," he said. "So you'll stand ready when your turn comes."

Anders could tell Hayn was about to send them away. He only had a few moments more to ask his question, but his patience had paid off—Hayn had given him the perfect opening. "Is there any way we can watch for them?" he asked. "Is there an artifact to help us find the dragons?"

"There was," Hayn replied. "Fylkir's chalice. But it broke long ago."

Anders's heart sank. Another dead end. "You can't repair it?" he asked.

"We can't repair broken artifacts," Hayn replied. He gestured at the workshop around them. "Updating or improving an artifact is one thing, but once the magic is gone, that's it. The artifacts you see here are broken now." He walked over to a pair of metal sculptures of plants, runes running along their leaves. "These used to keep a greenhouse at a perfect temperature, so we could grow fruit and vegetables all year round. Now they're just statues."

His hand lifted to brush down the frame of a huge mirror, taller than he was, and almost as wide. It had a pair of dragons forged into the frame down one side of it, and a pack of wolves running down the other. "This used to be a larger version of the small communication mirrors we use. We could reach all the way to Drekhelm with it. These days, it doesn't even show you your own reflection. It's just black, and silent."

Anders couldn't believe the chalice he needed had existed, and now it was gone forever. "You can't . . ." He searched for words, for ideas. "Carve the runes on Fylkir's chalice again, try to fix the artifacts that way?"

Hayn shook his head. "It would be too dangerous. An improperly repaired artifact could literally kill people. We would need the dragons' expertise, and we don't have it." He looked at both their sober faces and seemed to remember in that moment that he was talking to first year students. "Well, you'd better get to lunch," he said, suddenly businesslike, as if he regretted telling them the story he had. "Thank you for the help carrying the books."

Anders swallowed his disappointment as the big wolf showed him and Lisabet out of the workshop. To have come so close—to have learned the name of the artifact he needed, only to learn he could never use it—was a bitter disappointment.

But one small question still teased at his brain.

If the wolves couldn't make any new artifacts, and they couldn't repair the old ones, then what did Hayn do in his workshop? Why did he say he was still a designer?

Was there more to the broken artifacts than met the eye?

Anders decided that if he could, he was going to find out.

CHAPTER TWELVE

AFTER LUNCH THEY HAD PHYSICAL FITNESS WITH Professor Ennar. Despite Mateo, Jai, and Sakarias all warning him not to eat too much—and when Sakarias told you not to eat, you knew it was serious—Anders was nearly sick in the first ten minutes. Ennar didn't seem the least bit sympathetic as they ran until he thought his lungs would burst, and he had no chance to think over what Hayn had said.

When it was time to transform, though he'd been finding it easier and easier, he struggled to catch at the seed of the wolf inside him and manage the transformation. Around him, he noticed many of his classmates were just as slow.

"It's the weather," Sakarias said, running a hand through his reddish-blond hair and pointing at the window. "Sun's out."

Anders blinked. "Does that make a difference?"

"Pack and paws, does it ever," Lisabet muttered, scowling in concentration, then abruptly sliding into wolf form with a surprised yelp.

"Warm weather makes us weaker," Sakarias replied, as nearby Mateo successfully wrangled himself into wolf form, completing his transformation with a soft, annoyed growl. "Sun's not good for ice, after all. It's easier to channel essence in cold weather."

Anders wondered if that was why he had felt so muddled, struggled so hard to think, around the waves of heat rolling off Rayna in her dragon form. They had felt *wrong*, almost scary. If the heat was affecting his wolf blood, that explained why.

"Wolves prefer cold, and dragons are stronger in the heat," Ennar said, suddenly behind them. They both jumped. "Once you're ready," she said, a little pointed, "you can complete your transformations and begin your next series of laps. Days like today are good reminders of why we need training."

Nobody's transformation was pretty. Sakarias looked like he was going to make it, shifting most of the way to wolf, when suddenly he sprang back into human form like a ball bouncing off a wall, landing flat on his back and blinking up at the ceiling.

Anders laughed helplessly at his expression, and nearby Jai leaned on Det for support, wiping away tears of laughter, while Mateo's tongue rolled out in amusement. Even Viktoria cracked a smile, though she tried to get rid of it immediately.

"I hoped for more from you, Viktoria," Sakarias protested, gazing up at her and pretending wounded dignity. "I'd like to see you do better."

Viktoria sniffed, haughty all over again, her expression turning to a deep frown of concentration. She closed her eyes for several seconds, then slowly but surely made her transformation. Then she turned and trotted away to Lisabet.

"Viktoria is *intense*," Sakarias complained, rolling over onto his hands and knees to try again. "She can even intimidate *herself* into doing things."

By the time Anders and Lisabet made their way to the library for his tutoring session that night, he wanted to lie down under the table and sleep, not work on improving his reading.

He slowed down as they reached the glass cases of artifacts just inside the library door, mostly to delay sitting down and getting to work. He'd been wondering since he first saw them if any of them could help with his search.

They might not be as useful as the chalice Hayn had mentioned, but even something that could narrow his search area would be worth a risk.

"Why are these artifacts shut away?" he asked. He was pretty sure he could pick the lock in under ten seconds and slip an artifact out of one of those cases before anyone looked his way. He'd been watching for a chance, but it had been harder than he'd expected to find a time without librarians around. They moved so *silently.*

Lisabet looked down at the displays. "They're broken," she said. "And without a dragonsmith to fix them, they'll stay that way. It's only going to get worse, as more break, but like Hayn said, *apparently* it's better than risking letting the dragons back into our lives."

Anders didn't feel like getting into an argument about dragons. Lisabet was kinder to him than anyone at Ulfar, but just now, surrounded by yet more useless artifacts, he wasn't in the mood to hear about her views on dragons. Those same dragons had kidnapped his sister and were going to sacrifice her in a few weeks, unless he got there first. So to change the subject, he pointed at the metal buttons he'd seen the first time he looked at these cases. "What's that one?"

Lisabet made him help her read the labels, so he ended up in a kind of tutoring session anyway, but the answers were interesting. It turned out the buttons were for old people whose hands were too stiff to fasten their own. If you stitched the buttonhole with essence-infused metal thread, the button would do itself up without any help when you spoke the right command.

The boxes—back when they had worked—allowed their owner to store things much larger than the box itself inside them.

But it was the engraved metal picture frame that stopped Anders in his tracks. "It's a locator frame," Lisabet said, reading from the card. "I mean, it was. It says here that if you put it on top of something somebody owns, the canvas in the middle will show you a picture of that person."

Anders had to draw in a shaky breath before he could speak. "You mean, show them wherever they are?"

"I think so," she said. "But it says here it barely works anymore."

Anders could hardly keep still. If it *barely* worked, then perhaps, just once, it might. But the next moment, his heart crashed. Where was he going to get something Rayna owned?

He'd have to get out of Ulfar to check all their hidey-holes and see if she'd left anything behind. Which meant breaking the rules.

He'd find a way.

He fought to keep himself from giving anything away to Lisabet, forcing himself to turn away from the locator frame. "Let's do some proper work," he said.

That day they were starting a basic history primer, and Lisabet took him through it paragraph by paragraph, helping him figure out each word and writing down the ones he struggled with.

"It'll help it stick in your brain," Lisabet promised. "That's what I do."

"I feel like I'm taking up too much of your time," Anders said, chafing at the lesson, and not just because he was tired. This was of no use to him—nothing he was learning here got him closer to Rayna. "Isn't there something else you should be doing?"

"Not really," she said, gazing down at one of the books. And there it was again, for just a moment. That hint of something—of loneliness, maybe—he'd spotted when she'd argued with Sigrid in Military History, and more than once since. For all she sat with Viktoria and Sakarias at meals, and talked to the others in their class, something about Lisabet kept her a little bit solitary.

"Do you have any brothers or sisters?" he asked on an impulse.

"No," she said. "Just me. What about you? You said that first night you didn't have anyone, but did you ever—"

"Just me," he said, echoing her words and ignoring the pang inside. He wasn't denying Rayna. He was protecting her.

"You have the pack now," she murmured, and he knew she intended to be comforting.

"What do you think it's like for people who had a big family outside, before they came here?" he asked, hoping to divert her from thoughts of his family.

"Depends on what it was like," she said, considering. "Sakarias missed his a lot at first, but they were very poor. There's more for them with him here, and he has opportunities here he never would have had otherwise."

"Viktoria must have given up a lot," he said.

Lisabet smiled. "Why do you think she's the only girl at the Academy to still have long hair? She refused to cut it, had a huge argument with Dama Lindahl about it. In the end, the rules don't say it *has* to be short until you join the Wolf Guard, so she got to keep it. To be honest, though, I think she'd cut it now if she could. She was just upset about having to leave her home." She paused. "She's less spoiled than people think. Just . . . used to things a certain way. It doesn't mean she doesn't know how to work hard."

"I know," Anders agreed. Despite her tendency to wrinkle her nose, Viktoria had never really been unkind to him. She was worlds better than the ones who still whispered when he went by, about his lack of ice spears.

Lisabet paused again, but she didn't pick up their progress on the paragraph. Instead, she continued, more tentative still. "Do you miss your old life, before you came to the Academy?"

He considered the question. So much for causing a diversion. It was hard to talk about his life without talking about his twin, but more than that . . . it was difficult to put the answer into words. "It was different," he said eventually. "I mean, a lot of things are better here. There's always enough to eat. I know where everything will come from. There are people to help us, when we need it."

He hadn't expected to say that last part—he sounded like a wolf, always going on about *pack*—but he realized it was true. It felt different, having so many people to watch his back. It might even feel good, if he wasn't so scared of what they might find out about him.

"And some of it's not so good?" Lisabet guessed.

He couldn't exactly say that it wasn't as good because he was missing his sister like he was missing half his heart. That he was afraid, after what Hayn had said, that there was no way they could possibly even be related.

But there were other answers he could give. "I miss being able to move around as much as I like. It's amazing, up on the city rooftops. There are flowers as far as you can see, this time of spring. It's like your own world up there."

"Where's your favorite place?" she asked, smiling.

"I . . ." He hesitated, the words caught in his throat. The Wily Wolf was his secret place with Rayna—not a person alive knew about it except for the two of them. When they'd found the hatch by accident, it clearly hadn't been opened in generations. It felt like a secret he shouldn't share—it was the place they could always go to shut out the troubles of the world. It was as close to a home as they'd had since they left the orphanage. Just thinking of it now, his chest tightened a little. He wished so hard he were back there, lying in the warm dark with Rayna, making a plan for a new day.

Lisabet was watching him, her chin propped up on one hand, but when he looked at her, her gaze flicked away, her smile gone. "You can tell me," she said quietly. "It's not like I have other people I'd tell."

And there it was—this time not just the pang of loneliness he'd seen in Lisabet before, but a proper stab. The sadness that made her look serious whenever she wasn't smiling. Lisabet's brains, or her dangerous ideas about dragons, or her devotion to books and learning—something about her separated her from the rest of the pack.

But Anders liked her smile, he liked her generosity.

She was trying so hard to help him catch up, when there was nothing in it for her. He felt like maybe, even though she was surrounded by wolves, she wouldn't have minded a friend.

For sure, he could use one.

"There's a lookout point where you can see all of Holbard," he said, thinking back to the night before he and Rayna had transformed. "It's a tavern called the Wily Wolf, on top of the hill. It's a building just a little taller than the others, and it has a pointed roof, with a hoist for pulling supplies up to store in the attic. If you climb up, you can see every roof in the city, all the meadows spread out, the people down below, all the way to the port. It's like all of Holbard belongs to you." His mouth felt a little dry just speaking about it, as though he'd broken a promise to his sister. "It's my secret," he said. "It's . . . it's my special place. Nobody else in the world knows about it." *Except Rayna.*

"I won't tell," she promised gravely. "I'd like to see it one day. Maybe next time we're allowed out."

Anders blinked, abandoning thoughts of the Wily Wolf. "When are we allowed out?" This could be his chance—a way to find something Rayna had left behind in one of their hidey-holes.

"Didn't anyone tell you? Once a month we get an

afternoon out in the city, to do whatever we want. The next one isn't for a couple of weeks, you just missed the last. They come more often once you're senior, but because we're only first years . . ."

Lisabet was still talking, but inwardly, Anders was dancing a jig. If he couldn't find a way out earlier, then at most it would be two weeks—plenty of time before the equinox—before he managed to get outside. He could spend the whole afternoon searching for anything at all Rayna had left behind, and then with any luck at all, he could coax the locator into working and see where she was.

He was startled back to the present moment by Lisabet saying his name.

"Anders, can I ask you a question?"

"Sure," he said, still mentally planning.

"That girl," she said. "The day you transformed. The girl who transformed into the scorch dragon. Do you know who she is?"

"I—what?" He winced inwardly. *Not smooth, Anders, not smooth.*

"The dragon," she said. "She said the two of you were there for the Trial of the Staff, I heard her. And I just thought, if you knew who she was—"

"I don't," he said, interrupting her. His brain wanted

to shut down, but he forced it to keep moving, to try and generate some sort of reply. Lisabet had been one of the wolves to track him after he'd run from the square. She'd been at the docks. She'd seen Rayna's transformation, and his. She might have seen a look pass between him and his twin, she might have seen him panic when Rayna transformed. She might have seen anything. *She suspected.*

"No," he heard himself say. "I mean, like I said to Hayn, I'd seen her on the streets, but I don't know who she is."

Lisabet kept trying. "I just think if there was a way to talk to a dragon, perhaps we could prove—"

"Lisabet, stop!" His voice was louder than he'd meant, and they both froze as the librarian looked in their direction. Only once she was sure they were done shouting did she continue shelving books on the other side of the library.

He wanted so badly to trust Lisabet. She'd been nothing but kind to him, from the moment she'd picked him up from Sigrid's office and rolled her eyes to make him feel better.

She was the only one at Ulfar who showed even a hint she could ever trust a dragon, or at least listen to one. Anders personally wouldn't trust a dragon as far as he could throw it—but Rayna wasn't a *dragon*, not like the others. She wasn't one of them. She'd been kidnapped by them. Either way, Lisabet might be willing to hear her out.

But Lisabet was loyal to Ulfar Academy, however many questions she asked. If she knew about his connection to Rayna, she might turn him in.

Or just as bad, she might try and use his connection to Rayna to further one of her arguments. He knew Lisabet felt passionately about convincing the other wolves to think differently about the dragons, to question the Fyrstulf's determination to keep them away from Holbard at all costs.

He couldn't trust her not to think winning her argument was more important than protecting his sister.

"I just thought, well, you knew that boy who took my cloak, the day you ran away," she said, sounding a little apologetic for bringing it up. "I thought maybe you knew other children who grew up where you did as well."

Anders shook his head. "I hope they catch her," he said. "She's dangerous."

Lisabet nodded slowly, and she didn't ask again.

CHAPTER THIRTEEN

Anders left Lisabet behind in the library as usual, to finish up her own homework and research. Her constant presence there had made searching the Skraboks difficult, but now that he finally had a plan, he felt better than he had in days.

When he got back to their room, he found Viktoria alone.

She was sitting cross-legged on the end of her bed, staring down at something in front of her, her sleek black hair falling around her face. Her head jerked up when he opened the door, and he pretended not to notice as she hurriedly swiped her forearm across her eyes, rubbing away what he was pretty sure were tears.

"I thought you'd still be studying with Lisabet," she said in a snappy tone that suggested he *should* be studying.

"We finished our homework," he said, setting down

his books and looking over at her bed. The thing in front of her was a fan with a delicate wooden frame, blue-and-gold silk stretched across it. It was intricate, beautiful. "That's . . . wow. I've never seen one like that." Which made sense, of course—Viktoria had grown up rich, of naturally she had nice things.

"Well, you probably won't see one like it again," she said, sniffing, still staring down at it.

He was about to give up when she spoke again. "It belonged to my grandmother. She brought it with her when she came from Ohiro, when she was young. She came here because she fell in love with my grandfather. She was a doctor, he was a Vallenite sailor." Her fingers ran over the delicate silk. "I've always liked that she brought it with her. It wasn't a practical thing to choose, so it must have been important to her. Anyway, my parents wrote to say they think I should give it back to the family, for my sister to have it." She paused, squaring her jaw in her determination to keep her voice steady. "Because apparently my transformation means I've left the family."

Anders let out a slow breath and walked over to sink down onto the edge of her bed, keeping to the other end—because even when you were trying to comfort her, Viktoria was still Viktoria.

"They're wrong," he said. "You found a new family when you became a wolf—that's what they're always saying here, that we're a pack. But having a new family doesn't mean you give up the old one. Just because you're adding something to who you are doesn't mean you have to give up who you used to be."

Viktoria looked at him like he'd grown a new head, and he swallowed, wondering if he'd said something completely stupid. It was how he felt—it was what he desperately wanted to be true. He might be a wolf, but he was also Rayna's twin, and nobody could change that connection between them.

"Huh." Viktoria nodded slowly. "I didn't expect you to say something that smart."

Anders nearly laughed. Trust Viktoria to say something insulting, even when she was giving you a compliment. "I guess everyone's right once in a while," he said.

She showed him how the fan worked and let him hold it—the blue silk was smooth under his fingers, the gold thread gleaming where it was woven through—until the others arrived and it was time to get ready for bed. Then she quietly slipped the fan into a drawer, and neither of them said anything more about it.

Later that night, as Sakarias muttered things in his sleep—he really *never* stopped talking—Lisabet's question from the library echoed in Anders's mind, chased by his own words.

The girl who transformed into the scorch dragon. Do you know who she is?

He couldn't help wondering if he actually knew the answer to that. After two weeks in their midst, the history of the wolves was bearing down on him. They told stories that were centuries old. They had records that went back endless generations. Hayn said that he'd never heard of a wolf and a dragon sharing a family—and he was an expert on Ulfar's impossibly big library.

He was so sure Rayna was his twin . . . except the odds seemed vanishingly small.

He wasn't sure what Rayna was, and he wasn't sure what *he* was, *who* he was. Never had he wished so hard to know who his parents had been.

What he did know was that the answer to that question didn't matter when it came to finding a way to rescue her. His words to Viktoria had been absolutely true.

He and Rayna were each other's family, one way or another. Becoming something new didn't take away the old.

But the question still nibbled at him, however hard he tried to push it away.

* * *

Over the next two weeks he pushed his way through classes, lost in a maze of textbooks he couldn't read without a struggle and ice spears he couldn't throw. The equinox was drawing closer, and the students were saying the Wolf Guard was patrolling the city more carefully than ever. There were stories about more dragons seen overhead, and of two kidnappings of children from Holbard, of scorch marks at their homes.

And those were only the children somebody would report—Anders knew that if any of the children he knew from the street went missing, no adult would ever know. But when the first years asked their professors about the rumors, they were told to focus on their studies. Anders was used to being able to see what was happening all around Holbard—he felt so cut off, shut inside the Academy walls.

He tried to sneak to the library when he could, but Lisabet was so often there. And to make matters worse, suddenly the senior students had exams coming, and they were sitting in every corner, studying the very books he wanted to look at. Even when he did manage a few moments with the Skraboks, he took forever to read even one page.

He began to worry more and more about what would happen if he couldn't find something of Rayna's on his rest day out in the city. Or what would happen if after he did, the locator frame wouldn't work, and wouldn't show him a picture of where she was.

He would simply have to slip away—there would be no other choice. Perhaps if he could find a dragon aerie by searching the mountains, it would lead him to Drekhelm. Perhaps Rayna would be there.

Perhaps he would be small enough to sneak in and find her. If he could get inside and transform into a human, hide his amulet, perhaps they might think he was one of them.

Except it was a terrible plan. It was perhaps upon perhaps upon perhaps, and any one of them might be wrong. But he couldn't wait forever. If he didn't learn something soon, he'd have no choice but to go.

* * *

Finally, finally, the rest day came.

"Pack and paws, Viktoria, hurry up!" Sakarias was dancing from one foot to the other around their room, wriggling so hard it was a wonder he didn't transform so he could wag his tail.

Viktoria was taking her time winding her scarf around her neck, getting slower and more serene as Sakarias grew more frantic.

"Why aren't you putting on your cloak, Anders?"

asked Lisabet, who was fastening hers.

Anders started, looking up from where he was sitting on his bed, going over his homework. His plan was to wait until the others had left, then sneak out alone, so he could search his and Rayna's hideouts. "Oh, I think I'm going to keep on with my homework," he said. "There's nothing I need to see, and I don't have any money."

All three heads swiveled to look at him.

"But you get an allowance," Viktoria pointed out, tossing her hair.

"And we need you to be our fourth," Lisabet said.

"And *everyone* needs a day off," Sakarias added.

"We're only allowed out in groups of four," Lisabet continued. "It's the rule. Come on, you've been doing homework all morning. Come out for a couple of hours."

Anders's heart sank. He *knew* the Ulfar students only ever came out in groups of four, but in his eagerness to get out of the school alone, he'd forgotten. He hesitated, wondering if it was better to go now and try to slip away from the others, or wait and try and sneak out the gate on his own.

"Come on," said Sakarias, shoulders dropping, one hand lifting to lay along his head, imitating wolf ears gone flat with disappointment. "They've canceled the Trial of the Staff this month because of what happened at yours.

We're lucky they're letting us out at all."

"There isn't anybody else who can be the fourth?" Anders asked, helpless.

"There is," Viktoria said. "But . . ."

"We want *you* to come," Lisabet finished for her.

Anders looked around at the three of them, his cheeks warming as he registered their solemn faces. They actually wanted his company.

Did that make them his friends?

His pack?

"Well, I can . . ." He was only halfway through his concession when they started cheering, even Viktoria. They bundled him into his boots and cloak, Lisabet fastening it at his neck while Sakarias tied his laces, and Viktoria supervised.

"We get our allowance from the supply room," Lisabet explained as they headed there to collect their copper coins from Dama Lindahl before departing. "Once you're a student, you don't take anything from your family anymore."

A few minutes later Anders stared at the thin coins lying in his palm, designs stamped on them to show their value. Money, all his own, for no particular reason other than that he might want to buy something. It seemed an impossible, illogical luxury, and none of his roommates—his friends—seemed to think it unusual at all.

All his life he'd seen the quartets of Ulfar Academy students making their way around the city. All his life he'd watched them, knowing they had everything they needed and more, and now he was one of them, in his white-trimmed gray uniform. Part of the pack.

As they walked through the gates, a stab of guilt speared him. What was he doing, thinking about pack, about family, without thinking about Rayna? He bit his lip, promising himself he'd slip away from the others as soon as he saw a chance.

"Can we go to the apothecary first?" Viktoria asked as they cleared the gates, stepping out into a brisk cold that seemed almost to threaten snow, later on.

Sakarias and Lisabet groaned, but the four of them turned right along Ulfarstrat, and Viktoria gave a little skip of excitement that was as animated as Anders had seen her.

"Just remember we're hitting the sweet shop after-ward," Sakarias reminded her, falling into step with Anders. They walked down the street as a group, passing by a pair of adult Wolf Guards on patrol, inspecting every-one who made their way down the busy street. Everyone stopped obediently, but Anders noticed many of them scowled when they were safely past the wolves.

He and Rayna had always dodged the patrols, worrying their shabby clothes and dirty faces might land them back in an orphanage, but it looked as if Holbard's honest citizens had their own frustrations.

The four students made their way past the patrol without being checked at all, and where a few weeks ago Anders would have been carefully weaving through the crowd, now he found they gave way for him—now, when a woman in a dark green dress and coat bumped into him, she apologized, stepping out of his way.

She caught his eye and stared a moment too long, and he found he couldn't look away, backing after the others so he could keep his gaze on her. Why was she staring?

Did she recognize him?

She was digging in her pocket, and as Anders watched her, she pulled something out, holding it up as if to show it to him. She was ten steps away now, and a man passed between them, but she was still waiting when he was gone. She had something in her hand, but he couldn't quite make out what it was. And then the sun glinted on copper between her fingers.

All the air went out of him. *Was that one of Rayna's copper hairpins?*

Rayna would *never* have given anyone her hairpins.

They must have taken them from her.

He opened his mouth to shout the alarm—this woman had to be a dragon spy, and if the wolves could capture her, she might be able to tell him where Rayna was. This woman confirmed everything the wolves suspected—that dragon spies were in Holbard every day, walking unseen among the humans.

But the next moment, he snapped it shut. What could he possibly say? He couldn't admit he knew Rayna, let alone knew what her hairpins looked like. If that even *was* one of her pins the woman was holding.

So how could he explain he knew this woman was a dragon? One half of him wanted to find a way to talk to her alone, to find out the truth and demand she give him news of his sister. The other half was terrified of letting her near him.

The woman stared at him, and he stared back. Then Sakarias grabbed his arm to stop him from walking into another pair of adult Wolf Guards. "What are you looking at?" his friend asked cheerfully.

Anders glanced across at his friend, and when he looked back, the woman was gone.

His head was still spinning when they reached the apothecary, and he kept one eye out for the woman in the green dress even as he talked to the others. Maybe he could get away if he saw her again—she seemed wary of groups of wolves. She had reddish-brown hair and light brown skin, and didn't look much older than the final-year Ulfar students. If he saw her again, he'd recognize her.

He, Sakarias, and Lisabet waited out of the wind as Viktoria ducked inside the low-ceilinged shop, wooden beams strung with dried bunches of herbs. Huge, stoppered bottles filled with liquids and colorful powders were shoved onto every possible inch of the shelves.

"Does she need something we don't have at the Academy?" Anders asked, risking looking away from the street for a moment to press his nose against the window, where faded gold lettering spelled out the name of the shop. Inside, he could see an artifact machine pressing out new batches of pills without anyone touching it or directing it, then tipping to pour them into a couple of the hundreds of wooden drawers that lined the wall of the shop.

"She just likes to look," Lisabet said. "The apothecary shows her the new shipments of herbs and medicines, if she comes in when things aren't too busy."

"And then we like to visit the sweet shop," Sakarias said, jingling the coins in his pocket. "Where we do a lot more than just look at what's on the shelves."

After a few minutes Viktoria emerged. "His plant pressing machine has broken," she said with a frown of concern. "It was an artifact."

"They're breaking everywhere," Lisabet said quietly.

"He did have some new arrivals, though," Viktoria said.

"Only you could find a shriveled-up plant interesting," Sakarias told her, but she linked her arm through his, and he stopped teasing her after that.

Anders craned his neck, looking for the woman in the dark-green dress as they made their way along Jurtirstrat, dodging piles of half-melted snow. If he saw her again, he'd make an excuse to get away from the others, find some way to speak to her.

He had to—she was the best lead he could possibly get on Rayna. *And*, he suddenly realized, *if he could just get Rayna's hairpin from her, he could try and use it with the locator frame.*

They reached the confectioner's, where they bought chunks of salted chocolate the size of their fists, wrapped up in waxed paper. "Pack and paws, we earned this, running those endless laps around the combat hall," Lisabet insisted around a huge mouthful.

Anders could have laughed, if he dared. The idea that you got what you earned—that working hard meant you automatically got something—could only have come from a wolf.

He and Rayna knew that some days you worked hard

and ate nothing, and nobody showed up to make sure you got the things you deserved. Lisabet had been lucky never to learn that lesson, he supposed. He shouldn't begrudge her that luck.

Now, with his curls cut short, in his gray uniform with the Ulfar crest on his chest, he was as lucky as she was. He was pretty sure that if any of his old acquaintances saw him, they'd walk straight past without a second glance. Unless you were keeping out of their way, you paid no attention to wolves—it wasn't worth drawing their attention.

Sakarias led them down Sykurstrat next, to see if the new drawing pencils he wanted had arrived on the latest ship from Allemhäut, and Anders racked his brain for a plan to get away from his friends and go hunting for the woman in the green dress. And then when he glanced over his shoulder, there she was.

She was still trailing him, but as a group of older students made their way along the crowded street, she faded back into the crowd. He thought for a heart-stopping moment he'd lost her, but as soon as they were gone, she was there again. She *was* wary of the wolves, he'd been right.

Of course she was—she was a dragon. And no doubt she was supposed to be reporting on them, not revealing herself to them. Except for him. For some reason, she clearly didn't mind his seeing her. She seemed to *want* his attention, in fact. Surely that meant that if only he could talk to her, she'd have some news of his twin.

That realization confirmed it. He had to get away from the others if he was going to chase her down.

"I'm getting such a headache," he said as they approached the corner with Ulfarstrat, which led up to the Academy.

"Did you drink enough water?" Viktoria asked, immediately sympathetic. "Maybe you needed more after yesterday's Combat class, it probably left you dehydrated."

"That's probably it," he agreed.

"Do you need to go back?" Sakarias asked, and though the other boy didn't hesitate to offer, Anders knew he wanted to go and buy his pencils. It was starting to get dark, and if the others had to walk Anders back and then find a new fourth party member, it would be dusk before they could make it to the shop.

"Just a moment," Lisabet said. "I think I spy a solution."

There were a group of final year students making their way up Ulfarstrat toward the Academy, and when Lisabet asked, it turned out one of them was happy to switch groups and stay out a little longer, so Anders could walk back with her companions.

"There," said Lisabet. "Everybody's happy."

"Go to the infirmary if it doesn't go away," Viktoria said.

"And definitely go to the infirmary if your head suddenly explodes," Sakarias said, causing Viktoria to elbow him in the ribs.

Anders let the final years talk around him as they made their way back up to the Academy, keeping his head down and trying to stay at the back of the group, so he could get away right after they entered the Academy gates.

He was still twisting his head around every chance he got, looking for the woman as they made their way up Ulfarstrat. The gates loomed in the distance.

He dropped to one knee, tugging his bootlace undone, then slowly tying it in a knot, letting the gap between him and the others grow. They kept talking as they walked away.

It was just as he prepared to come to his feet that the siren atop the Academy walls started wailing.

CHAPTER FOURTEEN

THE FINAL YEARS ALL WENT STILL AHEAD OF
him, staring up at the Academy gates at the end
of the street. Then the tallest, a slim girl with short-cut
brown hair and dark brown skin snapped into action. "It's
an alert, we have to go!"

"What about the first year?" the boy beside her asked,
whirling around to jog back toward Anders, grabbing his
arm to pull him to his feet.

"Don't care," she said. "We're on the ready list, do you
want to explain where we were?"

Other wolves were already pouring out the gate, all
transformed, a sea of gray fur in every possible shade rolling down the street toward them, humans jumping out of
the way. There must have been a *hundred* of them.

"Quick, transform," the girl ordered Anders. "There's
an emergency."

His three companions became wolves in the blink of an eye, and Anders threw himself into wolf form faster than he ever had before. The scents of the city rushed up to meet him, and then the wave of wolves from the Ulfar gates was upon them, and he was running with the pack.

Somewhere nearby had to be the woman in green, but there was no possible way he could extricate himself from the pack of wolves that surrounded him. *What was the emergency? Dragons?* Some tiny part of his mind wondered if there would be a way to follow them back to Drekhelm, or at least to see which direction they flew in.

His body seemed to take over, knowing just how to steer him along with the wolves all around him, and he knew that even after just a few weeks with Professor Ennar, he was stronger and fitter than he'd ever been before. His wolf's body, which at first had felt so strange and terrifying now felt *right*, and as he swung his tail to help him turn a corner, he felt a wild kind of joy at being with his pack. It was almost dark now, and the air was cool as it rushed past him.

They ran the length of Ulfarstrat, the pack narrowing when the streets did, and he realized they were heading for the docks.

A growl rolled through the wolves around him—were there dragons ahead? Anders shivered but didn't break stride. They raced past humans who were running on foot, some toward the docks and some away, who smelled of sweat and desperation and fear. For a moment a whiff of wood smoke drowned out everything else, and Anders's heart thumped harder, and then they were arriving at the port.

And it was like his nightmare come to life.

The tall, colorful houses along the edge of the port were burning, pure white flames racing along the wooden shutters and window ledges, and even as Anders watched, the fire jumped from one house to the next like a living thing. Golden sparks showered from it.

Howls came from the pack, and though to the humans they must have sounded like a chorus of discordant notes, to Anders the word was perfectly clear: *Dragonsfire!*

The pack slowed as it entered the square, many heads lifting to scan the skies, though it was too dark to know if dragons were circling above them.

They had been here, that much was certain—the pure white flames and golden sparks replacing the red and yellow of everyday fire told him that. The dragonsfire had taken hold now, and it wouldn't relinquish its grip on the docks without a fight—without the essence-infused ice spears of the wolves.

There was a howl from the rear of the pack, and Sigrid

came pushing through, growling orders, snapping her teeth to get her troops moving. There were some human firefighters gathered around, lowering huge hoses down into the harbor and setting up pumps, but they fell back at the arrival of the wolves—water was a poor weapon against dragonsfire, but the ice of the wolves might be enough.

The wolves spread out in a semicircle around the burning buildings, Anders stumbling back out of their way, his ears flat with uncertainty, tail low. He had no training, and he didn't belong to any of the squads here. Suddenly, he was realizing he shouldn't be here, no matter what the final years had said.

He swung around, scanning the crowd, hoping against hope the woman in green had come this way too—but he was low to the ground, and his wolf vision dimmed the colors, and dark had fallen completely by now. It was impossible to tell. Could he get away, try to track her from where he had last seen her? But how would he know which scent was hers?

Ideas and questions jostled for space, but his thinking became clearer, crisper, as around him the wolves pounded their paws against the ground, sending ice spears hurtling toward the heart of the fire.

With a great hissing the spears immediately began to

melt, sending up steam, creating billows of white smoke against the night sky as golden sparks rained down on the cobblestones of the square.

"They'll never put it out!" a voice screamed behind him—a soot-stained woman, no doubt watching her house go up in flames. "The dragonsfire has a grip, they'll never—"

Before anyone had a chance to respond, there was a high, metallic squeal from behind her in the darkness—from the direction of the wind arches.

Brace yourselves, Sigrid howled, and an instant later, a huge gust of wind came barreling through the port. The humans hadn't understood her message, and they staggered against it, the wolves crouching low to the ground, eyes squeezed tight shut. The wind brought with it all the force that had been pent up behind the arches, and in the heartbeat before it was gone again it fanned the flames higher. Screams rang out around the square and bright golden sparks fell like rain.

The fire was fiercest at the lower stories of the houses, where perhaps it had started. Up above, families were appearing through the windows, and as the wolves cast ice spears again, the humans around them were finding ladders, pulling scaffolding from the cranes by the docks, doing anything they could to build a path down to the ground for the ones trapped above.

Anders paced behind the wolves, helpless—*useless*, without an ice spear to throw. Abruptly a stack of wooden crates that had sat in a thin alleyway between two houses collapsed, their bottoms burned out, sending a cascade of smoldering wood and embers out into the dock square itself.

Anders leapt out of the way, a pile of timber landing so close behind him the fur on his tail was singed, and as he whipped around to check nobody was caught beneath the debris, he yelped his horror.

He knew these boxes. There was a wide street behind the houses around the port, so the street children needed their own makeshift ladder to make it all the way up to the roof of these particular buildings, where many of them liked to sleep. They'd climb down the wall, and then use the boxes for the final descent—but now the bricks of the wall were burning hot, and the boxes were alight.

He backed up several steps, craning his neck, whining softly under his breath as he tried to see past the people, the flames, the smoke. *Please no, please, nobody be up there.* The words beat a rhythm inside his head.

But now he was looking, the picture suddenly came into focus, and he realized there were familiar shapes up on the roof. He could see Jerro up there, two figures that were probably his little brothers, and half a dozen others behind them, all children he'd grown up with on the streets. They were waving wildly, and he could see their mouths moving, but the noise of the square drowned them out.

On the roof! he howled, trying to make himself heard over the noise. But the wolves were busy fighting the fire, and none of the humans could understand him. A scream came from above as the flames licked higher, clouds of smoke enveloping the children.

Hurriedly he forced himself back into human form, pain shooting down his arms and legs as the heat of the fire made the change almost impossible. Almost, but not quite. He ran forward to where two men were positioning a ladder, pushing it up against the house and nearly knocking a second ladder out of the way in their haste. He grabbed at the nearest man's arm. "We need it to go higher," he shouted, pointing up.

The man's eyes widened, and he looked up, squinting through the smoke. But a moment later, he shook his head. "They have their ways down," he said. "They always have a way down. Otherwise how'd they get up?"

"They don't," Anders protested. "There's nothing behind these buildings—if they could, they wouldn't still be up there!"

But the man shook him off, sending Anders staggering

back as the crowd swirled around him. He had to do something! There were two ladders jostling for position to help the people at the windows, and only one was needed. If he didn't find a way to help Jerro and the others, they'd burn.

He straightened his back and marched back up to the man. "Listen," he said, hoping his voice wasn't trembling as hard as his insides were. "I'm from Ulfar, and this is an order. Get that second ladder up to the roof!"

The man looked at him again, this time taking in his uniform. He opened his mouth like he wanted to protest, and Anders glared at him, thinking as hard as he could of Sigrid, of Ennar, of Viktoria, of Rayna in a bad mood, and putting it all into his gaze.

And it worked.

The man turned away, speaking to his neighbor, and the two of them pushed the ladder in closer to the wall, so the top rungs would reach higher. In an instant a string of children were climbing down it, half sliding in their haste to reach the ground.

Anders was waiting at the bottom to help them. Jerro was in Lisabet's old cloak, now dyed black, and he came first. He nearly ran straight past Anders before he did a double take. "Anders!"

He flung his arms around Anders, and a moment later, two other pairs of arms wrapped around the pair of them, then more, and more, with Anders at the middle. He felt something at his hip, and he was pretty sure someone was picking his pocket, but he knew it was just habit, and he didn't mind.

"You should get out of here," he said quietly. And they all knew he was right—next thing, somebody would be asking where their families were.

With whispered thanks, they peeled away in ones and twos and disappeared into the dark. When Anders was alone, he realized the wolves were winning the fight—the buildings were badly damaged, but the fire was nearly out.

Perhaps this was his moment to slip away—to make one last attempt at tracking the woman in green. At finding out what she knew about Rayna, and why she had Rayna's hairpin. If he followed his own tracks back the way he'd come, she might be somewhere along that route.

He could hear Sigrid's voice ringing in his ears, her words from the night he'd arrived at Ulfar: *Fleeing once is understandable. I would not be so sympathetic a second time.* If he ran and didn't make it back to Ulfar in time, what would happen?

He didn't know, and it felt wrong to leave the pack, but he had to try.

But when he turned, he found himself ringed by a dozen townspeople. He was the only wolf in human form, and they were all watching him, waiting for him to say something.

"Our home," a woman cried, as a girl rocked her back and forth. "Everything's in there, everything's lost!"

The girl's mouth was set in a hard line, and Anders could see all of them were struggling not to give way to panic or despair or both. "I'm sorry," he said helplessly. "We came as fast as we could."

"We know," she wept. "Isn't there anything to be done? Everything we owned was inside. We have nothing. What will we do now?"

She stared at Anders, her words hanging in the air, and Anders wished desperately he knew what to say in reply.

He knew what it was like to have nothing.

Sigrid's voice sounded behind him. "The mayor's office will provide for you."

Anders turned his head, and there she stood, back in human form, her white face smeared with soot, her immaculate blond hair turned gray with ash. "I'm sorry we were too late," she said, her voice more gentle than he had ever heard it before. "We'll save what we can. Perhaps some of your belongings will still be inside. This was dragon work, make no mistake. This was dragonsfire."

Her voice lifted so all those in the crowd could hear, and they gathered close. "What they want is for us to be afraid. But we will *not* fear them. The ice wolves will protect you!"

The crowd murmured, a sound that was half fear, half gratitude, most of them gathering closer, some of them looking up at the sky.

Her voice was hard again, but there was a note of compassion there that Anders wasn't used to. Sigrid truly cared for the people of Holbard. She shared their anger.

And, he realized, so did he. What could drive the dragons to do a thing like this?

One thing he knew for sure—Lisabet was wrong. She was trying to understand the dragons, and there was clearly only one thing that needed to be understood. The dragons meant to harm the people of Vallen any way they could.

Leaving behind wolves to watch the embers of the fire and make sure it didn't return, and to start salvaging what they could of people's belongings, the rest of the pack left to return to Ulfar. Anders fell in with them, but though he knew both Sigrid and Professor Ennar had spotted him, neither had come to ask him what he was doing there.

The group of final years he'd been with before the alarm came to find him, and all three of them walked with him. "We'll be lucky if we don't get in trouble for dragging you along," one of the girls said. "We're certainly not losing you now."

Which meant he'd lost his chance to hunt for the woman in green. Or to slip away and find something else of Rayna's he could use to try and locate her.

He wanted to howl his frustration. He had been *so close* to the woman with the hairpin, so close to finding out more. And tonight, he'd been so close to slipping away to find something, before Jerro and the others had needed him.

How was he supposed to be both a wolf *and* her brother?

The pack approached Ulfar, some human, many on four legs. He found he could understand most of what they said, even when they were in wolf form.

A man with curly gray hair and a grim expression spoke louder than most. Like Sigrid, he was covered in ashes, his skin turned nearly as gray as his hair. "I've never wished so hard there was a way for us to find Drekhelm. To find the dragons. Those cowards, setting a fire and running, attacking at night."

A murmur of assent went through the group, the wolves growling and snapping their agreement, but Anders was watching Sigrid and Ennar, who were just a little way ahead of him. The two women turned their heads to look at each other, their eyes locking.

It wasn't just a look they exchanged. It was a *look*.

One that had Anders stumbling over a cobblestone, catching his breath in shock. Did they know something the others didn't? Something even Hayn didn't?

Did they have a way to track down the dragons?

He had to find out.

CHAPTER FIFTEEN

H E LAY AWAKE MUCH OF THE NIGHT, AND BY breakfast, he'd made up his mind. He grabbed a seat opposite Lisabet and spoke quickly, before Sakarias and Viktoria finished arguing about the amount of bacon on his plate and came to join them. He'd come up with an idea just before dawn—a way to get Lisabet's assistance without lying to her about what she would be doing, but without telling her exactly why she would be doing it. It was as honest as he could figure out how to be.

"Lisabet," he said quietly. "I need your help."

He immediately had her attention.

"Do you remember the locator frame in the library?" he said. "The one in the glass case?"

"Yes," she said, puzzled.

He told her about needing something belonging to the person he wanted to find, and she listened intently.

The only place he changed his story was the name of the person he was looking for. "I have a friend called Jerro," he said. He'd had the idea after seeing the other boy last night during the fire. "He's the one who helped me get away, the first day I transformed, when I was afraid. We always looked out for each other on the streets, and I'm really worried about him." He at least didn't have to fake his expression when he said that part—he had plenty of worries, and he was sure they showed up on his face more often than not. "Last night, at the fire, I saw some of the kids I used to know. And they said . . . nobody knows where he is. And I'm trapped in here, so there's nothing I can do—not that I'd know where to look anyway. They've tried all the obvious places."

"And you want to try the frame," she said, leaning in to keep her voice down. "But we'd need something of his. It's worth a shot. It would be difficult to break out of the Academy at night and go searching for something he owned, but not impossible. Before we take the risk, though, I think we should see if there's any chance it works. Try it on someone whose belongings we already have."

Anders stared at her. He felt like a fool for not thinking of that himself—of course, they could use something belonging to one of them, or a friend, and find out quickly enough if the locator frame was completely broken or just

219

unreliable. He'd gotten ahead of himself, trying to find something of Rayna's to use first.

They had to stop talking then, when Sakarias and Viktoria slid in next to them, and Sakarias began a long and involved story about a time he got chased by a cow at his family's farm.

Anders thought it was meant to make him laugh—that his friend could see he was worried—and he tried to pay attention as best he could. Viktoria said it was a classic example of Sakarias not paying attention and paying the price, but Anders saw a hint of her smile as she told Sakarias this.

That evening, Anders and Lisabet slipped away to the library after class. Everyone was used to them going there to do their homework together, so nobody seemed to notice. They took with them Lisabet's favorite bracelet, a scarf of Viktoria's, and a couple of Sakarias's pencils.

"If it matters how much time the person spent with the thing, the pencils will be a good test," Anders said as they made their way in through the big double doors.

Lisabet's job was to distract the librarian, so she wished him good luck and went off to get started.

Anders took his time unpacking his books, and soon Lisabet and the librarian had set off on a long and complicated search of the far shelves, for obscure books that only

Lisabet would know how to ask about.

He waited until he could hear Lisabet's voice at the far end of the library, and then picked up the pencils, the scarf, and the bracelet, hurrying over to the glass case. He just had to hope nobody came in for the next minute or two, and that the lock was as easy as he'd hoped. Lisabet hadn't thought to ask how he was going to handle it.

But when he got to the glass case, he stopped short. The metal locator frame and its blank canvas were *gone*.

In its place was a small, folded white card, with a message neatly printed on it. He read it as quickly as he could. *This artifact has been temporarily relocated to Hayn's workshop.*

His heart sinking, he went back to sit with his books and wait for Lisabet. The same question he'd had last time he left the workshop was echoing in his mind again. If there was no way to repair artifacts, why would Hayn take this one?

When Lisabet came hurrying back a few minutes later he slowly shook his head, and her face fell.

"It didn't work?"

"I didn't get to try," he said, and told her what had happened. It was one thing to ask her to distract a librarian, and completely another to ask her to help him break into a workshop. But Lisabet didn't hesitate.

"We'll have to figure out how to pick the lock on the door," she said. "It'll be much more complicated than a simple glass case. I'm sure I can look it up."

There was an awkward pause before Anders made himself speak. "Uh, I can probably do it," he admitted, reaching into his pocket to feel the hairpins he'd taken from Viktoria's bedside table. His cheeks felt hot. It was as good as telling Lisabet he'd been a criminal before he came to Ulfar.

But she didn't say anything, and they wasted no time, heading straight for the workshop. When they arrived at Hayn's workshop, Anders quietly knocked, then knocked again more loudly when there was no answer. All was silent inside, so he crouched in front of the lock while Lisabet stood guard.

He'd never felt quite right about pickpocketing, or about stealing out on the street so they could eat, though Rayna had always reassured him. Now, though, he didn't feel the slightest hesitation. What he was doing was important, and it was the only way to save his sister.

Usually Rayna did this job, though never with her precious copper hairpins, for fear of breaking them. He wasn't nearly as quick as she was, but he bent the first pin and carefully slid it in, finding the spot he wanted and pressing down as he inserted the second. Out of the corner of his eye, he could tell Lisabet was still keeping watch, but he couldn't help wondering what exactly she was going to do if somebody did come around the corner and catch them.

And almost as if the thought had conjured up company, he heard Lisabet suck in a quick breath. His head snapped up, and he saw their classmate Jai rounding the corner, red hair unmistakable, followed a couple of steps later by Hayn.

It was like time slowed down. And it couldn't have been more obvious what Anders was doing.

He didn't even have time to think—he just lifted his right hand, made a fist, and extended his thumb to touch his ear. The street signal for *help me, it's urgent*—the signal nobody could ignore. The signal he'd taught his classmates at the table in the dining hall.

He didn't imagine for a moment Jai would remember it, but their eyes widened, and without a moment's hesitation, they whirled around and smacked straight into Hayn.

"Hayn!" Anders heard Jai's voice ring out with false cheer down the hallway, as they herded Hayn back around the corner, not giving the big wolf even the tiniest chance of resisting. "I have something to show you, I was just looking for you! Uh, come this way!"

"Wow," Lisabet whispered, looking at the place where they'd vanished. She hadn't been at the dinner when Anders had taught Jai that signal, but she knew a distraction when she saw one. "Nice one, Jai. Hurry, they won't be able to keep Hayn away for long."

Anders did, and a second later the lock clicked. At *last*, something was going his way.

They slipped inside the workshop, which looked just as it had the last time they'd been there, dimly lit by the strings of lights. The Skraboks they'd carried in had been replaced by a new stack of books on Hayn's desk, and beside them sat the metal locator frame they'd come looking for. They hurried over.

Anders started with the pencils, which he thought had the best chance of success, placing them under the frame and watching it intently.

It did absolutely nothing.

He ran a finger around the rim of it, tracing over the runes, but they might as well not have been there for all the difference it made. The surface didn't so much as swirl, let alone show him a picture of where Sakarias was.

Grimacing, he removed the pencils, and tried with Viktoria's scarf, checking the frame from every angle for a message that would tell him his roommate's location.

Nothing.

Finally he tried the bracelet. Lisabet was standing right beside him. He held his breath, hoping against hope to see an image of her freckled face inside the frame. Even if it was weak, if it had any life in it at all, it should be able to tell him where she was.

But again, it was still and silent as they both stared down at it.

"Perhaps it wasn't forged well enough, and the essence slowly left it," Lisabet said quietly.

"We should go," he said, trying to ignore the pressure in his chest. He'd wasted so much time waiting to get out into the city and retrieve something of Rayna's, and he'd never had any chance of succeeding.

"Just a minute," she said, looking down at the papers on Hayn's desk. "He's making notes on the locator frame." She began to flip through the books, opening them to pages Hayn had marked with little scraps of paper. Most of them were ancient, sending up clouds of dust every time she moved them. Anders coughed, wondering just how far into the library Hayn had gone to find them.

He shoved the scarf and the pencils into his pockets and walked over to stand by the huge, broken communicator mirror by the door, straining his ears for the sound of approaching footsteps. The lack of reflection in the mirror was unnerving.

"Listen, Anders." Lisabet was reading out loud from one, the handwriting on its pages spindly and ancient.

The essence in weaker artifacts may be boosted at the times of the solstices and the equinoxes, for at those times essence floods the natural world and can be channeled in the greatest amounts.

Anders closed his eyes. He couldn't afford to wait for the equinox to try the frame again—Rayna could be dead by then.

He pressed his ear to the door. If the locator didn't work, there was no point in being here—though his curiosity at the work Hayn was doing still tugged at him. "Lisabet, if Hayn catches us here—" he said.

"Anders." She had turned another page, and her voice was a whisper. He hurried over to see what had shocked her. "This is a picture of the chalice Hayn told us about, the one he said was broken." Her finger rested on a sketch of a large goblet. The base was flared, decorated with round medallions on which intricate runes were engraved. It had a thick metal stem, and what looked like a wooden cup at the top, braced with bands of engraved metal. Still more runes circled the rim of it—it was one of the most complicated artifacts Anders had ever seen, and its name was written beneath it.

Fylkir's chalice.

Her voice got softer and softer, until he could barely hear her. "Look here, this is Hayn's writing, he's written on the actual book, he must have been very excited. He's written '*Can it be made to work?*' What do you think that means?"

"I think it means he's wondering if he can make the chalice work," Anders replied, trying to sound casual, though his heart was doing backflips. He'd told her he was only looking for Jerro—Lisabet was the one who wanted to know more about dragons, and he had to pretend he wasn't interested.

"But you can't fix broken artifacts," she whispered.

"Then the answer is no," he made himself say. "It can't be made to work." He couldn't afford to give away how hard his heart was thumping. "We should go, before Jai runs out of excuses."

She nodded, and together they carefully put everything on the desk back where it had been when they arrived, working as quickly as they could. "This means something," Lisabet said quietly. "This means there could be a way."

Anders was close on her heels as they hurried out, but the words were echoing over and over in his head.

There could be a way. *There could be a way to find the dragons.*

It confirmed his suspicions about the look he'd seen pass between Sigrid and Ennar after the fire.

If there was a way, he was determined to find it.

The bell rang overhead, and they were both quiet as they walked to the dining hall for dinner, lost in their own thoughts. Anders barely noticed what he put on his plate or where he was sitting, until Jai slid in to sit opposite him, blushing almost as red as their hair.

"Do you have *any idea* what an idiot I just made of myself?" they hissed. "I didn't have any distraction ready! Pack and paws, I ended up showing the most famous designer alive Mateo's *marble collection*! Hayn had no idea why he was there, and I was all 'oh hey, look at this one, it has a blue swirl in it.'" They buried their red face in their hands with a groan. "I'm never living it down."

"We owe you," Anders promised.

"You *know* you do." Jai snorted. "What were you doing, anyway?"

Anders and Lisabet exchanged a long look. Neither of them wanted to lie, but neither of them wanted to tell the truth either.

"Nothing bad," Anders said eventually. "I mean, we weren't supposed to be doing it, but it wasn't wrong."

Jai was silent a long moment, then nodded. "Well, I hope it went well," they said. And that was it. No more questions.

Anders was fumbling for something to say, some way to tell Jai that it meant a lot, to have friends—pack—who'd back you up without needing to know the reason why.

But he didn't know how to say it, and in the end he was saved by Sakarias, who thumped down beside Jai and started boasting about his double helping of pie, not even noticing as Jai stole a forkful.

* * *

Anders tried twice over the next two days to get back into Hayn's office, to look for more information about how Hayn planned on trying to make the chalice work, or even to search for the chalice itself, but he had no luck.

The designer might not have known who had broken into his office, but he clearly knew something was up— the lock had been replaced with a much bigger, much more robust version, and there was no chance Anders could pick this one.

He lay awake at night going over what he'd seen in his mind. Hayn had only written *"Can it be made to work?"* He hadn't said it could, or even that he *had* the chalice. Just that he had an idea.

Still, Anders couldn't see what his choices were, except to watch Hayn like a hawk, or to simply make a run for it and head to the nearest mountains alone. After that, he'd have to hope he could find a dragon—any dragon—and somehow use it to track Rayna. While not getting dropped from a great height or roasted alive.

But there was less than a week left until the equinox, and he was running out of time to make any other choice.

The third night after they'd broken into Hayn's workshop, he was watching the designer at dinner. Despite his size, the big wolf moved quietly, making his way through the world without causing anyone much trouble. Tonight, Hayn sat at a table against the wall with several of the professors and a few members of the Wolf Guard.

Anders was on the far side of the hall, with Sakarias and Mateo chatting about tonight's dessert from either side of him, and Viktoria, Det, and Jai discussing that day's class across the table. Lisabet had already left to head to the library—to research something to do with the chalice, Anders was sure.

Without any fuss, Hayn, Sigrid, and Ennar rose to their feet, nodding good night to the other adults, and walking out of the dining hall together. Only Anders noticed—because Anders was making it his job to watch Hayn as often as he could.

Without really thinking about it, he murmured a good night to his friends and slipped out after them.

"I'll finish this pie for you," Sakarias called after him.

Anders kept his footsteps quiet as he followed them into the corridor leading to Sigrid's office, but there were only a handful of other people around, and he knew in a few moments he could find himself following them alone. And what, exactly, was he going to do? Stand outside her office with his ear pressed against the door? That wouldn't be suspicious *at all*.

He needed a distraction—some way to get them to take the long way around to the office, so he could get there first. He could picture it in his mind's eye. There was plenty of room to hide behind the couches, if only he could just get a minute's head start. There had to be something nearby that he could use.

He knew he should be scared, but all he felt was a rush of determination. *What would Rayna do?*

And then he knew.

He dodged right down a corridor, tearing along it at top speed, then swinging left to circle around to the junction where the class bell hung. If he rang this, every other bell in the school would start ringing madly. Sigrid and Ennar would come to see who was ringing it, no question. And they had Hayn with them, an artifact specialist. He'd have to come too.

He grabbed the rope of the bell pull, shaking it back and forth, the clapper inside the bell ricocheting off its sides and setting up a deafening ringing that seemed to go on and on and on.

For a moment he stared up at it, amazed by the sheer volume of sound he'd produced. Then he turned to run for it. He had to get to Sigrid's office, and hope he could find a way in, before she and Ennar gave up on finding the culprit.

He knew the office by the tapestry hanging outside it in the hall, the long mural of the last great battle between the ice wolves and the scorch dragons. The hallway was empty, and with his heart in his mouth he knocked gently on the door, just in case she'd gone inside, instead of to investigate the noise. When there was no answer he knocked again, hand shaking, this time pressing his ear to the wooden surface. Silence, except for the fading sound of the bell's echoes.

He tried the door handle. *Surely it would be locked.*

Except it swung open at his touch, revealing the Fyrstulf's empty office waiting for him. Wasting no time,

Anders slipped inside and closed the door behind him. It was just as he remembered—the shelves were lined with books and artifacts, and the two couches sat along the sides of the office, facing each other.

He slipped between the left-hand couch and the shelves, and started to work his way along them, examining each artifact in turn, just in case there was something he recognized from all his studies.

Then the door handle rattled, and he had only a second to duck down behind the couch, pressing himself to the floor, before it swung open and three pairs of footsteps walked inside.

"I thought I locked that." Sigrid was speaking, and he could hear the frown in her voice.

"I suppose you didn't." That was Professor Ennar's voice, and she didn't sound happy to be there. "But, Sigrid, we need to talk."

"We do." Sigrid sounded grim. "We can't afford to wait much longer."

"Especially after that fire," Ennar agreed, sinking onto the couch above Anders.

"I . . . find the fire strange," Hayn admitted, sounding like he was over by Sigrid's desk. "It's such a busy part of town. I can imagine a dragon spy changing back to human form and getting away on foot, but they must have *been* a dragon to set the fire—the flames were white, it was dragonsfire. In fact, it should have taken more than one dragon. Why didn't people see them?"

"It was dark," Sigrid said quietly.

"Even so . . ." Ennar murmured.

"I've noticed the humans are protesting the patrols less after the fire," Hayn said, his tone neutral.

They were all silent a long moment.

"The truth matters, Sigrid." Ennar sounded troubled.

Anders hardly knew what to make of the discussion. He held his breath, trying to keep perfectly still. He hoped his hunch hadn't been wrong—he needed them to discuss a way to find the dragons, not just whether Holbard was ready for an attack.

Sigrid had a growl in the back of her voice when she replied. "What matters is that we are powerful enough to protect Holbard—to protect *Vallen*—if the dragons come again. *When* they come again. Ennar, you of all people, a veteran of the battle, our own combat instructor, cannot lose sight of that. And you, Hayn, you know what it is to lose family to those creatures. Do either of you deny there are dragon spies in the city?"

"We know there are dragon spies here," Hayn said. "We know we have to be ready for whatever they're planning."

"And it's not that the fire hasn't helped convince the humans the threat is real," said Ennar. "It's just . . ."

Anders tried carefully to adjust his position, so he could sink down to lie on the floor. His knees were hurting, crouching like this.

He rested his head on the ground, looking across the intervening rug to where Sigrid's boots were visible.

And then he went completely still, his breath freezing in his throat.

Lying on the ground behind the other couch, *Lisabet* was staring straight back at him.

CHAPTER SIXTEEN

FROM BENEATH HER COUCH, LISABET WIDENED her eyes as if to tell him to shut up, and he widened his right back to say he already knew that. She was supposed to be in the library! What she was doing here instead, he couldn't imagine. Apart from hiding, just like he was.

Sigrid was speaking again. "Tell us about your progress with the chalice, Hayn."

Anders went so still he was pretty sure he could hear his own heartbeat. He could only hope nobody else could.

"I . . . have a theory," Hayn said. "It's only that."

"If we can make it work, we can attack before they have any reason to think we're coming," Ennar said. "Right now, the dragons believe we have no way to find them. They will have become complacent, thinking themselves safe."

"They *are* safe," Sigrid snapped, frustrated, a hint of a wolf's growl creeping into her voice. "Because we *can't* find them."

Anders watched Sigrid's boots walk over to the wall, and she came into view down the side of the couch, taking a picture off the wall to reveal a safe behind it. All she had to do was look to her left, and she'd see him lying on the floor behind the couch.

She drew a wrought-iron chalice with a wooden cup from the safe, like a thick-stemmed wineglass made of metal and covered in runes. It looked exactly like the picture they'd seen in Hayn's book.

She lifted a jug to pour water into it until it was full. Then she removed what looked like a needle from where it was clipped onto the stem of the chalice and dropped it in, walking over to show the result to Ennar and Hayn. "Useless. It just spins endlessly. It's supposed to point, like a compass. Tell us your theory, Hayn."

"At first," said Hayn, "I thought it stopped working because the dragons moved the location of Drekhelm, after the last battle. But it was never designed to point to Drekhelm. It pointed to the largest group of dragons in Vallen, and that *was* Drekhelm. If they'd been somewhere else, it would have pointed there."

"Then why did it stop working?" Ennar asked.

Anders strained for the answer. This was an artifact that could solve everything. It could help him find the dragons' capital, and find Rayna. Underneath the opposite couch, Lisabet was staring at him.

"My theory is that a number of factors combined to stop it working," Hayn said. "It's become weak, just like many of the artifacts that need maintenance. The essence is fading from it. But it may not have faded completely, which is what we originally assumed. Maybe we were wrong."

"What happened instead?" Sigrid asked.

"I've been out to the farthest shelves of the library," Hayn said. "You know I've been going through the old texts for years. My theory is that there's too much dragon blood in the city. Every month at the Trial of the Staff, we see children who have enough wolf blood to claim the right to test, but they don't transform. There must be dragon descendants in Holbard too, people who don't know they have that blood but confuse the chalice all the same, surrounding it with too many weak signals. The same way a compass gets confused if you surround it with too many lodestones."

"You mean it's picking up so many signals, it spins around to try and point to all of them at once?" Ennar asked.

"Yes," Hayn said. "That, and it really is starting to break down. It won't work in Holbard, but I have a theory that if we can get it away from the city, and at a time when the essence will be strongest . . ."

"The equinox," Sigrid said.

"Yes," Hayn agreed. "And we know almost all of the dragons come together then. That would give the artifact the greatest chance of working and the largest possible target."

"We have to try it," Sigrid said. "And it's only a few days until the equinox. We can't afford to let any dragon spies in the city see one of us departing alone. We'll need a cover story."

Anders and Lisabet lay still as Sigrid walked back to return the water to the jug, and the chalice and the needle to the safe.

Anders's heart sank, and he shut his eyes as the safe closed firmly. He'd been desperately hoping Sigrid might leave the chalice on her desk. Even giving it to Hayn would have been better—he could have tried to find a way into the workshop.

"I have some ideas," said Ennar. But the three adult wolves were walking for the door, and if she said what her idea was, Anders didn't hear it before the door closed behind them and the lock clicked into place.

Anders let out a slow breath, rolling onto his back, but both he and Lisabet waited a full minute before they crawled out from behind the couches to meet on the rug.

"Are we locked in?" he asked, picking an easier question than *what are you doing here?* to start with.

"I have a key," Lisabet said, patting her shirt pocket.

His eyes went wide. "How did you get a key to the Fyrstulf's office?"

Lisabet shrugged, dodging the question. "Bet you're glad right now I did. Otherwise we'd still be locked in here when she arrived in the morning, and I don't think she'd have a sense of humor about it."

"You're why it was unlocked when I tried the door," he realized.

"I jumped behind the couch when you knocked. I didn't know it was you until you hit the deck too."

Anders swallowed. "Lisabet, what were you doing in here?"

"I wanted to look on her desk," she said. "Remember those notes Hayn wrote in the book in his workshop? I wanted to see if he'd written a report for Sigrid." She paused, then continued more gently. "And why were you here?"

Anders opened his mouth and closed it again. He'd been over this in his head so many times. He didn't dare trust Lisabet with the truth about Rayna.

He wanted to learn about the chalice to rescue his sister.

Lisabet wanted to learn about it because she thought the same dragons who'd kidnapped Rayna and set fire to the port could somehow be reasoned with.

Their goals weren't the same, and he couldn't afford to have her trying to make friends with Rayna's kidnappers.

"I'm still trying to figure out how to find my friend Jerro," he said. "I thought maybe the Fyrstulf would have some kind of artifact in here I could use. She keeps the Staff of Hadda in her office, so I thought if there were other powerful artifacts . . ." He trailed off to a shrug, hoping she'd believe him.

"I don't think so," Lisabet said, glancing at the shelves. "Most of these are pretty well known. It was a good idea, though."

Anders was looking at his friend, but behind him and to his left was the picture covering the safe, and inside the safe was the chalice, tugging at his thoughts. He might not get into the office again, so he couldn't leave without trying to get to the chalice itself. How, though, with Lisabet watching?

Without thinking, he turned his head toward the picture, and Lisabet followed his gaze. "They want to find the dragons again," she said, shaking her head. "Just so they can attack them."

"Do you think the chalice really could work?" he asked, trying to sound casual.

"Hayn does," she replied. "If anyone knows, he would."

"Maybe . . ." He chose his words carefully. "Maybe we could get it out of the safe."

She blinked. "You'd help me with that? But you don't agree with any of what I think about the dragons. Nobody does."

"Well, it . . ." He couldn't bring himself to say the obvious thing. *Of course, you're my friend, I'll help you try and make friends with dragons if you want.* Because she *was* his friend, and using that to lie to her was more than he could bear. "I mean, maybe I can use it to find Jerro. It's a locator, isn't it?"

"Only for dragons," she replied. "Unless he's an undercover dragon, it wouldn't help at all—and even then, it only detects large groups of them."

Right. Terrible cover story. He swallowed hard. No matter how flimsy it sounded, he had to somehow try and get the chalice. "Let's try anyway."

She looked at him carefully. "Anders, what's going on?"

"I want to find Jerro is what's going on," he said, trying to remember Rayna's tips on being convincing. *Don't blink too much. Don't blink too little. Keep eye contact. Don't stare.* He was pretty sure he just looked like his face was melting.

"But the chalice won't help," she said again, much more slowly this time, as if she was trying to figure him out.

"Well, I mean, you want it too," he said desperately. He *couldn't* leave the office without trying. What if he never got back in? "Let's just see if we can get it out, and we can worry about using it later."

"That's a combination lock," she said quietly. "And we don't know the combination."

His heart sank to his boots.

"Anders," Lisabet said, taking a step closer. "Seriously. *What* is going on?"

Warring impulses tugged at him. On one hand, Lisabet was his friend. He knew she cared about him. And if anyone was going to believe Rayna wasn't terrible just because she was a dragon, it was Lisabet.

But on the other hand, she was so determined to chase her ideas about dragons that she might use what he told her about Rayna just to prove her point.

"What would you do?" he asked. "If you got the

chalice, and it pointed at Drekhelm, and you could find the dragons?"

"I don't know," she admitted. "What I *do* know is that if we had peace with the dragons once, it might be possible to do it again, and it doesn't seem like our leaders want that. *The truth matters.*" Her hands made fists as she repeated the words Ennar had spoken to Sigrid.

But even if the dragons hadn't always been the way they were now, Rayna had still been kidnapped. *Today's* dragons were capable of kidnapping his sister, and who knew what they'd do with a dragon that had been born and raised in Holbard.

If she'd made the mistake of falling for their cunning, of admitting she was related to a wolf, things might be even worse.

He swallowed. "You're so determined to prove what you think is true. I'm afraid if I tell you, it'll just be one more thing you can use in your fight."

Her mouth fell open. "Anders, you're my friend!" She leaned forward, reaching for his hands so she could gaze straight into his eyes. "I would never hurt you. I would never put you in danger. Didn't I help you break into Hayn's office already? Haven't I been there every night to help in the library?"

Something in Anders's chest tightened. She *had* helped

him, and he'd lied to her about why. Lisabet wasn't like the other wolves. Lisabet was his friend, and Lisabet had doubts about everything she'd been raised to believe.

He'd wanted to trust her more than once already, and now, he knew he had to. "I was here to find out about the chalice too," he said slowly. "I need to figure out where the dragons are as well, but not for the same reason you do." Lisabet nodded, and he forced himself to go on. "She was my sister," he heard himself say. "*Is* my sister. The dragon who transformed the day I did. Her name's Rayna."

He was shaking, desperately afraid despite his trust that Lisabet would look shocked, would run straight to Sigrid. He was related to a *dragon*.

But she simply nodded, as if this confirmed something she'd already decided.

Anders stared at her, trying to process the fact that she didn't look surprised. "She had no more idea it was coming than I did," he said. "She's not loyal to the dragons. She didn't mean to transform on the dais, and she didn't mean to do it the second time in the street. She doesn't want to be part of any battle, and she doesn't want to kill wolves. She wants to get away from them, and I'm the only hope she has of getting out. I'm afraid they want her for the equinox sacrifice, and I'm running out of time."

"Pack and paws, the equinox is nearly here," Lisabet whispered, pale beneath her freckles.

"And the chalice might point to wherever Drekhelm is now," he said. "If Hayn's research is right, it could still work. It would be my best chance of finding her. You have to believe me, Lisabet. She's not the way they say she is."

"I do," said Lisabet slowly. "It fits in with everything I've been wondering. You're my friend, Anders, and I trust you."

Anders just stared at her. He'd grown up with a set of simple rules—*you do something for me, I do something for you*. Lisabet had only known him a few weeks, but then again, she'd grown up safer than he'd ever been.

"If you vouch for Rayna," she said, "then I'm prepared to believe you."

"Just like that?" he said quietly.

"Just like that," she agreed. "I'd believe you because you were my friend, but it just adds up. Think about what Hayn was saying the other day—that there are rules about dragons and wolves sharing a family. Here's my question: If dragons are so awful, why is there even a rule? Why would a wolf ever even *think* about falling in love with a dragon? I think it's just one more piece of evidence that we got along, some time in the past."

Anders's head was a whirl. "Do you really think that's possible?" he asked.

"It would explain why a rule was there," Lisabet replied. All Hayn could say was that he'd never heard of different elementals sharing a family. He couldn't say it was *impossible*."

Anders took a shaky breath. Was she right? It didn't seem real that he and Rayna could be something so uncommon that Hayn had never heard of it in all his research . . . but as Lisabet said, it wasn't *im*possible.

"I'll help you find her, if we can," Lisabet promised. "I'll help you rescue her. Even if we did get along with the dragons once, we haven't since the last battle, and now less than any time since then. Whatever I think about things being the way they are, even *I* know we can't just hope she'll be all right. I hope I'm right about the dragons, but I could be wrong."

"Nobody can know about this," he warned her. "If Sigrid found a way to get hold of her, I don't know what she'd do to her. Kill her, maybe." But despite the shiver of fear that went through him at those words, he realized he was feeling lighter. Finally, he wasn't alone.

"Nobody will know," Lisabet said. "We could be exiled if they found out we're trying to help her. We have to get the chalice. It's our only hope of finding the dragons. And that means getting it out of Sigrid's safe."

They both turned to look at the picture that hid it, and Anders winced.

"Do you know anything about safe cracking?" Lisabet asked.

"Nothing," he admitted. "I never stole things like that. Just food." Embarrassment washed over him even admitting that much. Wouldn't she hear that she was trusting a criminal?

"We'll figure it out," Lisabet said. "They're not telling the truth to us about the dragons, and this will prove it— and even if it wouldn't, friends stand by friends. We'll get the chalice, and we'll find your sister, and we'll get her to safety. I promise."

* * *

Over the next couple of days, he and Lisabet kept on trying to come up with a plan to get into the safe. He watched Sigrid every chance he got, wondering if she had any way of telling someone had been in her office. But though he caught her looking his way a few times, she never seemed to look any sterner than usual. It didn't seem she thought of him as anything other than a new student.

His and Lisabet's plans grew wilder and more desperate as the equinox drew nearer. Without the safe combination they had no chance of opening it.

So they wondered about trying to get out of the

Academy, finding a criminal who *did* know how to crack safes, and smuggling them back in again. But they weren't even sure how to manage step one, let alone find the kind of person they were looking for.

Then they tried to think up ways to get Sigrid to take the chalice out of the safe *for* them. It was when Lisabet wondered how big a fire they'd have to set to have the Academy evacuated—hopefully forcing Sigrid to take the valuable chalice with her—that they knew they were close to failure.

Anders barely slept, turning it all over in his mind, trying to think through everything he'd learned. And when he and Lisabet walked into their next Combat class, he wondered if Professor Ennar had been sleeping either. She had shadows under her gray eyes and a twist to her mouth that warned the class she wasn't in a good mood.

He couldn't help staring at her while she gave them their briefing. She was keeping Sigrid's secret about the existence of the chalice, but she did seem to care—both about her students and about the truth. *The truth matters*, she'd said.

"Go ahead, Anders."

He blinked back to the present, and realized Ennar was addressing him, the whole class looking at him expectantly. "What was that, Professor?" he tried, wincing inwardly.

"I asked you to repeat the instructions I just gave the class," Ennar said, her mouth a thin line of disapproval. She'd spotted him daydreaming. Behind her, Sakarias was dancing about and making gestures, presumably trying to convey by charades what she'd been saying.

Anders stared at Sakarias for a moment as the other boy pretended to walk down an invisible flight of stairs, then grabbed at something imaginary in the air, starting to wrestle with it. Anders had to force himself to tear his gaze away.

"I, um." He searched for an excuse, but there wasn't one, and Professor Ennar was still staring at him. "I'm sorry, Professor, I wasn't listening."

"In which case you were wasting my time, and now that of your classmates," Ennar growled. "Anders Bardasen, never has it been more important for you all to pay attention to this class in particular. Dragons are here, in Holbard, and as the humans who live around the port learned only days ago, nobody is safe. I will do whatever it takes to keep my students safe, but at a bare minimum, you need to listen when I give you instructions."

"Yes, Professor," he mumbled as his classmates made faces from sympathetic to disapproving. *Whatever it takes,* his mind echoed. *Does that include lying? Does that include killing? Killing my sister?*

He pushed the questions from his mind as they began drills. They practiced fighting opponents in large numbers, tracking a human on foot, and tracking a wolf. They talked about ways to track a dragon—the signs of an aerie, how to tell from the clouds whether the air was favorable for flying, how to tell which mountains might hold the volcanoes that created the warmth the dragons needed. By the end of the session, Anders was practically buzzing with excitement despite his exhaustion—all this was exactly what he needed to learn if he wanted to find Rayna.

As usual in Combat, however, something was waiting around the corner to kill his mood. Next, they practiced with ice spears, and a few of the students who had made their transformation nearly a year ago, and were nearly ready to move into second year, practiced summoning cold as well.

All around him his classmates cast jagged ice spears and summoned clouds of cold mist that would weaken a dragon's ability to channel essence into its fire. His thoughts were clear and his body felt strong as the temperature dropped.

But as usual, he couldn't sense the water around him,

let alone make it do what he wanted.

As usual, he failed to raise even a hint of frost. He knew there were still those in his class who smirked when he got things wrong, who chose to sit at the other end of the table or make sure they didn't partner with him for combat. To them, he was still the boy who came from the streets, who wouldn't even say how he'd come to be part of the pack.

Mostly he could just ignore them, and focus on the friends he *had* made—on Lisabet, Viktoria, and Sakarias, on Jai, Mateo, and Det. Focus on the job he had to do, which was more important than anything else. But at moments like this, it was much harder to push his worries away.

And what was he going to do, if he came up against dragons at Drekhelm? He was the worst chance of rescue anybody had ever had.

At the end of the class, as they were preparing to turn toward the change rooms and get out of their tunics and into their uniforms, Ennar called for them to gather around. "Tomorrow we're trying something different," she said. "I'm taking the class out of Holbard, on an overnight camping excursion. Some of the pack is out on the plains today, caching supplies for us so we can travel in wolf form, without worrying about needing to carry anything. Be ready to leave immediately after breakfast tomorrow—we'll be back the following night."

Everything else melted away as she spoke, and Anders realized what her words must mean.

The class chattered excitedly as it peeled away, and in a moment Lisabet was at Anders's side, squeezing his arm. "You know why we're going," she whispered, eyes gleaming.

The same thrill was going through Anders. "I'll bet my tail she's taking us out as cover, so she can test the chalice," he whispered. "Making it look like a class trip, so the dragon spies in the city won't know they're up to something."

"And that," murmured Lisabet, "means the chalice won't be in the safe in Sigrid's office."

"This is it," he whispered. "I can't believe it, Lisabet, this is it."

"Now all we have to do is steal it from Ennar," she said, though she was smiling too. "And hope it actually works, and get away from the rest of the class without getting caught, and locate the dragons, and rescue your sister. Oh, and the equinox is just a few days away. There are a few steps left between here and success."

"Who cares?" he whispered back, gleeful. "We're on our way. That's what matters."

That was exactly what Rayna would have said in this moment, he realized. And for once, when he thought about her, he smiled.

Rayna, I'm coming.

CHAPTER SEVENTEEN

THEY ASSEMBLED THE NEXT MORNING AFTER breakfast in warm clothes, different from their regular school uniforms. They wore thicker trousers that tucked into their boots, and looser shirts of coarse material with quilted jackets over the top, all still edged in white to show their status as students.

"We'll be warm enough in wolf form, but we'll need layers whenever we change back, like when we eat dinner," Viktoria said, smoothing down her jacket and checking her amulet at her throat.

"Speak for yourself," Sakarias replied, grinning. "I want to go hunting. I hope she'll let us."

Anders began to pull a face at the thought of hunting, and of raw meat, when suddenly he realized his mouth was watering. His mind might not like the idea, but his body had no problem with it.

Jai and Det started dancing around at the idea of hunting. One after another they transformed into wolf form and starting a wrestling match, which lasted about a minute, until huge Mateo jumped on top of both of them and pinned them to the ground.

Professor Ennar was similarly dressed when she arrived, and she carried a satchel over one shoulder. It was covered in a fine metal mesh that glinted in the sun. All it took was a soft growl in the back of her throat—even in human form—and the wrestlers were back on their feet and back in human shape.

"That bag Ennar has is an artifact," Lisabet said casually, when she saw Anders looking at it. "It means it'll transform with her, like her clothes." Her tone was innocent as she went on. "She must be carrying something she didn't trust the team building the cache to carry, or something she didn't want to leave out there all night and all day today."

"Must be," Anders agreed, a thrill of anticipation going through him. He kept one eye on that satchel, trying to imagine the chalice inside. It was certainly the right shape.

If only the chalice worked, they'd have their chance to make it to Drekhelm. The plan was to try and creep in unnoticed, and hunt for Rayna without being discovered—wolves were so small, compared to a dragon. Surely dragons' homes would be huge as well, with plenty of crevices and shadows to hide creatures as small as he and Lisabet.

They transformed as a pack, and Ennar, whose fur was as steel-gray as her hair, led them up Ulfarstrat and toward the city gates. Loping along in the middle of his class, Anders found himself enjoying the cobblestones beneath his paws, the breeze ruffling his fur. This was different from the mad dash to the fire at the docks in every way.

As they left Holbard and moved farther out onto the plains, they found there were still patches of snow covering the grass in places. The night's frost had yet to melt, edging the grass in silver and reflecting the early morning sunlight, and it seemed to Anders that the ground stretched away forever. He had never left the city before, and though he'd seen the plains from his perch high up on the roof of the Wily Wolf, being out on them was something else entirely.

Their breath fogged the air, and the ground stretched away in front of them, all the way to the forest at the base of the mountains, so far away it was only a faint line on the horizon. *The Great Forest of Mists*, it had said on the map. Tonight, Anders would have to find a way to steal the chalice, and to follow it, he hoped, to Drekhelm. The day after tomorrow would be the equinox.

But just now, he gloried in running.

Ennar lifted her head to howl her pure pleasure at being out on the plains, at racing along with her pack behind her, and as one, they lifted their heads to rally with her, an extra kick to their stride. Then she really stretched her legs, putting on speed and racing away, and the class spread out behind her to follow, losing themselves in the pace.

Now they were running as they couldn't in the city, with its tight streets and crowds. This, Anders could see now, was nothing like running laps in the combat hall.

This felt like being *alive*.

Eventually they settled into an easy lope that chewed up the miles, and as the morning sun melted the frost off the grass but never quite banished the last patches of snow, Anders let his mind fall into the rhythm of his limbs. The plains were so big, it was almost like being in the middle of an ocean—he felt he was moving impossibly fast, or perhaps standing completely still.

Every time his paws hit the ground, he remembered that each mile was one closer to that evening's camp. Each mile was one closer to the mountains, with their steep black sides and snowy tops. Finally, he was moving toward Rayna.

The grass of the plain was light and tufted, giving way frequently to patches of black, jagged-edged rocks that were the only remaining signs of long-ago volcanic explosions. Now they lay quietly, covered with a thick layer of golden-green moss that looked like fuzzy velvet, stretched thin where the black showed through at the sharp edges and corners.

Streams snaked across the plains, twisting and turning back on themselves, never straight, the water flowing quietly. From a distance, they looked like perfect silver mirrors, reflecting the pale sky above, and he took them all in as he ran by.

The pack stopped for lunch, arriving at a small structure built of stones on the bank of a stream, standing about waist-high to a human. Ennar transformed back to human form, barely breathing heavily, and the class followed her example, panting, leaning over to brace their hands against their knees.

The Wolf Guard had been through the day before to leave supplies for them, and Ennar pulled out dozens of rolls of rich, dark-brown bread, packages of cured meat and cheese, then a pile of tin cups that fitted one inside the other.

They dipped the cups into the stream to fill them with water and sat along its edge, pulling open the bread rolls and stuffing them full of meat and cheese.

"I'm starving," Sakarias said, taking a bite of his cured meat and chewing with relish. "Is it just me, or is the meat way more interesting than the bread and cheese?"

"That's spending the whole morning as a wolf," Viktoria replied. "Eat it all, though, it'll help you run this afternoon."

"I'll be tired by tonight," Lisabet admitted, stretching out her legs. "I always envied the older years when they got to head out overnight, but now I'm wishing I'd had a little more training."

"We'll all sleep well," Anders agreed as he exchanged glances with Lisabet. Hopefully everybody *would* sleep well, except for them.

Ennar didn't allow them much of a break, and soon enough they were loping across the plains once again. They did stop throughout the afternoon, though they never left wolf form, as she gave them quick lessons in tracking and showed them how to find the safest ways down to the edge of the streams, pawing at the soft edges where they threatened to crumble, then leading them to a firmer descent, so they could plant their front paws in the flowing water and drink in long, thirsty gulps.

The water itself was ice melt from the mountains, mouth-numbingly cold, and Anders's gut ached as he drank. But it revived him too, and a few moments later they were running once more.

That evening they made camp at a second cache, switching back to human form to unpack their supplies from the stone shelter. Neither Anders nor Lisabet missed it when Ennar stowed her satchel inside.

"They've spoiled us," their teacher said with a rare smile, as they discovered the adult wolves had hauled kindling for them from the woods, which were at least a couple of hours' run from here. "Someone must have had a friend in the patrol that came out this way."

Mateo admitted it was his big brother, and the others cheered as the group found turf to fuel the fire, and food to spare. As dusk fell they built up the fire near the river-bank, mixing together flour and water and a pinch of salt to make a rough dough, and wrapping it around the ends of sticks to hold it over the fire and toast it until it cooked. Anders quietly took a packet of flour and hid it under the pile of turf and kindling—it was about the same size as the chalice, and he hoped he'd need it later.

Ennar showed them how to ease the roughly cooked bread off the end of the stick, and fill the hole where the stick had been with berry jam, which quickly melted from the heat, running down their chins as they ate. Only a couple of the students—those who were about to move up into second year—had been out overnight before.

For Anders's friends, this was the first time, and they all seemed determined to have as much fun as possible. For his part, Anders was impatiently waiting for them to go to bed—he had to get away with the chalice tonight and find Rayna tomorrow, because the day after that was the equinox, and . . . his mind shied away from what might happen then.

Sakarias was the one who started the dragon stories, and by the time darkness had fallen completely, the whole group was huddled in close to the fire, and to one another, jumping at shadows.

Professor Ennar seemed more relaxed out here, and she let them go on until the stars were bright above them, scattered across the sky like the first snowfall of the year. Then she banked the fire, and the class transformed back into wolf form, piling together on top of one another, sharing their warmth as they settled down to sleep.

Where the ground would have been too firm for a human, every bone hurting where it stuck into the hard surface, and where their jackets wouldn't have been enough to keep them warm all night, Anders found that in wolf form he was perfectly comfortable. In wolf form they really should have been wakeful at night, ready to run or hunt, but the day's journey had taken its toll on everyone.

He and Lisabet took up positions at the very edge of the group, on the far side from Ennar, as near to the stone cache site as they could manage. The others were nearby,

Sakarias and Viktoria curled up in a ball together, Mateo somehow already gently snoring underneath a pile that contained Det and Jai.

Anders and Lisabet were careful to keep quiet, communicating in tiny whines, puffs of breath, flicks of their ears, like whispers for wolves.

A few minutes later, Ennar quietly padded by, conducting a head count, and checking in on each of the students. *Get some sleep*, she whined softly, when she saw the two of them lying there with open eyes, her tongue lolling out in a smile.

But she didn't seem to really mean they should follow her advice, for she eased down onto her belly beside them, her tail waving slowly, pleased. *I just spoke to Sigrid using a hand mirror.*

Anders tilted his ears forward for a moment, confused, until he remembered the day he'd arrived at Ulfar. Then, Sigrid had talked into a hand mirror, and someone on the other end had heard her and summoned Lisabet. He forced himself to keep still and not give anything away, but he wanted to tense up at the words.

If Ennar could communicate with Sigrid from out here, she had a quick way to summon help when she discovered he, Lisabet, and the chalice were missing. *Pack and paws, I hadn't counted on that.*

Ennar was looking at Lisabet as she continued. *She said to tell you that the lookout you suggested, on top of the tavern, the Wily Wolf, is so good that she's not even going to ask how you knew about it. She said you really can see the whole city from up there. She's posted a permanent guard.*

Anders went still with shock. *He'd* told Lisabet about that lookout atop the Wily Wolf, back when she'd asked him about his favorite place in the city. He'd shared that with her, his secret, after she promised he could trust her—and she'd given it to *Sigrid*? Without even telling him? *What else had she told Sigrid?*

Lisabet wasn't looking at him, and thankfully, neither was Ennar, because Anders knew he was showing how he felt now. Lisabet had called herself his friend, told him that she was honest with him.

She'd told him to trust her.

But passing information like that to the Fyrstulf?

It's nothing, Lisabet said to Ennar, uncomfortable. *Just something I thought of.*

Well, it was a good thought, Ennar replied. *Sigrid's proud of you, even if she's not very good at showing it.*

Anders, desperate for Ennar to leave—and desperate not to let his body language show her how hurt he was, how betrayed—closed his eyes and put his head down, and heard the professor's huff of breath as she pushed to her feet. Perhaps she said good night with a flick of her ears, but if she did, Anders didn't see it. He just heard the pad of her paws receding.

Once she was gone he opened his eyes, and found Lisabet gazing at him, misery in every line of her body, her ears flat, her tail low. *Anders, I can explain.*

Why you told her a secret you promised to keep? He growled, soft, in the back of his throat. *Did you share other secrets too?*

It wasn't just his sister who was gone now. Even the place they loved the most was gone. There were wolves there, keeping watch. Probably scaring Kess. Taking over the place that had been theirs, and only theirs.

Lisabet tried again. *Anders, I—*

But he pushed silently to his feet, turning his back on her so he wouldn't have to see the way her head tilted, so he wouldn't have to see her make an excuse, or lie.

Keeping his belly low to the ground, Anders crept over to the stone cache. He crouched behind it to transform back into a human, then reached inside, feeling around in the dark until he found Ennar's artifact satchel.

But before he had a chance to open it, Lisabet was crouching beside him, one moment a wolf and the next moment a girl. She was white as a sheet beneath her thousands of freckles. "Anders," she whispered. "You have to listen to me."

Frustration boiled up inside him. He didn't *have* to do anything for her. She sounded just like Rayna, telling him what he had to do. "I don't," he whispered back, as fierce as he could when he was speaking that softly. "Why don't you go talk to the Fyrstulf instead? She listens to you. She's *proud* of you, Ennar just said so."

"No she's not," Lisabet whispered. "She never has been. But I thought if I could get her to pay attention, get her to see I had good ideas, maybe she'd listen to me about other things. About the dragons. This was incredibly important, Anders."

Anders's fingers tightened around the satchel in his hand until the metal netting pressed into his fingers. "You told her about my secret place so she'd listen to your made-up ideas about making alliances with dragons?"

"They're not ma—" But Lisabet must have known they didn't have time for that argument right now. "Anders, I've spent my whole life trying to get her to listen to me, and for the first time, she's actually impressed with something I said. It's worth it if she'll listen to something more, and something more after that. We have to talk about the dragons!" Her voice threatened to rise above a whisper, and she quickly yanked it back down again. "Maybe this could even help Rayna."

But Anders was still stuck on the first thing she'd said.

"Your whole life?" he echoed. "But you've been a student less than a year."

Lisabet bit her lip, for once not sure what to say.

How would Sigrid have known Lisabet her whole life?

And in that moment of silence, it began to make sense. His thoughts whirled faster and faster, and with a series of clicks, different memories from different moments came together like clockwork.

Lisabet had a key to the Fyrstulf's office, and when he asked her how she got it, she'd dodged the question.

Lisabet argued with Sigrid in class, when nobody else dared.

Sigrid had spoken to the class, after she'd sent Lisabet out of the classroom. She'd said, "when you were all babies," not "ten years ago," as so many of the other wolves said. Like she remembered the time when Lisabet in particular was a baby. Sigrid had even *said* to Rayna, up on the dais on the day of the Trial, that she had a daughter Rayna's age.

Lisabet had been trying to impress Sigrid *all her life*.

Anders stopped breathing.

"Lisabet," he whispered. "Sigrid's . . . your mother."

Lisabet's face told him everything he needed to know. She had been lying to him all along.

Lisabet had had *so* many chances to tell him she was

connected to the Fyrstulf herself. She'd had so many chances, and she hadn't taken one of them.

Her mother was Sigrid, the one who'd have been leading the celebrations if they'd managed to spear Rayna straight out of the sky. And she'd told him to *trust* her? She'd literally stood with him in her mother's office and quoted Ennar to him. *The truth matters*, she'd said.

That had been a lie, and she'd told it at the exact moment she could have been telling him the truth. He couldn't afford to risk her doing it again. Not with his sister on the line. And he couldn't afford to waste time arguing with Lisabet about her betrayal, or about her lies.

His decision was settling in his gut like a heavy weight, but there was no question in his mind about what he had to do. He reached for the satchel, tugging the flap up. Inside, atop a small pile of medical supplies was the chalice he'd seen Sigrid holding in her office. Fylkir's chalice.

His breath catching in his throat, hands trembling, Anders pulled it free. The metal gleamed in the moonlight, rows of tiny runes marching along every available surface. He shoved his stolen bag of flour into Ennar's satchel in place of the chalice, to leave the bag looking as full as it was before, in case Ennar didn't open it for a while yet. Perhaps she wouldn't try and use the chalice until the middle of the night, or even until the morning, before the students woke.

"Anders," Lisabet whispered. "I'm your friend. I want to help. I thought if Sigrid would listen to me, decide I had reasonable ideas, she might listen when we tried to tell her about Rayna. There might be a chance she'd believe Rayna's a prisoner, not just another dragon."

"Then you should have told me that." His hand tightened around the chalice. "You should have told me she was your mother. And none of that matters now, anyway. There's no time to convince anyone of anything. I'm going to try the chalice, and if it points to Drekhelm, I'm going to find her."

"I'll come," Lisabet whispered immediately.

He shook his head. His thoughts were a whirl. How could he trust her to make saving Rayna her number one priority?

"I don't want you with me," he said. And even through all his hurt and frustration, through his anger, it still felt terrible to say it.

Her face fell, and her lips pressed together very hard, as if she was trying not to cry. Anders turned away before he had to look at her again.

He pushed himself back into wolf form and picked up

the chalice experimentally in his mouth. It wouldn't be comfortable, but he'd be able to carry it.

Keeping it clamped safely between his jaws, and slinking with his belly close to the ground, he left his friend behind, disappearing into the night.

CHAPTER EIGHTEEN

ANDERS CREPT AWAY FROM CAMP AND DOWN TO
the bank of the river they'd camped by, a wider version of the silvery streams they'd run past earlier that day.
Here, the air was crisp and cold, faint spray landing on his
fur as the water hurried along.

He trotted along the bank for a few minutes, putting some distance between himself and the camp before
he stopped. He set down the chalice to transform, and a
moment later he was a human, crouching on the river-
bank.

He did as Ennar had shown him a few hours before,
felt out a firm place to make his way to the water's edge
and carefully climbed down. The waters were wild and
churning, crashing against boulders midstream and sending up spray. He checked carefully before he rested his
weight on the soft ground of the bank.

He unclipped the needle from the stem of the chalice, holding it between his fingers as he dipped the cup into the running water to fill it. He carefully set the needle on the surface of the water, where it floated. It spun in an idle circle that might be no more than the current of the water, and it hesitated for a moment on him. Then it spun again, much faster, and pointed quivering toward the mountains to his west. It didn't move again.

Drekhelm. Drekhelm was to the west.

* * *

The river snaked from west to east, roaring along beside his path, its fast-running water glinting in the starlight. Anders was grateful there was barely any moon, though he knew his tracks would still be easy enough to follow. And by morning, Ennar would have tried to use the chalice, and more likely than not, she'd be on his trail.

He wasted no time as he loped across the dark plains, cutting a path through the silvery grass and the patches of snow, which grew more frequent as he made his way toward the forest at the base of the mountains.

He had to transform every so often, to check a more exact direction with the chalice, but it always pointed west, along the course of the river. His jaw ached, and breathing around the chalice wasn't easy.

It was a couple of hours before Anders reached the

edge of the Great Forest of Mists. He slowed to a trot as he slipped between trees that towered a hundred yards above him, their needles a thick carpet on the forest floor. There was much more snow piled here in the shelter of the forest. Out on the plains, the breeze had carried him the scents of faraway places, but here, the world focused in sharply to his immediate surroundings.

He found he could tell an old tree from a young one by the scent of its bark, could smell where a rabbit had crossed his path hours before, and which way it had been going. Every breath brought him new stories, added new depth to this place. As a human, he'd have thought a forest an exciting but dangerous place.

Now, *he* was the predator.

It was almost completely dark farther in, the trees seeming to lean over him to block the faint starlight, a faint mist clinging to the forest floor, swirling around his paws. Anders was grateful for his wolf's vision. He followed the river as it wound its way through the black trees, the world silent except for the faint crunch of his paws on pine needles and snow, and the sound of the water.

His limbs were beginning to ache after a whole day of running. He knew he was lifting his feet a little less, carrying his tail a little lower. A small voice in his head kept reminding him that what he was doing was nothing short of betraying the pack—the kind of action that deserved the exile Sigrid had threatened.

That same voice began to ask questions about Lisabet, as he scrambled up the huge trunk of a fallen tree, the rotting wood soft beneath his paws.

She didn't tell you who she was, the voice pointed out. *But you lied about who you were too. You didn't tell her about Rayna.*

He made it over the fallen tree and set the low mist swirling as he landed back on the bed of pine needles, starting out once more. The voice didn't stop. *She told your secret when she shouldn't have*, it said. *But you said the locator frame was for helping Jerro, you didn't tell her about anything you were doing.*

I did eventually, he pointed out to the voice. *I chose to trust her, and she was never going to tell me about Sigrid.*

The voice had a ready reply: *You took your time telling her. Perhaps she was just taking her time telling you. Hoping you'd still be her friend afterward.*

He sighed, making his way across a large patch of snow. What Lisabet had done had been wrong—she'd shared a secret, she'd lied to him, if only by not telling him something she should have. But he'd done the same, and he knew how it felt to wonder if anybody would still want him, once they knew the truth about him. He wished now that he'd said something different before he left.

Still, perhaps it was best she was back at the camp. If he got caught, if he got exiled, at least she'd be safe.

About an hour into the woods the wild river finally split into two, swinging north and south. He had no option but to cross it, if he wanted to continue west. Anders pushed himself back into human form to check the chalice. As he drew closer to the mountains he was finding every change harder than the last, each time requiring more concentration. Tiredness, he supposed.

The river was running faster and fiercer now, and Anders was careful as he edged his way down the steep, boggy bank, keeping firm hold of a tree root as he leaned down to dip the chalice into the current. The water nearly snatched it from his hand, numbing his fingers with cold in an instant, and he snatched it back, water slopping. There was enough, though, and he made his way up the bank to safety, dropping the needle into it. It swung instantly west. There was nothing for it but to cross the river.

He'd only swum a few times, as a human. On hot summer days in Holbard the street children would launch themselves into the harbor, throwing down cork buoys stolen from fishing boats to help themselves float. Paddling around in the harbor, though, was a very different thing to throwing himself into this rushing torrent. He knew his wolf's body would be stronger, and his instincts told him he'd be able to swim, but the current was roaring past him like a living thing, waiting to grab him and drag him down.

He forced his body into wolf form once more, pacing the riverbank, studying the far side in the gloom. There was a place downstream where he could land, perhaps. The bank looked less steep there, which gave him a better chance of scrambling up. If he started upstream and tried to swim across as the current swept him down, he should hit it. He hoped.

Beyond that landing place the banks towered above the river for as far as he could see into the gloom. If he missed it, he'd lose his chance to climb out of the water before the cold and the current exhausted him, and he would be dragged under.

He let himself imagine, just for a moment, that Lisabet was with him. He'd felt so alone, walking up to Hayn the day he'd enlisted at Ulfar. But now, having found friendship, he was more alone than ever without it.

The water below was freezing and churning, racing downstream like a wolf pack across the plains. Jagged rocks made dark islands down its center, white spray standing out in the dark around them. Hesitating wasn't making this any easier. He picked up the chalice in his mouth and edged his way down to the water.

The current rushed past the bank, and Anders braced himself to jump, swaying back and forth, trying to summon the courage to make the leap. There was only one way to Rayna, and that was across. And then suddenly, before he knew he'd made the choice, he was in the water.

The cold hit him like a huge hand wrapping around his ribs and squeezing tight, forcing all his breath up into his throat, then wrapping around that to squeeze too.

He clenched his jaw shut around the chalice's handle as the current swept him along, the shock sweeping through his body and driving every thought from his mind.

As the river swung him around he caught a glimpse of the landing. The sight galvanized him, and he remembered what he was supposed to be doing, scrambling to swim across the current to reach the shore. Keeping hold of the chalice forced his mouth open, and as water splashed down his throat he had to clamp down on the urge to cough.

As he struggled for breath, the current swung him around in a circle, the rocks and the rushing water and the shoreline blurring together as one. *I'm not going to make it.*

The whole of his body slammed into one of the rocks in the middle of the river, pain overtaking the frozen numbness for an agonizing moment, foam and spray surging up over his head. Then he was past it, desperately holding onto the chalice, watching the landing place as he swept by it.

He gasped another breath, simply trying to keep his head above water as the banks grew taller and steeper. *If he hit another rock it could knock him out.* He'd drop the chalice, or simply slip beneath the surface and drown. He found more strength, frantically clawing at the water, dragging in breaths when he could manage it.

Then over the rushing of the water he heard a high, piercing howl from the shore. He wrenched around in time to see *Lisabet* racing along the far bank in wolf form, her dark fur glittering with frost, leaping over a fallen log to keep pace.

He glanced off another rock, sending a sharp pain through his ribs, spinning around again. As she came back into his field of view she transformed seamlessly from wolf to girl without breaking stride, suddenly a human running a few steps ahead of him.

She leaned down to grab a branch, pivoting and swinging it out into the river with all her might. She kept hold of one end as she pushed the other into the current. With the last of his strength Anders forced his legs to work, surging toward it, and crashed into it with a force that reverberated through his body.

He tangled his legs around it, the water grabbing at

him with ice-cold fingers to try and tug him free. Above him, Lisabet used the current's force to swing the branch in parallel to the steep shore.

Anders sunk his front paws into the soft mud there, hooking one around a tree root, and Lisabet frantically dragged another branch into place to make a bridge up for him. With the last of his strength he scrambled up. Lisabet reached down to grab at the scruff of his neck and helped him up the steep, boggy incline, until they both fell in a heap in the snow at the edge of the river.

He finally released the chalice, trembling as he coughed up water in great, heaving gasps.

Lisabet was still wrapped around him, half underneath him, still holding him, as if even now he might slip away beneath the surface of the furious river.

Even if he'd been human like her, he couldn't have spoken, still caught up in coughing. But he turned his head, and between gasped breaths, he pressed his wet nose to her cold cheek in thanks.

It was a little while before either of them spoke, and eventually it was Lisabet who broke the silence. "I'm sorry," she whispered.

He had to reply in wolfish, with a flick of his ears and a soft whine. *I'm sorry too.*

Her face was nearly hidden in the dark, but he knew

she understood him. "I should have told you. I just . . . everyone judges me by my mother. I liked making a friend who didn't. I wanted you to trust me. And you *can* trust me."

And he knew now that she was right. He whined another question. *Do the others know?*

"Most," she admitted. "But they know I disagree with her on a lot of things, so they don't bring it up. They don't forget either, though."

That explained the loneliness he'd sensed in her, he realized. The isolation.

"I'm not the daughter she wanted," Lisabet continued, still in a whisper. "My father should have been a powerful wolf. Instead, he was a mercher from Baseyda who was back on a ship before I was born. I'm not sure he even knows I exist. If she ever imagined having a child, it wasn't like that. It wasn't me."

Anders wondered whether that was why Lisabet tried so hard, was always top of the class.

"It's like because I don't behave the way a daughter of hers should, because I ask so many questions, she has to be the most *wolf* she can possibly be," Lisabet whispered.

Anders knew a thing or two himself about not measuring up, and he was quiet, considering her words. *I lied to you as well,* he said eventually. *I didn't tell you who my sister was. I didn't tell you what I was trying to do. I was afraid to tell anyone.*

"We both had reasons," she said quietly. "Some of them were good, some of them were bad. But I know we never meant to hurt each other."

In the end, Lisabet had been there—been *here*—when he needed her most. She'd acted like a friend, even when he'd thought she wasn't.

It turned out he still had one after all.

He thumped his tail against the ground, because it was like the cold water had washed away his anger. *I should never have left you behind. Forgive me?*

"Let's forgive each other," she said, picking up the chalice. "And let's keep heading for Drekhelm."

CHAPTER NINETEEN

AFTER ANDERS COULD BREATHE A LITTLE MORE normally, he rolled in the snow to shed as much water from his coat as he could, trying to ignore the growing aches and bruises all over his body. He was lucky he hadn't broken anything.

They made their way on in the direction he'd been traveling, Lisabet still in human form. They paused when they found a small stream feeding the river, and she used that to fill the chalice and check their course. "That way," she said, pointing away from the river and on toward the mountains.

How did you get across? he asked, looking back, thinking of the roiling current as she poured the water out of the chalice.

"I found a place farther up," she said. "But mostly, I wasn't trying to carry the chalice in my mouth, so I could actually breathe." She set down the chalice and braced her hands against her knees, shivering in clothes as wet as their fur had been after their swim. "It's so hard to transform."

Anders whined his soft agreement, watching as she gathered herself to try.

"I don't know how I did it just now, except I was terrified," she continued. She looked down at the snowy ground beneath her feet. "I don't think it's that I'm tired either. That doesn't usually stop me. We're getting closer to the mountains. There's lava down there somewhere. Our bodies know it. It makes it harder for us to change, even when we're in the snow."

She drew a deep breath and whined softly as she stretched out in wolf form, pushing her paws ahead of her and bowing for a long moment.

He tipped his ears toward her, and she pressed in against him, nudging his nose with hers in reply. It felt good to be a "we" again.

They were leaving a clearer path behind them as they headed out once more, the cover of the trees preserving the snowdrifts that had melted out on the plains and at the edges of the forest. Lisabet had left shortly after Anders, and though Ennar hadn't worked out that the chalice was missing by then, with half the night gone, surely she had by now.

They couldn't afford to stop and rest. So they took it in turns, one carrying the chalice while the other carved a path ahead through the banks of snow, their heads hanging lower and lower as their exhaustion grew.

It was some time later when Anders nearly walked straight into Lisabet's tail, and he blinked awake, realizing he'd been dozing as he walked. The sky behind them was starting to grow lighter, pinks and oranges creeping up above the horizon as dawn prepared to make herself known. They'd been awake almost twenty-four hours.

The trees were finally thinning out, and Lisabet had stopped because they had their first clear view of the mountains, soaring up into the clouds above. They had steep sides of black rock, sheer in some places, with tiny, silvery waterfalls tumbling from great heights to fall hundreds of feet to the ground. Snow sat higher up before the peaks disappeared into the clouds, and huge boulders littered the slope, as if they'd been carelessly thrown there sometime in the past.

The path Anders and Lisabet were on—the path the chalice still insisted on—led straight up the steep slope ahead of them.

So Anders took his turn to lead, and he kept on climbing. Somewhere up there was the largest gathering of dragons in Vallen. Somewhere up there, he hoped, was Rayna.

The lower foothills of the mountain sloped gradually, and for a few minutes Anders thought the ascent might not be so bad. He weaved his way through boulders and past the last few thinning clusters of trees. The ground turned to scree, loose pebbles sliding beneath their paws, but he found when he stayed low to the ground he could get a better grip.

Both he and Lisabet craned their heads back every so often to look for dragons, but though the sky on the horizon behind them was pink, it was still a velvety dark blue up ahead, and he knew he had little chance of warning if they came down from Drekhelm.

So he simply focused on finding safe footholds, moving up the mountain as efficiently as he could. And eventually, he realized he'd stumbled upon some sort of path. Between the patches of snow he could see it worn into the rocks, and after an hour or so, he found four steps carved into a particularly steep ascent.

Someone had intended that this place should be approached on foot, once upon a time. A long time ago, judging by the way the weather had worn the steps.

There was a huge boulder up ahead that seemed like it would provide some shelter from the growing wind, and he decided he'd stop on the far side of it to mention the steps to Lisabet—though he knew she really couldn't have missed them. It was an excuse for a rest.

He rounded the moss-covered sides of the boulder, pausing a few paces around its curve when the wind only seemed to worsen—it wasn't just racing down the mountainside now, but seeming to batter him from above, and he was forced to crouch as a gust nearly knocked him sideways. It was as if the wind really was coming from—oh *no*.

From above.

He backed up abruptly until his tail hit the boulder, yelping a warning to Lisabet. She lunged forward to his side with a growl of her own, and suddenly the pink and orange of the sunrise seemed to come to life and streak across into the darkened skies, as three dragons appeared to hover above them.

Their scales ranged from the orange of the dawn to the dark red of blood, streaked through with copper and gold. They took up a position directly above the two wolves, and the downdraft of their wings pushed Anders and Lisabet back against the boulder, forcing them lower to the ground.

One of them sent a gout of flame soaring up into the sky, and even from where he crouched, Anders could feel the heat of it, the roar of the hot air crashing into the cold.

Beside him, he felt Lisabet shift her weight, ready to

bring down her front paws and create an ice spear, but he felt her uncertainty too. Which one would she aim at? And what would the other two do next?

He dropped the chalice into the snow at his feet, frantically casting his exhausted mind around for his next move. He couldn't throw a spear. He couldn't fight. The dragons didn't look like they were in the mood to listen, even if he could think of something to say. His plan had been to stay unseen, because he was totally useless in a fight. Running or hiding were his only options.

Perhaps they could run, find some place to squeeze into that the dragons couldn't follow? But even as he thought it, two of the three dragons descended to the ground, the wind from their wings buffeting the two wolves and forcing them back against the rock behind them. Once they'd landed they smoothly transformed, shrinking down and shifting into a boy and a girl about his own age.

The boy reminded him a little of Sakarias, but his hair was a deeper copper, and longer, more tousled. His smirk had a harder edge than the wolf's friendly grin, and where Sakarias's green eyes always danced with a joke, this boy's were more calculating, their deep brown standing out against his pale skin.

She was a little more suntanned than him, her blond hair pulled into two braids. She was bigger and broader than the boy, and moved with an ease that told Anders she was strong. Both of them were clad in fur-lined cloaks and gloves, but they didn't wear a uniform like the wolves.

The girl folded her arms across her chest as the boy sauntered toward the two shivering wolves, his gait relaxed. And why shouldn't it be? He had the girl right behind him, a dragon circling in the air above him, and they outnumbered the two exhausted wolves.

Anders was going to fail Rayna and get Lisabet killed in the bargain.

"Well," said the boy, lifting one eyebrow. "To what do we owe this very great honor? We weren't expecting visitors." His smirk didn't budge one inch.

"And we don't want any," the girl added from behind him. "Explain yourselves."

Anders racked his tired mind for one more idea.

There had been moments when he'd almost begun to believe Lisabet—to wonder if there was more to the dragons than the wolves were telling him. Now, looking at their satisfied, unfriendly faces, he felt that uncertainty fall away. They were hostile. They were *amused* by his fear.

He tried to think back over the path they'd taken, calculate how long it would take to run for the woods, where they might at least have some cover. *Too long.*

He wondered if Lisabet would run for it, if he ran

forward to distract the dragons. But she wouldn't. She'd try to help him. And she clearly had no more idea than he did of what to do, crouching beside him.

"Forgotten how to transform, Wolf?" the boy asked, amused.

Anders made his racing heart slow. He had to speak to them. He had to find the right words. It was the only way to save Rayna—and himself and Lisabet.

He reached inside himself and found the kernel of a human, and tugged at it, forcing himself back into that shape.

Beside him, he felt Lisabet changing as well. Even though he was taller than a wolf when he was in human form, he still had to look up the mountain to where the dragons stood above him.

His clothes were still clammy, damp from his plunge in the river and sticking to his freezing-cold skin, and he was shivering the moment he was human. But the cold of his clothes felt *wonderful*. The dragons were radiating heat, and the wet fabric helped keep his skin cool—he felt stronger, even as he shivered. Perhaps there was some way he could talk his way out of this.

"Just give me a chance to explain," he said, his voice hoarse with tiredness. "I can explain."

"Go on," said the girl, tugging up the fur-lined hood

of her cloak as the breeze picked up around them once more, sending a shiver through Anders and Lisabet. "I'm fascinated to hear."

But before Anders could try, the wind buffeted them again, pushing him into Lisabet, and then throwing them both back against the rock. The world overhead became a whirl of red, and he realized the last of the dragons was descending, forcing the boy and girl before them to stumble out of its way.

It landed with a swing of its tail, and a moment later it transformed, shrinking down to a figure in a red-brown coat. Anders could make out a shock of black, curly hair, but the swirl of snow still settling after the dragon's landing obscured the face beneath it.

Anders's feet were moving before his brain understood what he was seeing, the information arriving in a jumble.

Ahead of him was *Rayna* running down the slope, sliding on the stones in her haste, and in the same instant he was running toward her, scrambling over wet and icy rocks.

They smacked together in a tangle of arms and legs, his sister squeezing his ribs as tightly as the frozen river had done.

Relief crashed over him, pushing away the pain he should have felt when she hugged him right over his bruises, and his knees threatened to give way as he wrapped his arms around her in return.

"What are you *doing* here?" she demanded, refusing to let go. Her skin radiated heat, but he didn't care.

"I—" he tried, but with the air squeezed out of him, he couldn't make a sound. Over her shoulder, he could see the boy and the girl walking slowly toward them, and he had no idea what Lisabet was doing behind him. He shoved weakly at Rayna, and with a laugh, she let him go.

"What are you doing here?" she repeated, looking him up and down, her eyes widening as she took in his uniform. "And wearing *that*?"

"We came to get you back," he said quietly and urgently, hoping the two other dragons wouldn't overhear. "The equinox—"

"You didn't join Ulfar, did you?" she said, talking straight over the top of him. It was the same voice she always used—*tell me you didn't mess things up again*, it said.

A flash of pure frustration flowed through Anders, hot and quick. She thought him joining Ulfar Academy was the problem? Rayna was the one who'd been herded away by dragons, flown out of sight against her will and not heard from since. Rayna was the one who'd transformed into a *scorch dragon*, one of the creatures that had killed their parents.

Lisabet came up to stand beside him, leaning in to

press her shoulder against his in silent understanding, and answered for him. "The equinox is tomorrow," she said. "We had to get to you before . . ."

Rayna was looking at them blankly. *This* was why she was busy telling him off, Anders realized. She had no idea what was coming. The dragons hadn't told her—of course they hadn't. Why would they warn her?

His sister's gaze flicked across to Lisabet, and her eyes narrowed for a moment, weighing the other girl. Anders knew what that look was—Rayna wasn't used to Anders being a "we" with anyone other than her.

A shiver went through Anders, so sharp it hurt the bruises all along his ribs where he'd hit the rocks in the river.

Rayna's face softened. "You're wet," she murmured. "That was no way to say hello, I'm sorry. Here, have my coat." She peeled it off and handed it over, and Anders took it without a protest, pulling it close around him. The wolf in him liked the cold, but his human body couldn't take much more.

Some tired part of his brain was still working overtime, trying to figure out how he could convince Rayna to come away with him and Lisabet, with two dragons standing right there behind her.

The warmth left by Rayna's body in the coat's fur-lined

interior sank blissfully into his skin as Rayna took his hand in hers again.

The girl and the boy—*the two dragons*, his brain corrected him—were still watching them, brows raised. The girl spoke, her voice cutting across their reunion. "Are you going to introduce us, Rayna? Or shall we just set them on fire and save everyone the time?"

Anders nearly stopped breathing, but Rayna didn't seem to take it seriously.

"This is my brother, Anders," she said. "And that's . . ." But she had no introduction for Lisabet.

"Lisabet," Anders supplied. "My friend." *Better not introduce her any other way. Like mentioning her mother.*

"Your *friend*?" Rayna said, sounding surprised, as if she had no idea how Anders had come by such a thing in the short time since they'd parted.

"He can't be your brother," the girl said with a sniff. "He's a *wolf*."

"He looks like her," the boy said, thoughtful.

"But he *can't* be," she argued, as if that settled it.

"Well, he is," Rayna told them, curling her hand around Anders's. She didn't seem to have any of the doubts he'd harbored, or if she did, they didn't show on the outside. Then again, Rayna's doubts never seemed to. "We're twins."

The girl snorted. "Impossible."

Anders's head was spinning. Rayna was acting like anything but a prisoner. Clearly she had no idea about the sacrifice, and the dragons intended on keeping it that way. He had to find a way to warn her.

"We should take them straight to Drekhelm," the boy said. "The Dragonmeet will want to see them immediately. They'll want to know what wolves are doing in our territory when all our leaders are here."

"They're spying," said the girl, backing up several steps. "We'll take them in as spies." Before either of the wolves could reply or protest, she dropped to a three-point crouch, the fingertips on her right hand pressed to the ground, dropping her head.

She suddenly swelled, morphing in seconds to the sunrise colors of her dragon form, limbs lengthening, neck growing, until she settled into her new shape. She exhaled with a low rumble, breathing gold-and-white sparks.

Drekhelm? How would they ever get out of Drekhelm, once they were surrounded by dragons?

Lisabet spoke behind him. "We didn't come to spy. We came for Rayna."

The boy shrugged. "Well, now you'll come with Rayna to Drekhelm. Rayna, you take your brother, I'll take the girl."

Anders looked across at Rayna, his mouth dry. She didn't look much more comfortable than he was.

"Don't try and run away," the boy called, backing up the slope to make room for his transformation. "I'd hate to have to roast you, but I'll do it." He jerked a thumb over his shoulder at the sunrise-colored dragon. "And Ellukka here wouldn't even hate it."

"It'll be okay," Rayna whispered, letting go of his hand to back up with the other dragons, moving into the space up the mountainside so she could change without colliding with the group.

"What are we going to do when we get up there?" Lisabet whispered once they were out of hearing.

"I have no idea," Anders whispered in reply. "They can't let us go, we could show Sigrid the way to Drekhelm. And I'm not even sure Rayna *wants* to go back." Frustration surged through him for that admission. After everything he'd done, everything he'd risked, Rayna was just charging on past him like she always did, without bothering to stop and ask what he wanted. How he felt. Taking over yet again. "She has no idea about the equinox. I have to find a chance to get her alone and tell her."

Lisabet nodded. "They're not as friendly as I'd hoped," she admitted, and though the words were mild, Anders could tell from her face that she was beginning to realize just how much trouble they were in. Just because she wanted to talk didn't mean the dragons wanted to listen.

"I don't think we have any choice," Anders said eventually. "They'll catch us if we run. We have to go with them."

Ahead of them, the boy transformed to a dark-red dragon, and Rayna crouched, turning to the reds and bronzes of her dragon's form.

Once the transformation was complete, Anders and Lisabet made their way up the slope, Anders buttoning his borrowed coat tightly, each heading to the sides of the dragons who would transport them. Rayna crouched, pushing out her foreleg so Anders could use it as a ladder.

Up close she radiated heat, like the sun shining straight on his face in the middle of summer. Her scales were a rich red color, and the streaks of copper and gold he'd seen the other times she transformed were in every overlapping scale, a marbled patina of different metallic shades, glinting at him in the dawn.

The sight of a dragon so close—even one that was a person he loved—shot shivers straight down his spine that had nothing to do with the cold. It was as if he could hear the crackle of the white dragonsfire and the screams of people around him, see the golden sparks raining down around him, smell the smoke. As if his dreams were surging to life.

Rayna rumbled encouragement deep in her huge chest, and Anders forced himself to reach out and lay one hand on her foot. He'd expected the scales to be hard, like a seashell or a bone, but they radiated warmth through his hand, and there was a yield to them, despite their toughness. He didn't reach out to touch her claws, but he knew they'd be as hard as he expected, and as sharp.

Careful of hurting her, reminding himself that this wasn't just a dragon, it was his sister, he lifted his foot to step up onto her paw. She twisted around to watch him, her dark eye half the size of his whole head. She didn't seem bothered by his weight, so carefully he climbed up her leg to her elbow, and from there to sit astride her back.

He'd been wondering how he'd stay in place without anything to hold on to, but he found that he fit pretty well into the spot where her neck met her shoulders. He could notch his legs in front of her shoulders and shove his body between two of the ridges that ran the length of her back, wrapping his arms around the one in front of him.

There was a surge as Rayna leapt, his stomach lifting for a moment right up into his throat, and then another as she brought her wings down in a long sweep, soaring off the side of the mountain. She spiraled around in a dizzying ascent, and Vallen spread out beneath them like some kind of incredible miniature model, complete with snowy slopes, winding rivers, and dark forests.

There was no turning back now—they were headed for Drekhelm.

CHAPTER TWENTY

THE SKY WAS LIGHTENING AHEAD OF THEM AS they glided out over the valley, gaining height as dawn took over the sky. Anders could see the forest, and the glint of the river tumbling through it in the early morning light, and beyond it a dim hint of the plains. With the sun rising now, he wondered if out on the plains Ennar would be able to see the dragons around the mountain, or whether the distance and the clouds would hide them.

Then they were wheeling around, and the mountain rose before them. Rayna flew in formation with the other dragons, following them up and up and into the clouds, where the freezing-cold air bit at his exposed skin, numbing his nose in seconds. He knew they must be moving, because Rayna was still pumping her wings, and he could feel the wind in his face, but in the pearly cloud around them it looked like they were perfectly still.

She tilted to wheel sideways, and he chanced a look down—then found himself staring. Through a gap in the clouds and a gash in the side of the mountain he saw fire—was it a dragon breathing flame?

But no, it wasn't fire. It was lava, bright and hot, like a living thing in the belly of the mountain. This was the lava Lisabet had told him was somewhere beneath them, making it harder every moment to transform from wolf to human, or back again.

The dragons turned as one, arrowing straight ahead, and as the clouds parted he realized they were heading for a cliff. Rayna's speed didn't flag, and Anders's heart began to kick up, hammering wildly in his chest as they flew directly toward the rock face.

He tightened his grip on Rayna's neck ridge, ducking down close to her body, as if that would somehow shield him when they plastered themselves flat against the mountain.

At the last possible moment the dragons fell into single file, and one after another they swooped in toward a black spot on the mountainside that suddenly resolved itself into the mouth of a cave. The opening swallowed them whole, and Rayna flared her wings to slow their flight, then landed with a couple of skipping steps, stumbling and stopping, jolting the breath right out of Anders's lungs. It was a comfort to see there was *something* about being a dragon she hadn't perfected yet.

The cave was enormous, with room for several dragons to land at once, the ceiling so high and perfectly smooth that he couldn't decide if nature had made it that way or if it had been somehow carved. There were huge doors that could close off the cave mouth where they'd flown in, and underneath them, doors sized for humans. Both stood open, offering a view of the snowy mountain beyond.

Grand tapestries lined the walls, some with sections still to be completed, and up at the end of the hall farthest from the mountainside was the human-scaled section. A long, ornate metal table on a raised platform was surrounded by chairs, and several doors led off in different directions.

Every place at the table was taken, and its occupants were pushing back their chairs to stand or twisting around to get a better look at the newcomers. Some of the people staring at them were silver-haired, but a couple of them looked young, perhaps no older than the final years at Ulfar. They were as varied as the wolves at the Academy—old and young, tall and short, with skin ranging from the deepest brown to as white as Lisabet's, some with stern faces, others simply serious.

But what they all had in common was that they were staring straight at Anders and Lisabet.

Anders climbed down Rayna's side, hitting the ground with a tired thud and leaning against her for a moment.

Lisabet was dismounting nearby, and once the two wolves were clear, Rayna and the other two dragons suddenly seemed to shrink in a way his eyes couldn't quite follow, diminishing rapidly until they were just three humans, crouching in formation, one hand pressed to the ground.

Up at the fancy metal table, a man who reminded Anders of the girl they'd met on the mountain with suntanned skin and a blond braid, broke the silence. "Who are those humans?"

An instant later, a woman was pointing at Anders, then Lisabet. "Wolves!" she shouted. "Those are wolves!"

It was the woman in the green dress—the woman he'd seen in the streets of Holbard with Rayna's hairpin. Other people—other dragons, they must all be dragons—were standing now, a low murmur going through them. The man standing at the head of the table pushed back his chair and rose more slowly to his feet, walking several steps closer to look at the newcomers thoughtfully.

He was fit and strong, with a shock of red hair and a neatly trimmed beard, and ruddy cheeks, as if he was outdoors a lot. He had a politely interested expression that was hard to read, though Anders wished he could.

Rayna took hold of Anders's hand to lead him forward, but Anders could hardly make his feet move. This was Drekhelm. These were dragons themselves staring down at him, and he was utterly helpless—there was no way he and Lisabet could make a run for it.

And the equinox was tomorrow.

Rayna yanked on his hand, and he stumbled forward beside her.

"Leif, this is Anders," Rayna said to the redheaded man, as respectful as he'd ever heard her sound. "And his friend . . ." There was a pause as she hunted for a name. "Elsabeth," she said after a moment, triumphant.

"Lisabet." That was the copper-haired boy who'd carried Lisabet, speaking from somewhere behind him. Anders could still hear that same smirk in his voice.

Rayna ignored him. "Anders, this is Leif. He's the Drekleid, the head of the Dragonmeet."

The Dragonmeet must be the group gathered around the table, Anders thought—though some of them were young, they all had an air of assurance around them, of power. They were in charge of the dragons, he was pretty sure.

But even the members of the Dragonmeet fell silent, waiting for their Drekleid to speak. He didn't for several heartbeats, gazing down at the five of them, looking at something behind Anders—Lisabet, probably—before his gaze fixed on Anders himself. "And what," he said finally, "brings you to our territory?"

Anders drew in a careful breath, trying to make sure his voice didn't shake. "My sister is here," he said. His voice did shake a little.

"That is unlikely," Leif said quietly.

Rayna squeezed his hand and raised her voice beside him. "Leif, *I'm* his sister."

A ripple of shock went through the room—some of the adults at the table just laughed, and not kindly, others waved away the idea, or turned to their neighbors to raise their voices in denial. A voice rang out from the group, a big man with a bushy beard. "He's a *wolf*, he's no dragon's brother. He's a spy."

"I give you my word as a dragon!" Rayna shouted, raising her voice over the crowd.

"What good is that?" the man scoffed. "You've only been here a few weeks, we barely know you. This could have been your plan since the moment you arrived. The wolves got you young, turned you against us, and now you've brought them right to our home. It's *impossible* that he's your brother."

Voices rose all around them, shouting and arguing, and Anders tightened his grip on Rayna's hand. At this rate, the dragons weren't going to wait until tomorrow to start sacrificing people.

"Leif—" he tried, raising his voice. But the redheaded man didn't answer. He was busy watching the others argue, and it probably didn't matter anyway. Anders didn't know what he would have said if he had got the Drekleid's attention.

Another woman was shouting now. "The Dragonmeet is all gathered in one place; the equinox is tomorrow, it's the perfect time for the wolves to attack."

Then Leif raised his hand, and one by one, everybody fell silent. The whole room was looking at him now, waiting. "Anders, was it?" he said, looking down at Anders.

Anders swallowed hard and nodded. The way the Drekleid spoke, so quietly, was actually *more* intimidating than the Fyrstulf's growl, he decided.

"Very well," said Leif. "We will speak to you first. Rayna, please take your other guest through to the reception room."

Rayna squeezed his hand tightly, and in just the same way as he knew what the wolves were saying, even when they didn't make a sound, he understood his sister. They were a pack of a different kind, and they had been learning to speak the same language their whole lives.

I'll be nearby, she was saying. *I'll be listening for trouble.*

I'll come running if I hear a thing.

Anders desperately didn't want her to leave, but he couldn't think of a single way to have her stay, so he nodded and made himself unpeel his fingers from around hers one by one.

She and Lisabet turned to walk across the hall, both casting anxious, backward glances at Anders as they went. He was pretty sure neither of them would have chosen him to speak on their behalf if they'd gotten a vote, and he didn't blame them.

The boy and the girl who had brought them in both bowed to the members of the Dragonmeet and turned to disappear through a door in the opposite direction.

And then Anders was alone with twenty-five adult dragons.

Pack and paws.

Leif was the one who broke the silence. "Anders," he said, gesturing for the others to take their seats. "Why have you come?"

"My sister," he said, his voice sticking in his throat. He took a breath and tried again. "Rayna is my sister. I came because you . . ." *Pack and paws,* said a little voice in his head. *Just say it.* "Because you kidnapped her," he said, louder than he meant to.

"We *rescued* her," a woman shouted from the other end

of the table to Leif. "She was under attack!"

"And she's not your sister," the man with the bushy beard added. "That's impossible."

"How convenient," said Leif quietly, and Anders noticed that everyone hushed when he spoke, "that we have an expert on the impossible. We have more important questions to answer just now. Anders, how many other wolves are coming?"

A part of Anders desperately wanted to bluff—wanted to tell the dragons that every wolf in Ulfar was right on his tail. But they'd find out soon enough he was lying, and what if they just killed him before they flew out to battle? "None," he said quietly. "I mean, my professor might try and follow me, I stole— But nobody, I don't think."

Even if Ennar had followed them up the mountain, she'd find the place where their paw prints met the dragons' footprints, and surely she'd assume the worst. That they'd been killed, or that they were traitors.

"So you have come alone," Leif said, thoughtful. "That was unwise."

Anders swallowed hard again. He was so very, very tired—he hadn't slept since he'd left Holbard, a full day before—and even Rayna's coat felt heavy right now. "The equinox," he said. "I came to try and get to her before the equinox."

Everyone was silent, several of the men and woman around the table squinting at him thoughtfully. It was one of the youngest members of the Dragonmeet who broke it, a girl who looked no older than eighteen. "I'm missing something," she said. "I mean, it's a *great* party, but . . ."

Anders's patience broke. *Were they just playing with him for fun now?* "I know about the sacrifice," he blurted out. "Please, I'll do anything! You can have me, but please let Rayna and Lisabet go. Please . . ." It was as if he were watching himself from the outside. *Had this been his plan all along? To offer himself up, if he got caught?*

Leif's mouth fell open, his calm expression completely gone. "I take it you're not talking about sacrificing lots of delicious food," he said eventually.

Anders shook his head.

"Put your mind at ease," Leif said. "I would very much like to know how that story got started. We do not sacrifice anybody, Anders, at the equinox or at any other time."

"But the stories—"

The bearded man cut him off, pushing to his feet to shout again. "Is this what the wolves are telling their young? Telling the humans? That we sacrifice children?"

The hubbub started to rise around the table again, but Leif once again cut it off by raising his hand. "Anders," he said gravely. "We dragons are often not of one mind. We are individuals. We disagree, we tread our own paths. We spread ourselves all over Vallen, and when we do come together, there is often much debate. There are many who do wish to take action against the wolves—who will see your presence here as reason to do so."

Anders swallowed, shoving his hands in Rayna's pockets so nobody would see them shaking. How many of those dragons who wanted to hurt wolves were here right now?

But Leif was still speaking. "However, I give you my word as the Drekleid, there is no truth to this story. Not an ounce. We do take children from Holbard at the time of the equinox, but it is not to sacrifice them. It is because they are of dragon blood, and the scouts we have sent to the city tell us they are ready to transform. We must bring them here and help them, or they will die."

Anders stared at him, searching his face for the tiny, telltale signs he was lying. And even as he tried desperately to guess the truth, his friend Det's story came back to him.

Det had grown sicker and sicker in Mositala, until he came to Vallen for the Trial of the Staff.

And the story on the street was that the dragons always kidnapped the sickest children.

Leif's gaze was steady, and though the outraged shouting around the table hadn't abated yet, as he ran his eyes over the Dragonmeet he grew surer and surer. His wolf sensitivity to body language was delivering a thousand different messages to him, and they all said the same thing.

Leif was telling the truth.

Relief flooded through him like rain sluicing the streets of Holbard, carrying away all the mess and confusion, and leaving him cleaner, clearer in its wake. Sure, he was still trapped in a remote mountain with the twenty-five most important dragons in Vallen, but at least nobody was planning to sacrifice his sister tomorrow. He decided to count it as an improvement.

The youngest woman spoke again. "What's being said in Holbard, Wolf? What are they saying about dragons?"

Anders considered how best to answer—he didn't want to provoke them by refusing, but he didn't want to give away information on Ulfar either. "That there are dragon spies in the city," he said eventually. After all, the dragons already knew that.

The Dragonmeet were murmuring among themselves once again, and Anders stood and waited, unsure of what to say next.

Leif solved his problem by nodding at the door Rayna and Lisabet had gone through. "Thank you, Anders," he said gravely. "Please go and wait with Rayna, and send the other wolf out. I think we'd better speak to her next."

CHAPTER TWENTY-ONE

ANDERS MADE HIS WAY THROUGH THE PAINTED green door Rayna and Lisabet had gone through, accidentally banging it against Rayna's head as he pushed it open. She squeaked, stumbling back, one hand rubbing at her temple, looking at Anders like he should have known better.

"She was eavesdropping," Lisabet said from farther down the short hallway, where she was nursing a steaming mug, and had a blanket around her shoulders.

"'Course I was," said Rayna, leading him down the hall and into a small room lined with bookshelves and couches, probably a place designed for people to wait. She pulled a lever just inside the door and a trapdoor in the ceiling opened, lowering down a tray suspended by four metal cords, one at each corner. On it sat a second mug of what smelled like cocoa, which she handed to Anders.

"Kept your drink warm for you," she said.

"They have artifacts and machinery we've never even seen," Lisabet told him, somehow looking excited despite her exhaustion, and the fear in the back of her gaze. That was Lisabet. Trying to understand and learn, even now.

"They want to speak to you," he said quietly.

She nodded, took a deep breath, and let herself out.

And then it was just Anders and Rayna in the little room. Silently she wrapped both her arms around him, careful not to jostle his mug, and pulled him in for a gentle hug.

Anders closed his eyes, tilting his head sideways to rest it against his sister's, drinking in the heat of her skin that had never been there before, and the faint scent of her that always had been, though now there was a sweet note to it, like cinnamon.

"Rayna," he murmured. "I was so scared. I thought you were a prisoner here. I was imagining . . . all kinds of things. I didn't know what was happening to you."

"Me too," she whispered. "I was scared at first, but once I realized I was safe, I had a screaming match with them about getting back to you. They were teaching me to patrol when we found you, but I was looking for a chance to run for it to Holbard, if the cloud came in enough. I was so worried about you."

"I didn't know what they'd do to you," he murmured.

"I saw a woman in Holbard, she had one of your hairpins, but I couldn't get near her. She disappeared every time she saw other wolves."

"I convinced her to try and give you a message," Rayna said. "Though I didn't tell them you were my brother. She found Jerro, and he told her you were at Ulfar, so she waited by the gates."

"When I saw her, I didn't know what she'd done to get the pin from you," he said quietly. "Or what they'd do to you next."

"Nothing," she said, as confident as usual.

"You don't know everything about dragons," he told her. "There's no way you can be sure. Our parents *died* battling dragons. There are still scorch marks all over Holbard from battling dragons. How can you be so sure they're safe? We're their prisoners."

"Not if we don't want to be," she replied. "And I've made friends, Anders. The boy and the girl you met with me, their names are Mikkel and Ellukka. I *like* them. You could fit in here too, you know. We could talk to Leif. He could win over the Dragonmeet."

"What?" He drew away from her in shock. "You just said you were getting ready to run for it, and now you're saying I should move in with dragons?"

"Well, the wolves tried to kill me in Holbard," she

pointed out. "And it's not Mikkel's and Ellukka's fault the Dragonmeet said I had to stay here. This place isn't anything like the stories."

"And what will I be if we stay here?" he asked. "The odd wolf out?" He didn't want to leave Rayna. But he wasn't a dragon, and he knew nothing of this place. He couldn't begin to imagine living here, away from his pack, stranded among dragons who thought he was the enemy. Drekhelm wasn't built for him, for anyone without wings. He couldn't come or go, unless he wanted to brave the long, treacherous path up from the valley below.

Though he'd fought every day since they were separated to get to Rayna, he'd never really known what would happen after he reached her. And now he was here, it turned out he still didn't know.

"I'm just so glad to see you," she murmured, and he felt himself soften. He knew what she said was true, but it wasn't like her to actually voice something like that, unless she was comforting him over his latest mistake.

"Me too," he said. "We'll figure something out, and we've got Lisabet as well, she's smart, we can—"

Rayna cut him off. "Anders, I'll handle it. Promise. I always do."

His temper surged. "I handled plenty of things while you were gone," he snapped. "I got myself into Ulfar, I figured out how to find Drekhelm, how to find *you*. I can do things myself, Rayna."

She stared at him, mouth open, and he realized his was open too.

Had he just said that?

He waited for her temper to flare in return, for her arms to cross and her scowl to sweep across her face. But instead, she just kept staring at him. Eventually, she spoke. "I know you can," she said stiffly. "I know you can do things for yourself."

"You don't know that at all," he shot back. "You've never let me make a decision."

"You never *wanted* to make a decision," she replied, her voice rising close to a shout.

"Well, now I do," he snapped. "I've changed."

And he hadn't realized how much until this moment, when he'd found himself back with Rayna, her telling him she'd handle everything, expecting him to fall into line as he always had.

Well, he wasn't going to.

In the weeks they'd been apart, Rayna and he had both seen things and learned things the other hadn't. They'd never been separated before, and now it seemed that in such a short time, their paths had diverged more than he'd ever imagined they could.

"You look cold," Rayna said eventually, her tone conciliatory. "Drink your cocoa?"

He knew it was her version of an apology, and he sank down onto one of the couches, taking a slow sip, then another. His frustration faded out. He knew he should feel lots of things, should be trying to think his way out of this.

But right now, all he felt, all he could think, was that he was afraid—afraid for Rayna, afraid for Lisabet, afraid he'd never be able to keep everyone he cared for safe.

"Listen," said Rayna, thoughtful. "Perhaps we can—"

But she got no further. A deafening crash sounded from the great hall, and above it, a chorus of screams, and the bellowing roar of a dragon.

Together, he and Rayna ran for the door. They burst out into the hallway, and were nearly at the green door to the great hall when they heard a new sound rise above the chaos beyond it.

It was the howl of wolves.

CHAPTER TWENTY-TWO

TOGETHER THEY PUSHED THE DOOR OPEN, AND Rayna grabbed him just in time to slam him to the floor as an ice spear came flying straight at their heads. Pain rattled through his body as his knees and elbows connected with the stone. They crawled along the wall, away from the doorway, so used to escaping tight situations together that they instinctively turned in the same direction.

All around them was chaos. Three full-size dragons dominated the hall, twice the size Rayna had been, at least thirty feet each. But there was no room for any more—they were surrounded by a throng of bodies, human and wolf alike, all locked in battle. In an instant Anders spotted Professor Ennar's steel-gray pelt, and moments later he was picking out his classmates.

Those dragons in human form were fighting however

they could, swinging chairs, a few brandishing knives—they had overturned the huge table, which must have been the crash he heard, and some were fighting from behind it. The wolves were fighting with teeth and ice spears, his classmates acting with trained precision.

As Anders crouched against the wall an ice spear crashed into the shoulder of one of the dragons, who let out a bellow of pain. For an instant its red scales turned gray and blue around the injury, jagged like frost, and it staggered back, nearly crushing wolf and dragon alike. The spears weren't just inflicting wounds—it was like the cold was doing some kind of other damage to the dragons.

The injured dragon exhaled a shower of white-and-gold sparks, but though it swung its head this way and that, wolves and those dragons still in human form were mixed everywhere, and it could find no safe target for its flame.

"What do we do?" Rayna screamed above the chaos. "They'll kill each other!"

But Anders was paralyzed—he wasn't sure which side he was supposed to be fighting on, his friends' or his sister's, much less how to help.

He saw Mateo run by, as bulky in wolf form as he was as a boy, disappearing down a hallway, followed by Jai. Turning back to the crowd, he saw Viktoria and

Sakarias together, snarling as they backed a pair of human dragons up against the wall, snapping at them when they brandished poles that had once supported tapestries. His classmates might be young, but Ulfar Academy knew how to train its soldiers, and they were winning. Would one of them be forced to actually kill a dragon?

A howl he knew grabbed his attention, and he saw Lisabet in wolf form by the overturned table. By her stood Leif, who remained a human. She was the one who had howled, and even in his human form, Anders understood her.

Stop, she howled. *We don't have to fight, we can talk to them!*

Some of the wolves ignored her, but Anders saw others hesitate, turning toward her to listen. Det paused, ducking a knife instead of striking back.

Sakarias wavered, and he turned his head. It was all the chance the human he was fighting needed—she swung the tapestry pole hard at him, connecting with his head and shoulder and sending him flying backward.

Viktoria ducked and shifted to human form to grab him, hauling him out of the fray, crouching over him and baring her teeth like a wolf when one of the dragons looked set to follow them. She glanced up at Lisabet by the table, then turned her attention to Sakarias, who was almost unconscious.

He had trusted Lisabet, and he paid the price for it.

Stop! Lisabet howled again. *If you kill their leader, there'll be a war!* But this time the wolves weren't listening. Behind her, Leif raised his hands, shouting some command to the dragons, looking out across the crowd.

He didn't see the ice spear flying toward his body.

But Lisabet did, launching herself up to intercept it. It crashed into her side, sending her flying back past Leif.

She crashed into the table and fell to the ground, limp and still. And suddenly Anders was moving, pushing to his feet to shove his way through the crowd, ducking weapons and flames, jumping over wolves and humans where they wrestled, teeth snapping and knives glinting.

A pair of hands grabbed him, yanking him down to the ground as a flame lit the air just above his head, burning where he'd been a second earlier. He looked around and found himself face-to-face with Professor Ennar. "Are you all right?" she shouted, looking over his shoulder for danger.

"I'm fine," he shouted back. "Please, you have to stop! They didn't kidnap me, my sister's here! My sister's one of them!"

"A dragon?" For a moment, Ennar was so incredulous, so confused, that she let go of him. Then a scream nearby yanked her back to the present. "I will do whatever it takes to keep my students safe," she growled, an echo of her words that day in the combat hall.

Suddenly Anders wasn't sure—had she come here to rescue him? Or to discover Drekhelm and tell Sigrid where to find it? Or both?

He tore free of her grip, ducking through the crowd again to get to Lisabet. The tide was beginning to turn in earnest—if the battle had been in the open, the dragons and their flames would have certainly had the advantage, but in here they couldn't understand the snarled commands the wolves passed along, and the ice spears seemed to be really hurting them, even when they barely grazed their targets. The dragons were disorganized, and the wolves fought as one.

"Keep moving," someone shouted in his ear, and suddenly he realized Rayna was beside him, helping him shove and fight his way toward Lisabet. "Anders, we   "

But she never finished the instruction—an ice spear caught her shoulder, knocking her back into the crowd, and she hit the ground.

She screamed, grabbing at her shoulder, arching her back in pain, and he lunged to grab her just as a huge dragon's tail came swinging around toward both of them, pulling her clear by her legs. There was no blood at her shoulder—it looked as if the spear had pierced her clothes, but not her skin—but her face was already turning from its usual warm brown to a completely unnatural shade of blue-gray, as if she were turning to ice right in front of him. She tried to move, to climb to her feet, and collapsed, her eyes rolling back.

Panic gripped Anders. Rayna was struggling to stay conscious behind him, and Lisabet was an unmoving heap upon the dais, where Leif was fighting three wolves at once, brandishing a chair.

He could see Viktoria trying to help Sakarias to his feet, dragging him toward the doors out of the cave. All around him were howls, roars, and shouts.

He didn't want his old classmates hurt any more than he wanted Rayna in danger, any more than he wanted Leif killed—because Lisabet was right. That would start a war, if they hadn't begun one already. A new generation would end up orphans, just like him.

He wanted to turn and check on Rayna, and he wanted to get to Lisabet. He wanted to run to Sakarias.

Perhaps as a wolf he could howl, make himself heard, convince his classmates to retreat. He crammed himself into wolf form, though every bone in his body screamed a protest, and every nerve sang with fiery pain. The scent of blood and sweat was suddenly crisp in his nostrils, and the bright colors of the world faded out for dimmer versions of their old selves.

And in the next heartbeat, everything seemed to slow down, a second crawling by at a snail's pace. He saw a huge dragon turn its head, draw breath, and send a pure white flame straight at Viktoria and Sakarias, where they were staggering toward the exit, his arm around her shoulder.

He saw a wolf's paws crash down, an ice spear flying straight at Leif's chest, sharp and straight and true.

He heard Rayna moan her pain behind him, heard the scrape of sound as she tried and failed to climb to her feet.

It built to a peak, his fear and his panic taking him over, each new sight hitting him one after another like a series of blows, until a rush came over him that felt like transformation, and yet nothing like transformation.

He only had a heartbeat to save Viktoria and Sakarias, and Leif.

He had never understood how the others sensed the water around them. How they drew it from the air, turned it to ice. He'd never even had a hint of that feeling.

But suddenly, his every nerve sharpened by fear, he *saw*.

There was water everywhere, in every breath of air.

It was all his—he could make it dance, he could make it fly, he could make it freeze.

And he could do more than that. He could draw in the air around him, so rich and so ready to breathe, and he could combine it with the water . . . and change it.

It was as if somebody had suddenly switched on a light, and a map was laid out in front of him.

He reared up, slamming his front paws against the stone floor of the great hall.

He made ice.

He made fire.

He saw it all, and he commanded it.

A great wave of blue-and-silver fire came pouring forth, arcing across the hall to form a barrier between the scorch dragon's fire and the ice wolf's spear.

The white fire and the ice spear both vanished into nothing as they connected with his blue-and-silver flames.

CHAPTER TWENTY-THREE

ANDERS FELT DIZZY BUT EXULTANT AS THE BAT-
tle surged around him, both sides momentarily
panicked by his silver-blue fire. The power to cast another
wave of it came rushing up through him, and as the wolves
cast new spears and the dragons breathed new flame, he
unleashed his own weapon.

Again the ice spears vanished into nothing as they
hit his fire, and the dragonsfire seemed to vanish as well,
becoming a part of his own flame. He heard a note of panic
in Ennar's growled command, and in the next moment a
dragon swung its tail around at full speed, sending Det
crashing into a wall.

Bereft of her weapons, Ennar tilted her head back and
howled the retreat, a note of panic in her voice that Anders
had never imagined he'd hear.

The wolves were snarling as they backed up toward

the mouth of the cave, readying to make their escape.

Mateo and Jai came racing out of the hallway they'd disappeared into, and though Anders saw that they each carried something in their mouths, he had no chance to see what it was.

He crouched beside Rayna, pouring himself back into human form so he could gather her up in his arms. Across the great hall Viktoria was still helping Sakarias, and his heart broke as he watched his friends limp away, injured and afraid.

Afraid of *him*.

"Let them go," Leif was shouting from where he knelt by Lisabet. "Do not follow!"

"They invaded our home!" A nearby dragon shouted, still brandishing a knife. "What do you mean, 'let them go'?"

"They are children," Leif replied, close to a snap. "What are you going to do, roast a pack of cubs who don't know any better than they've been taught? Where's a healer?"

A man came running across the hall to kneel by Leif and Lisabet, and as the dragons started to take stock of their wounded, a woman knelt by Anders and Rayna, carefully examining Rayna's shoulder. "She'll be all right soon," she promised. "The cold weakens us, but it will wear off in time. She needs to rest, is all."

"The others," Rayna whispered. Already her skin was returning to its usual brown, but she still looked terrible.

Anders wasn't sure what she meant, until he stood and realized that the boy Rayna had said was her friend, Mikkel, lay near Lisabet. His already white face was unnaturally pale now beneath his tousled copper hair, and his smirk was missing. The girl, Ellukka, was leaning over him. He must have been all right, because she was scolding him for something as she helped him sit up. They must have been waiting nearby for Rayna, and come running when they heard the battle.

Anders took hold of Rayna's hands, gently pulling her to her feet and draping her arm around his shoulder so they could make their way over to Leif and Lisabet and the others.

Leif was still kneeling by her, issuing quick commands to the dragons around him. "Saphira, take to the skies and watch them retreat, but do not interfere. Unnult, assemble teams to carry the wounded to the infirmary."

Together, Anders and Rayna dropped to a crouch beside the pair of them. "Is she . . ." Lisabet was still unmoving, and he couldn't make himself say it.

"Unconscious," Leif said quietly. "The cold didn't hurt her, but her head hit the ground. I think she stirred a moment ago, she . . ." He trailed off as Lisabet's eyelids fluttered. She was as snow-white as she'd ever been beneath her freckles, with a sort of dull gray sheen to her skin. After a moment, she subsided again, apparently not ready to wake up just yet.

"I've got her," said Ellukka, shifting over to sit closer to Lisabet and settling the girl's head in her lap. "We saw her protect you, Drekleid." And that, her tone clearly said, changed everything.

Mikkel leaned back against one of the table legs beside her, quiet.

Anders shifted to sit on the steps leading up to the dais, Rayna taking her place beside him, an arm around his shoulders.

He felt as though he'd been clobbered, his head spinning.

What had he done?

What was the silver-blue fire he'd thrown?

He was already forgetting how to do it, the knowledge slipping away like water through his fingers. But for one shining moment, it had been like Ennar and all the other wolves had told him—he only had to see what was in the air, and then control it.

But it seemed he saw something different in the air than everyone else. Was it just that he had only been looking for water all along?

"They've found Drekhelm again," a nearby dragon was saying, her voice close to despair. "They'll come for us here! We have two *wolves* here, they'll come back for them too."

"The Dragonmeet is here," Leif replied calmly. "We will discuss what to do."

Lisabet stirred and made a soft sound. Anders twisted around and met her bleary gaze. "Are you okay?" he whispered.

She considered the question for a moment, started to nod, then thought the better of it. "I will be," she murmured.

Rayna's arm tightened around him, and he felt a flash of pain for Lisabet. Whatever she thought of her mother, she was trapped away from her now, and Anders knew firsthand what losing family was like. He'd only just got his back.

Death or exile.

The words echoed in his head once more. Would Sigrid want Lisabet back, or brand her a traitor? It was hard to imagine the wolves ever welcoming them back to Ulfar, and Anders didn't want to be separated from his twin again, no matter how much he worried about his pack.

He should never have let Lisabet come with him—though "let" wasn't really the right word. Lisabet was unstoppable.

The adult dragons were still speaking. "*Do* we have two wolves here?" When Anders looked up, the blond man who looked like a relative of Ellukka's was pointing at him. "Leif, we saw him cast fire. Silver-and-blue fire. What kind of creature does that?"

"He's not a creature," Rayna said hotly. "He's—"

But Anders was ready to answer that for himself. For once, he didn't feel like everyone talking over him. "I'm a wolf," he said, his voice carrying and silencing those around them. "And my sister's a dragon. And you're welcome, by the way."

"He is a wolf," Leif agreed. "A particular kind of wolf. I believe what we saw today was icefire."

All around them now, dragons were staring at Anders with something like awe.

"Icefire is a myth," a woman said.

"Except we just saw it," Rayna replied. "And he's right, nobody's said thank you to him for driving the wolves out."

Guilt washed over him at her words. He hadn't just driven "the wolves" out. He'd driven his *friends* out. But at least Sakarias and Viktoria, Mateo and Det and Jai and Ennar and all the rest of the class were safely away. He'd done that too.

"The discovery of Anders's icefire has bought us at least temporary safety," Leif said. "The battle might have been far, far worse, save for his bravery."

Everyone was looking at Anders now. "I was only—people were in danger," he said. "My sister, my friends. It wasn't—"

"That is what bravery is," Leif said. "Doing what you must."

Anders sat quietly with Rayna, watching as a healer checked Lisabet over.

"I can't believe you did that." Rayna's voice startled him, pulling him back from his own thoughts, his own worries. "You were amazing, Anders."

"I was afraid," he said quietly.

"*Everyone* was afraid," she replied. "What you were saying before, about being able to do things yourself. I know you can. You're right, that's how you got here, and you just saved all of us." Her arm tightened around his shoulders. "I'll try and remember you can stand on your own two feet. Or your own four feet, some days."

"Do we know what they took?" That was Ellukka, who still had Lisabet's head in her lap, one gentle hand resting on her forehead to stop her from moving. "A couple of the wolves had something in their mouths when they left. They went farther into Drekhelm."

Everybody shook their heads. Anders suspected they'd find out soon enough.

Once Ennar was back in Holbard, Sigrid would know exactly where to find Drekhelm. And he knew she wouldn't be content to simply sit on that knowledge.

As the noise around them devolved into many smaller conversations and the dragons started to help their wounded to the infirmary, Anders looked around at his companions, old and new.

Rayna leaned in against Anders, her head on his shoulder. Ellukka had accepted a cold cloth from a healer, and was leaning in to lay it on Lisabet's forehead. Mikkel watched from his place by her side.

"Did anyone hurt you?" Lisabet asked Anders, looking up at him from under the compress.

"I'm all right," he said. Because despite everything he had to worry about, despite everything that had gone wrong, he was.

He had bought them time to think. And as he looked around at the company he was keeping, for the first time in a very long time, he felt like he'd done enough.

Nobody had won today, but he had saved them from injuries that could never be undone.

It was a start.

He had no idea what to do next. His friends and his sister were hurt, and his classmates were on the run, nursing injuries, and no doubt thinking he'd betrayed them.

He was exiled to a mountain full of dragons who didn't trust him, and didn't understand his icefire. He should have been ready to creep under a rock and hide there. But he wasn't.

If Leif was right, and bravery was doing what you must, then perhaps Anders was braver than he'd realized. He'd been doing things he didn't know he could for weeks now.

He'd spent all his life looking for something he could be good at, a way he could be useful, a place to belong. Now, for the first time, he was realizing that a place to belong—a home—wasn't a place you found.

It was a place you made. And though he hadn't done it yet, he felt as he never had before that, given time, he could.

"Let's get Lisabet to the infirmary," he said. "First things first."

And as they worked together to help her to her feet, he was even surer. Everything had changed, but this didn't have to be an end.

This could be a beginning.

ACKNOWLEDGMENTS

Writing this book has been a joyful experience, and I'm even luckier than Anders—I had a whole army of Lisabets to help me. I'd like to thank a few of them here.

Abby Ranger edited the first book I ever published, and working with her was such a joy that I jumped at the chance to do it again. Abby, thank you so much for your guidance, your encouragement, your good humor, and your friendship. It was a joy all over again.

I wasn't just lucky enough to have one incredible editor on this book—I've been lucky enough to have two. The wonderful Andrew Eliopulos stepped in to help with the end of this book, and to take on the next with kindness, humor, effortless expertise, and just the right amount of nerdiness for me. (By which I mean a lot.) I can't wait for the rest of this adventure.

Thank you as well to all the wonderful Harper crew, from sales and marketing to production to art and more. Thanks in particular to Rosemary Brosnan and Kate Jackson for their support, to Rose Pleuler for her wonderful editorial work, to Joe Merkel and Levente Szabo for my gorgeous cover and design, and to Virginia Allyn for a map of unsurpassed beauty. Thank you to copy editor Jill

Amack and production editor Emily Rader for saving me from myself, not once but many times.

Thank you to my incredible agent, Tracey Adams, who never fails to know exactly what I need—even when I don't. Tracey, I'm grateful for your smarts, your calm head, and your friendship. A huge thanks as well to Josh Adams, who's part of the pack on every book.

I've also had such wonderful friends to share this journey with, and I barely know where to start in thanking them. Meg Spooner—dedicating this book to you doesn't begin to express my gratitude for the ways in which you've changed my life. Thank you for all the road behind us so far, and I can't wait for all the road ahead. Marie Lu— when I wasn't sure, you told me to just jump in and take on this story, and you were right, as you always are. I can't imagine my life without you in it. Jay Kristoff—that bacon was the best investment I ever made. I'm so grateful for your friendship, your humor, your constant support, and all the miles we've covered so far. Leigh Bardugo—thank you, thank you, for being your marvelous self, for always having my back, and for reminding me in one incredibly timely email that first drafts don't need to be perfect.

On that note, a huge thank-you to Alison Cherry, who helped me get started when I was totally stuck, and read this book as it came to life—Alison, your amazing smile is your superpower, and it saved the day! Shannon Messenger proves herself a superhero on a regular basis—Shannon, thank you for all your enthusiasm, support, and cheerleading. I'm awash with wonderful authors who helped out at every stage—Sarah Rees Brennan and C. S. Pacat provided friendship, cheerleading, and a turning-point conversation about the link between my own fears and Anders's over the most valuable Korean meal I've ever had. The lovely Arwen Elys Dayton ran her expert eye over this book and it was all the better for it, and the ever-generous Garth Nix gave me a gentle push at just the right moment. Kiersten White showed up like a dream just when I needed her, Ryan Graudin somehow always knew just the right thing to say, and Lindsay Ribar always knows just the way to lift my mood. Alex Bracken, Sooz Dennard, and Erin Bowman—good things come in threes! To the authors who offered such generous words about this story, a huge thank-you—Shannon Messenger, Marie Lu, Margaret Peterson Haddix, Gregory Funaro, Claire Legrand, and the ever sparkly Alex Gino, I appreciate your collective kindness so much!

Michelle Dennis—for every walk, every talk and text, every evening, and just plain everything, thank you. Kacey Smith—I have no idea what I'd do without you, and I never want to find out. Nic Crowhurst—your heart is even bigger than your brain, and that's saying something. Kate Irving—we stick together though oceans separate us, but I'm so glad they no longer do. Soraya Een Hajji, who knew a punch in the nose could be a harbinger of such great fortune? Peta Freestone, you're a constant delight. Eliza Tiernan, you light up every room you're in. And to every member of Team Roti Boti—having exceptional friends like you is proof I'm as lucky as they come. (And look, I finally wrote something that won't scare your children!)

Every author has help from experts, and I'm no exception—as always, everything I get right is thanks to them, and everything I get wrong is all on me. Alexander Daly and Will Marney provided invaluable feedback and advice, as did Alex Gino, Anna Prendella, Becky Albertalli, Marianne Kirby, Dhonielle Clayton, Tempest Bradford, Nisi Shawl, and other excellent people as well. The staff of the Wolf Conservation Center in South Salem, New York, provided me with a research opportunity I'll never forget—thank you!

As ever, before I wrap up I want to thank the readers, reviewers, librarians, and booksellers who share my adventures with me, and then share them with others—without you, I'd still be telling these stories to my dog. If nothing else, he's glad you all give him a break sometimes. I'd also like to thank two teachers in particular. My primary school librarian, Joan Amiet, was the one who taught me something that Anders observes during this book: librarians have special powers. I'm so grateful you were mine. And my sixth-grade teacher, Di Rundas, always had time for my storytelling, and when I was Anders's age, she took me to Dromkeen, a trip that changed the course of my life. Thank you.

And finally, of course, my family. To my parents, Philip and Marilyn; my brother and sisters, Dean, Sacha, and Flic; my nieces and nephew, Maddy, Luca, and Bode; to Kay and Neville; Shannon and Adam; and all the extended Aussie, Irish, and American clans, whether they're my family by blood or by choice, thank you for every ounce of your support, which I never take for granted and always, always treasure. (And for once with my family thanks, I really must mention Sandy and Midnight, Charlie, Tarver, Flynn, Freddie, and Jack, generations of dogs who may or may not have provided a little wolfish inspiration.)

Now there's only one person left: Brendan, you fill my heart and my life with enough joy to make all my stories possible. You're my rock, my calm place, my perfect counterpoint, and I love you.

Turn the page for a
sneak peek at the next
electrifying adventure in
the Elementals series . . .

CHAPTER ONE

THE BATTLE BETWEEN THE DRAGONS AND THE wolves was over.

Now, less than an hour later, Anders sat between his best friend, Lisabet, and his sister, Rayna, both of whom were on makeshift beds amid the bustle of the infirmary.

All the scorch dragons were in human form—the crowded cave was deep inside the mountain, not big enough for even one actual dragon. As it was, bodies were packed into every corner as medics hurried back and forth.

Anders's attention was abruptly yanked away from the flurry of activity when Lisabet groaned beside him. Her pale skin was whiter than usual right now, and even her freckles didn't look like themselves. She'd hit her head hard defending the dragons from the wolves she and Anders had accidentally led here.

"Are you okay?" He leaned in to get a better look at

her, but the answer came from his other side, in his twin's dry voice.

"She tried to knock her brains out. She's probably not."

He turned to look at Rayna, who was curled up under a huge pile of blankets, only her head visible. Her warm brown skin had turned a dangerous gray when she'd first been hit by a wolf's ice spear, and though it was slowly coming back to normal, her cheeks were still unnaturally pale, the color of ashes. *Cold damage*, the healer had said.

One of his Ulfar Academy classmates had done that to her. He and Lisabet had come here to try and save Rayna, and his class had followed in pursuit. If *only* they hadn't followed, everybody would be safe right now.

During the long race to reach Drekhelm, Anders had been constantly afraid. Afraid Rayna was about to be sacrificed by the dragons. Afraid he wouldn't know how to save her even if he did make it. Afraid she wasn't his twin sister at all, since she could transform into a scorch dragon while he was an ice wolf, and everyone knew it was impossible to find both in the same family.

But instead of saving her, he'd found her settling in just fine. He'd brought danger right to her doorstep, and he'd made enemies of the wolves he'd just learned to think of as his pack. And now he was trapped at Drekhelm, the dragon stronghold.

"I'm okay." Lisabet's voice jolted him back to the present.

"The nurse said you'd have a headache," he told her quietly. "And you have to stay awake for a few hours more, in case there's any damage inside your head that they can't see."

"Rayna?" she whispered, and Anders and Lisabet both looked across at Anders's sister, who was still shivering.

"I'm fine," Rayna insisted. "It was just an ice spear, it'll wear off eventually. I'm lucky it only nicked me. I'll probably be walking around in an hour."

Anders felt a quick rush of affection, warming him from the inside out. That was Rayna, ready to get up and keep going, as she had been all their lives. He still couldn't quite believe he was by her side again.

But a nurse loomed up behind her, his hands on his hips. "You won't be going anywhere in an hour," he said firmly. "If you're lucky, you'll be discharged in the morning, and then it'll only be because we have others worse than you. As for you two"—and he nodded to Anders and Lisabet, his square-jawed face stern for the two wolves—"you can go to guest quarters. We've got an escort waiting to take you there. The Dragonmeet won't want to see you until the morning."

Anders followed his gaze and saw Ellukka, the blond

girl Rayna had said was her friend. She'd been anything but friendly at first, but right after the battle she'd seemed to feel a little differently. She'd seen Lisabet defending Leif, the head of the Dragonmeet.

Just now, she had her arms folded across her chest and was leaning against the wall by the infirmary door. She was bigger and broader than Anders, and with her arms crossed like that, she looked like she meant business all over again.

Anders turned back to Rayna. "I don't want to leave you here," he said, and his concern was *mostly* for his sister.

"They won't let me go until tomorrow," she said. "You know where to find me. Go and get some rest, I'll be okay."

His instincts still rebelled against leaving his twin, but he knew she was right. She had been safe up until now, and he did desperately need to rest. He'd run with the pack all yesterday across the plains, and overnight he'd crossed a river and climbed a mountain with Lisabet. It was late morning now, which meant he'd been on the move for more than a day straight.

"Tell them to call me if you get worse," he said to Rayna.

"If I were you," the nurse said to Anders, scowling, "I'd be more worried about myself right now. There are going to be a *lot* of questions for you tomorrow, and if you don't have answers the Dragonmeet likes, you can be sure they'll extract better ones."

"Leave him alone," Rayna snapped, pushing up on one elbow.

With one last significant look at all of them, the nurse stalked off to see to other patients, and Rayna turned her attention to Anders. "I'll make sure someone calls you if I get worse," she promised. "And let's deal with tomorrow when we get there. We'll make them understand."

Anders wasn't nearly as confident as she sounded—Rayna's version of talking their way out of things was what had started their transformation to wolf and dragon in the first place—but he knew there was nothing he could do today, not with his sister and his best friend both almost too weak to move.

So he helped Lisabet sit up, then stand, keeping an arm carefully around her. Ellukka pushed away from the doorway to lead them outside, but despite her improved opinion of Lisabet she didn't seem inclined to help keep her steady.

She led Anders and Lisabet down hallways carved into the dark stone of the mountain, all human-size rather than dragon-size. Anders wondered if, like the wolves, the dragons spent most of their time in human form.

The trio passed lamps that appeared to be made of solid metal, fixed to the wall by brackets. Whenever they came within a few steps of one, it began to glow softly, and when Anders looked behind him, the others had faded into darkness once more.

Lisabet was watching them as well. "That's actually happening, right?" she asked. "It's not just that I hit my head?"

"The lights?" Ellukka asked, looking over her shoulder. "Well of course. They're artifacts."

Now Anders looked more closely, he could see the rows of runes engraved around the sconces. Those runes meant the lamps had been designed by wolves and forged by dragons—before the last great battle ten years before, no doubt.

Ellukka stopped by a cupboard built into the hallway, pulling out mismatched clothes for them in blues and greens and reds—the dragons seemed to prefer bright colors, and even in the short time he'd been here, Anders had noticed they all dressed differently. The wolves all wore the same uniform—a sign of their pack, their togetherness.

"This is the guest area," Ellukka said, in answer to his questioning glance. "There are spare rooms, spare clothes, things like that."

"Do you have a lot of visitors?" he asked, trying to imagine who could possibly come all the way up a mountain. Trying to find a way toward friendly conversation with this girl who seemed to know his sister so well. He needed every bit of help he could get right now.

"Most dragon families and groups move around a lot," Ellukka said. "We live pretty spread out. There are aeries all up and down the Icespire mountain range—in mountains all over Vallen, actually—so we visit each other quite often. It's usually easier not to carry a lot of your stuff."

She stopped at a wooden door. Inside was a cozy bedroom with a bed on either side, each draped with a thick patchwork quilt. A rug covered the stone floor, and a glass-paned window peeked out onto the face of the mountain itself. There was another wooden door on the other side of the little room, and a water clock on the wall, a slow stream of liquid trickling through marked tubes to show the passing of time.

Good, Anders thought. They could use that to keep track of how long Lisabet needed to stay awake. And how far away morning was, and with it the Dragonmeet.

"It's warm in here," Lisabet said, and Anders thought immediately of the hot glow he'd seen deep inside the mountain as he'd flown above Drekhelm on Rayna's back. "And it was out in the hall too," she continued. "But there aren't any fireplaces. Do you use the lava?"

"What else?" Ellukka said, dumping the clothes on one of the beds and sorting them into two piles. "And some artifacts help with the temperature as well. There's a bath right through that door there, as much hot water as you want. I mean, I know wolves prefer cold, but I assume you don't want cold showers."

"Not when we're in human form," Lisabet agreed.

"Well, get clean," Ellukka said, folding her arms and backing up toward the door. "You smell like wet dog."

The door closed behind her, and Anders sank down onto one of the beds. Every muscle in his body ached, but he made himself lean over to unlace his boots, and then pull off socks that were still wet from the snow outside.

He realized he was still wearing his sister's coat. He turned his head and inhaled, and found it held that scent that was uniquely Rayna's, though now there was a hint of spicy sweetness to it that hadn't been there before. And even though it wasn't quite the same, the familiarity of it made his eyes ache.

He had done it. He was here, with Rayna. Whatever came next, he'd find a way through it, because he was with his sister again.

"You have the first bath," he said to Lisabet. He needed a few minutes to pull himself together.

She disappeared through the door, and he flopped backward onto the bed, staring up at the ceiling. It was smooth stone, just like the walls. *Because this room is inside a mountain*, he reminded himself. *Because it's inside Drekhelm.*

It was all really beginning to sink in now. He'd found his sister—done the thing he'd been afraid for weeks he would never manage. But nothing had gone as he'd hoped, or expected, or even as he'd feared. Guilt sat heavy inside him over the injuries his classmates had suffered—even now, as he sat in this comfortable room, they would be running across the plains to return to Holbard, to Ulfar Academy.

And fear sat heavy beside that guilt. What would the Dragonmeet say tomorrow? What answers did they want to extract?

How could he convince them to let him stay near Rayna, without betraying the wolves?

But despite the nurse's words and the fear they'd kindled, he also admitted to himself that the dragons weren't at all what he'd imagined. He didn't quite know what they *were* like yet, who they were, but the stories at Ulfar and in Holbard had always made them out to be blood-thirsty villains, living only to hurt those who weren't like them. And whatever the truth was, he now knew it was much more complicated than that. They had friends here, family. They had rooms for guests and debates about the right thing to do.

Rayna had found a home here in a way he'd never imagined possible. He wasn't sure what that meant for him, or for Lisabet.